BRIAN FL'
BLACK ED

BRIAN FLYNN was born in 1885 in Leyton, Essex. He won a scholarship to the City Of London School, and from there went into the civil service. In World War I he served as Special Constable on the Home Front, also teaching "Accountancy, Languages, Maths and Elocution to men, women, boys and girls" in the evenings, and acting in his spare time.

It was a seaside family holiday that inspired Brian Flynn to turn his hand to writing in the mid-twenties. Finding most mystery novels of the time "mediocre in the extreme", he decided to compose his own. Edith, the author's wife, encouraged its completion, and after a protracted period finding a publisher, it was eventually released in 1927 by John Hamilton in the UK and Macrae Smith in the U.S. as *The Billiard-Room Mystery*.

The author died in 1958. In all, he wrote and published 57 mysteries, the vast majority featuring the super-sleuth Antony Bathurst.

BRIAN FLYNN

BLACK EDGED

With an introduction by
Steve Barge

DEAN STREET PRESS

INTRODUCTION

> "I believe that the primary function of the mystery story is to entertain; to stimulate the imagination and even, at times, to supply humour. But it pleases the connoisseur most when it presents – and reveals – genuine mystery. To reach its full height, it has to offer an intellectual problem for the reader to consider, measure and solve."
>
> Brian Flynn, *Crime Book* magazine, 1948

BRIAN Flynn began his writing career with *The Billiard Room Mystery* in 1927, primarily at the prompting of his wife Edith who had grown tired of hearing him say how he could write a better mystery novel than the ones he had been reading. Four more books followed under his original publisher, John Hamilton, before he moved to John Long, who would go on to publish the remaining forty-eight of his Anthony Bathurst mysteries, along with his three Sebastian Stole titles, released under the pseudonym Charles Wogan. Some of the early books were released in the US, and there were also a small number of translations of his mysteries into Swedish and German. In the article from which the above quote is taken from, Brian also claims that there were also French and Danish translations but to date, I have not found a single piece of evidence for their existence. The only translations that I have been able to find evidence of are *War Es Der Zahnarzt?* and *Bathurst Greift Ein* in German – *The Mystery of the Peacock's Eye*, retitled to the less dramatic "Was It The Dentist?", and *The Horn* becoming "Bathurst Takes Action" – and, in Swedish, *De 22 Svarta*, a more direct translation of *The Case of the Black Twenty-Two*. There may well be more work to be done finding these, but tracking down all of his books written in the original English has been challenging enough!

Reprints of Brian's books were rare. Four titles were released as paperbacks as part of John Long's Four Square Thriller range in the late 1930s, four more re-appeared during the war from Cherry Tree Books and Mellifont Press, albeit abridged by at least a third, and two others that I am aware of, *Such Bright Disguises* (1941) and *Reverse the Charges* (1943), received a paperback release as part of John Long's Pocket Edition range in the early 1950s – these were also possibly abridged, but only by about 10%. They were the exceptions, rather than the rule, however, and it was not until 2019, when Dean Street Press released his first ten titles, that his work was generally available again.

The question still persists as to why his work disappeared from the awareness of all but the most ardent collectors. As you may expect, when a title was only released once, back in the early 1930s, finding copies of the original text is not a straightforward matter – not even Brian's estate has a copy of every title. We are particularly grateful to one particular collector for providing *The Edge of Terror*, Brian's first serial killer tale, and another for *The Ebony Stag* and *The Grim Maiden*. With these, the reader can breathe a sigh of relief as a copy of every one of Brian's books has now been located – it only took about five years . . .

One of Brian's strengths was the variety of stories that he was willing to tell. Despite, under his own name at least, never straying from involving Anthony Bathurst in his novels – technically he doesn't appear in the non-series *Tragedy at Trinket*, although he gets a name-check from the sleuth of that tale who happens to be his nephew – it is fair to say that it was rare that two consecutive books ever followed the same structure. Some stories are narrated by a Watson-esque character, although never the same person twice, and others are written by Bathurst's "chronicler". The books sometimes focus on just Bathurst and his investigation but sometimes we get to see the events occurring to the whole cast of characters. On occasion, Bathurst himself will "write" the final chapter, just to make sure his chronicler has got the details correct. The murderer may be an opportunist or they may have a convoluted (and, on occasion, a somewhat over-the-top) plan. They may be working for personal gain or as part of a criminal enterprise or society. Compare for example, *The League of Matthias* and *The Horn* – consecutive releases but were it not for Bathurst's involvement, and a similar sense of humour underlying Brian's writing, you could easily believe that they were from the pen of different writers.

Brian seems to have been determined to keep stretching himself with his writing as he continued Bathurst's adventures, and the ten books starting with *Cold Evil* show him still trying new things. Two of the books are inverted mysteries – where we know who the killer is, and we follow their attempts to commit the crime and/or escape justice and also, in some cases, the detective's attempt to bring them to justice. That description doesn't do justice to either *Black Edged* or *Such Bright Disguises*, as there is more revealed in the finale than the reader might expect . . . There is one particular innovation in *The Grim Maiden*, namely the introduction of a female officer at Scotland Yard.

Helen Repton, an officer from "the woman's side of the Yard" is recruited in that book, as Bathurst's plan require an undercover officer in a cinema. This is her first appearance, despite the text implying that Bathurst has met her before, but it is notable as the narrative spends a little time apart from Bathurst. It follows Helen Repton's investigations based on superb initiative, which generates some leads in the case. At this point in crime fiction, there have been few, if any, serious depictions of a female police detective – the primary example would be Mrs Pym from the pen of Nigel Morland, but she (not just the only female detective at the Yard, but the Assistant Deputy Commissioner no less) would seem to be something of a caricature. Helen would go on to become a semi-regular character in the series, and there are certainly hints of a romantic connection between her and Bathurst.

It is often interesting to see how crime writers tackled the Second World War in their writing. Some brought the ongoing conflict into their writing – John Rhode (and his pseudonym Miles Burton) wrote several titles set in England during the conflict, as did others such as E.C.R. Lorac, Christopher Bush, Gladys Mitchell and many others. Other writers chose not to include the War in their tales – Agatha Christie had ten books published in the war years, yet only *N or M?* uses it as a subject.

Brian only uses the war as a backdrop in one title, *Glittering Prizes*, the story of a possible plan to undermine the Empire. It illustrates the problem of writing when the outcome of the conflict was unknown – it was written presumably in 1941 – where there seems little sign of life in England of the war going on, one character states that he has fought in the conflict, but messages are sent from Nazi conspirators, ending *"Heil Hitler!"*. Brian had good reason for not wanting to write about the conflict in detail, though, as he had immediate family involved in the fighting and it is quite understandable to see writing as a distraction from that.

While Brian had until recently been all but forgotten, there are some mentions for Brian's work in some studies of the genre – Sutherland Scott in *Blood in their Ink* praises *The Mystery of the Peacock's Eye* as containing "one of the ablest pieces of misdirection" before promptly spoiling that misdirection a few pages later, and John Dickson Carr similarly spoils the ending of *The Billiard Room Mystery* in his famous essay "The Grandest Game In The World". One should also include in this list Barzun and Taylor's entry in their *Catalog of Crime* where they attempted to cover Brian by looking at a single title – the somewhat odd *Conspiracy at Angel* (1947) – and summarising it as "Straight tripe and savorless. It is doubtful, on the evidence, if any of his others would be different." Judging an author based on a single title seems desperately unfair – how many people have given up on Agatha Christie after only reading *Postern Of Fate*, for example – but at least that misjudgement is being rectified now.

Contemporary reviews of Brian's work were much more favourable, although as John Long were publishing his work for a library market, not all of his titles garnered attention. At this point in his writing career – 1938 to 1944 – a number of his books won reviews in the national press, most of which were positive. Maurice Richardson in the *Observer* commented that "Brian Flynn balances his ingredients with considerable skill" when reviewing *The Ebony Stag* and praised *Such Bright Disguises* as a "suburban horror melodrama" with an "ingenious final solution". "Suspense is well maintained until the end" in *The Case of the Faithful Heart*, and the protagonist's narration in *Black Edged* in "impressively nightmarish".

It is quite possible that Brian's harshest critic, though, was himself. In the *Crime Book* magazine, he wrote about how, when reading the current output of detective fiction "I delight in the dazzling erudition that has come to grace and decorate the craft of the *'roman policier'*." He then goes on to say "At the same time, however, I feel my own comparative unworthiness for the fire and burden of the competition." Such a feeling may well be the reason why he never made significant inroads into the social side of crime-writing, such as the Detection Club or the Crime Writers Association. Thankfully, he uses this sense of unworthiness as inspiration, concluding "The stars, though, have always been the most desired of all goals, so I allow exultation and determination to take the place of that but temporary dismay."

In Anthony Bathurst, Flynn created a sleuth that shared a number of traits with Holmes but was hardly a carbon-copy. Bathurst is a polymath and gentleman sleuth, a man of contradictions whose background is never made clear to the reader. He clearly has money, as he has his own rooms in London with a pair of servants on call and went to public school (Uppingham) and university (Oxford). He is a follower of all things that fall under the banner of sport, in particular horse racing and cricket, the latter being a sport that he could, allegedly, have represented England at. He is also a bit of a show-off, littering his speech (at times) with classical quotes, the obscurer the better, provided by the copies of the *Oxford Dictionary of Quotations* and *Brewer's Dictionary of Phrase & Fable* that Flynn kept by his writing desk, although Bathurst generally restrains himself to only doing this with people who would appreciate it or to annoy the local constabulary. He is fond of amateur dramatics (as was Flynn, a well-regarded amateur thespian who appeared in at least one self-penned play, *Blue Murder*), having been a member of OUDS, the Oxford University Dramatic Society. General information about his background is light on the ground. His parents were Irish, but he doesn't have an accent – see *The Spiked Lion* (1933) – and his eyes are grey. Despite the fact that he is an incredibly charming and handsome individual, we learn in *The Orange Axe* that he doesn't pursue romantic relationships due to a bad experience in his first romance. We find out more about that relationship and the woman involved in *The Edge of Terror*, and soon thereafter he falls head over heels in love in *Fear and Trembling*, although we never hear of that young lady again. After that, there are eventual hints of an attraction between Helen Repton, but nothing more. That doesn't stop women falling head over heels for Bathurst – as he departs her company in *The Padded Door*, one character muses "What other man could she ever love . . . after this secret idolatry?"

As we reach the halfway point in Anthony's career, his companions have somewhat stablised, with Chief Inspector Andrew MacMorran now his near-constant junior partner in investigation. The friendship with MacMorran is a highlight (despite MacMorran always calling him "Mr. Bathurst") with the sparring between them always a delight to read. MacMorran's junior officers, notably Superintendent Hemingway and Sergeant Chatterton, are frequently recurring characters. The notion of the local constabulary calling in help from Scotland Yard enables cases to be set around the country while still maintaining the same central cast (along with a local bobby or two).

Cold Evil (1938), the twenty-first Bathurst mystery, finally pins down Bathurst's age, and we find that in *The Billiard Room Mystery* (1927), his first outing, he was a fresh-faced Bright Young Thing of twenty-two. How he can survive with his own rooms, at least two servants, and no noticeable source of income remains a mystery. One can also ask at what point in his life he travelled the world, as he has, at least, been to Bangkok at some point. It is, perhaps, best not to analyse Bathurst's past too carefully . . .

"Judging from the correspondence my books have excited it seems I have managed to achieve some measure of success, for my faithful readers comprise a circle in which high dignitaries of the Church rub shoulders with their brothers and sisters of the common touch."

For someone who wrote to entertain, such correspondence would have delighted Brian, and I wish he were around to see how many people have enjoyed the reprints of his work so far. *The Mystery of the Peacock's Eye* (1928) won Cross Examining Crime's Reprint Of The Year award for 2019, with *Tread Softly* garnering second place the following year. His family are delighted with the reactions that people have passed on, and I hope that this set of books will delight just as much.

Steve Barge

PART ONE
The First Escape

CHAPTER I
Crisis

(From the Narrative of Stuart Traquair, M.B.)

Two things stand out in my mind every time that I look back on the day of the tragedy. The first concerns the poor devil whose maimed body was brought into my morning surgery. He had been knocked down by a fast-travelling car only a few yards from my place and directly I saw him I knew that I could do little or nothing for him. All that I could do, of course, I did. After sending for his wife—luckily they lived close at hand—I superintended his removal to the Commemoration Hospital. I got his clothes off him as well as I could, 'phoned for the Corporation's ambulance and saw them both off—the man as comfortable as my skill and attention could possibly make him, and the woman white-faced and tearful. Before they went I promised to do something further.

From what the woman told me, her husband made a living as what I may term an "extra hand" at funerals. That is to say, he was engaged at odd times by various local undertakers, when business from their point of view was flourishing and much pressure in consequence placed upon the staff, to stand at the back of one of the carriages or to walk at the side of the hearse, as occasion demanded. What worried the man and woman was the fact that on the following day he had an engagement with old man Morley, the leading undertaker of the district, and didn't know how he would be able to let the old man know that he couldn't come, or, alternatively, fix up to send along a substitute. Which procedure, I gathered from the woman, was quite ordinary amongst the men who followed this class of employment. To allay the woman's anxiety, I took the man's name and address and promised that I would 'phone Morleys' and explain the position to them. *That* was the first incident. The

BRIAN FLYNN

2 | BRIAN FLYNN

second I will describe later. Just after I saw the ambulance away from the front door, I heard a step outside and Madeleine came into the surgery.

"How was he?" she said.

"Pretty bad," I replied. "Touch and go for him, I'm afraid."

"How awful," she went on.

"Yes. Internal and multiple. *Inter alia*, a broken pelvis."

She shuddered at my words, and I think that it was at *that* moment my previous suspicions changed their condition and I *knew* for certain. I went suddenly very cold. I was dazed, too. So dazed, that her words, when she spoke to me again, seemed meaningless and I had to pull myself sharply together to understand them.

"Have you many calls to make, Stuart?" she questioned me. By this time I had just begun to collect myself, and luckily for me she hadn't been quick enough to detect my uneasiness. "Oh," I replied . . . "Fairish. Mrs. Casson, the two Bracegirdle boys, old man Dexter . . . and a call's come through this morning from Aldersmere—Claverton House. They're the only 'specials' that I can think of . . . everything else can wait. And is going to! Why do you ask?"

Her voice was hard as she answered and the blonde beauty of her seemed and looked to be lost on me. "Nothing. I was just wondering—that was all. Will you be wanting the car?"

I hesitated. Then I thought more clearly: "If I'm going out to Aldersmere, I shall. But if you want it for any purpose . . . I'll leave that call over until after lunch. It's up to you, Madeleine."

The words were mine, but all the time my thoughts were far away. I thought of Armitage and of how soon I could get to him. For to get him and have things out with him, I must. As it was, I had delayed too long, and was now facing stark realities which previously had been but nebulous fancies. My wife's voice softened this time as it had hardened before.

"It doesn't matter, Stuart. I'll stay in. What I wanted to do can be left until another time." She came close to me, half touched me on the arm as though she were about to say something, but then shook her head and turned away. I knew that my arm had stiffened involuntarily at the contact. When she spoke again she was standing by the door and had her back to me. "I shall see you at lunch-time then. Try not to be late." She turned and gave me a half smile.

"All right," I said. It was all that my brain could think of to say.

She closed the door behind her. I was left with my thoughts. It was, of course, to some extent, my own fault . . . but she was my wife . . . and I had trusted her. I should have remembered *all* that I knew of Rupert. It is no use taking anything for granted in this life. My own professional training should have taught me that, if nothing else! I went slowly to the garage, still a prey to conflicting thoughts. Beyond seeing Armitage and thrusting my knowledge at him I had no plan of campaign at all. And Armitage so far was but a name to me. To go to see him at this stage might well mean disaster. After all—I hadn't definite proof of anything. All that I had was the strongest suspicion. I wasn't ready. I got out the car and almost mechanically set it in motion. It purred away from the start and I could hear the menace in it as it devoured the roads as soon as I had left the town. I quickly reached fields. Then I ran up the ascent to Cheldersley Common and swung my car over the new bridge across the Brest towards Aldersmere. I could soon see the chimney-tops of Claverton Hall. I wasn't detained over long, finding just an ordinary hepatic disorder—and I was actually on the point of getting away to the Bracegirdle establishment when a woman, with part of her hair untidily down, came breathless and anxious right to the front of the car and spoke to me.

"Doctor Traquair, is it?" she said excitedly.

"That's right," I answered. "What's the trouble?"

"Oh, and indeed I'm glad to have caught you," she answered, her breath still coming in convulsive heaves. "Will you come along at once, please, Doctor, to Lockyer's Corner? We've a child there as poorly as can be. Oh, Doctor, it's glad that I am that I've caught you. It was indeed a stroke of good fortune hearing that you were here at the Hall."

"How far is it?" I asked laconically, for, if I tell the truth, I had never heard of this place that she called Lockyer's Corner. Actually I couldn't remember that I had ever been farther than Claverton Hall in this particular part of the country.

"About half a mile, Doctor," she replied. "Straight round by the road."

"Then you had better get in the car and come with me," I gave back to her.

She seemed pleased at the suggestion and with a quick bobbing movement of the body got in the car and we started off. She directed me with a series of sharp gestures and when we reached Lockyer's Corner I saw that all there was there was a row of straggling, rather tumbledown cottages. "This is the one," the woman cried, pointing to the end one of the row, and she whisked from the car with me soon on her heels. In a bed within a small room lay a small girl. I saw quickly that it was a diphtheria case and the child about as bad as she could be. The false membrane had already begun to spread into the air passages and there was, of course, the resultant risk of asphyxiation. I came to a quick decision. The girl was very young, so I resolved to try intubation. It would be an easier matter than slitting the trachea. So I soon had the woman busy preparing me the necessaries to the best of her resources and utility, took a short metal tube from my bag, and by way of the youngster's mouth pushed the tube into the larynx. I got the silk thread in position and made a good job of the entire business. "She should be better in time," I said to the mother (at least I suppose it was the mother). "That will keep an air passage open for her."

She nodded blankly, but I could see the gratitude in the woman's eyes. The intubation operation has the advantage, in practised hands, of being performed within a few seconds and of being done without cutting of any kind. It is not as efficient, in the great majority of cases, as tracheotomy—not, as I said, well worth trying in an emergency like this. I asked the mother several questions, made a few notes on the case generally, and promised that I would come over to Lockyer's Corner again that evening. She thanked me profusely. When I took my departure from the cottage I looked at my watch and saw that at the best I was going to be very late for lunch. So I thought matters over.

On this particular day I had no special desire to be late for lunch. Also, I wanted quietude, tranquillity—solitude almost. I wanted in addition to think one or two things out. I determined therefore to turn the car in the direction of Grantley, which is a good-sized town, and have lunch in a pub when I got there. Then, I thought, I'd do Mrs. Casson and Dexter on the way back and return to the surgery at my leisure in time for the evening's interviews and consultations. I put this idea into effect. When I reached Grantley I pulled up at the "White Hart", had a wash and brush-up, and lunched off the half-crown ordinary in a very comfortable and well-appointed dining-room. The girl brought me a coffee after the sweet and I sat there with a cigarette and tried to think things out. I could not be sure as to how far she had gone with Rupert . . . and then I cursed myself mildly for having married her. If it were only my own destiny and career that were at sake! Was a man justified at a time like this, and faced with a problem of this kind, in taking matters into his own hands and adjusting them? The mere contemplation of all the possibilities sent me alternatively hot and hold.

I smoked cigarette after cigarette and thus I stayed until closing-time. When I left, however, I was no nearer to the solution than I had been when I started my essay in reflection. I even found myself recalling everything: my medical training, my scientific bent, my meeting with Madeleine. . . . Rupert had introduced me to her in the first place . . . it was usually like that . . . and my setting up in my first practice at Wrack. I paid my bill, got the car going again, called on Mrs. Casson (atrophy of the heart) and old man Dexter (tuberculous cystitis), and eventually ran the car into the mews at the back of my surgery a few minutes before six o'clock. It was just getting dark and a most unusual time for me to arrive home. Usually I was either much earlier or about an hour later. I went in the back way through the little room next the surgery where I used to make up most of the medicines (I had a sink there) and walked rather silently upstairs to the room that Madeleine and I always used as a lounge. I wasn't creeping about the house deliberately. . . . I just didn't happen to make much noise—that was all. When I was about half-way up the flight of stairs I thought that I heard voices . . . so I stopped on my way up . . . and listened. I was right. I could hear Rupert's voice. He seemed to be reading something out aloud, very carefully and deliberately . . . the phrases measured to a nicety! I heard him stop reading and lower his voice. I strained to hear what he was saying.

". . . he must be got rid of . . . when the time comes". I finished my journey up the stairs and opened the door.

CHAPTER II
TRAGEDY

(*Stuart Traquair's Narrative*—continued)

RUPERT Halmar was sitting with his arm across Madeleine's shoulders. She paled as I entered and I knew then that neither of them had heard me as I had come up the stairs. Madeleine hastily turned to hide something from which they had been reading. Her movement in itself told me everything that I wanted to know. My suspicions, which had flared up during the morning, blazed now into a flame of absolute certainty. Madeleine knew everything. My secret and all that it meant to me, to her and to all. In some way, that I had known nothing about, she had gained access to my private drawer and had read my private papers. I steeled myself to the inevitable ordeal that was close at hand.

"Hallo!" I said quite casually. "I had no idea that you were here, Rupert. Madeleine didn't tell me that you were expected. How are you these days?"

His handsome, swarthy face flushed a little, but in a second he had recovered and had himself under complete control. "Oh, pretty fit, Stuart, thank you. I was at a loose end this afternoon . . . and I hadn't been over for some time . . . so I came along. How are you? Living the strenuous life . . . what?"

"Yes," I replied, "more or less. I'm certainly tired, if that's anything."

"I'll ring for tea," said Madeleine coldly and quietly. "I presume that you've lunched . . . somewhere. I waited half an hour for you."

There was reproof in her cold tones. Madeleine had always possessed a flair for turning the tables . . . I knew that, none better.

I flattered myself that the revelations of the day had come to me before it was too late.

"I'm sorry," I replied to my wife, "but I was called farther away than I had anticipated. To Lockyer's Corner. A diph. case. I had to operate, it was the kid's only chance. As I was well on the road I went on to Grantley and had lunch there. I couldn't have reached here in time for you. Sorry if I put you out at all."

"No," she was saying impersonally, "a doctor's wife can never really be inconvenienced. She learns that early in her married life. If I were to—" She was interrupted by the maid bringing in the tea-things. There came a silence into the room. Rupert Halmar was now sitting with his back to the door and every now and then he would twist his body round to look at one of us. The maid arranged the tea-wagon as Madeleine instructed her and then went out again. Madeleine poured out tea and passed the first cup, I remember, to me. Then Rupert began to talk. All through his speeches I knew that he was warning me. The insistence upon the pronoun "we" . . . he scarcely ever said "I" . . . held a sinister significance for me that I should have been mentally blind to have ignored.

The inner meaning of little things began to come home to me. Trivial things that had meant but nothing to me when they had occurred. As you come down the main staircase of my house the hall is more or less exposed to the eye of the descending person. I remembered coming down some few weeks back when we were throwing a little supper-party and finding Madeleine standing by the fireplace in the library, on the left-hand of the fireplace. Alone— although some of our guests had already arrived. As I had descended she had been bending down, looking into the red heart of the fire, so that her back was towards me.

When she heard my step on the stairs she had turned suddenly . . . eagerly . . . and looked up. Then had taken a step or so towards the staircase. When she saw that it was I who was descending she had come to an abrupt stop and an emotion very much akin to acute disappointment had showed on her face. But there was watchful-ness in her eyes, too . . . all these points came back to me now. I had engaged her in conversation at the time and her uneasiness had grown all the time that I was with her, until the sound of a door shutting somewhere upstairs had floated down to us, followed by the tread of another step upon the stairs. Madeleine's awkwardness had then come to its greatest height and she had jumped up with a semi-apology to me for her too-evident inattention.

"Forgive me, Stuart, I'm afraid that I'm not very bright to-night . . ." and there had been a curious loudness of voice and an unusual stressing of the name . . . "Stuart". The sequel had been that the man who had been descending had . . . shall we say . . . understood—and gone back. Ascended the stairs again and beaten a retreat. Rupert's face, however, half an hour afterwards, had been, when I scanned it, quite inexpressive and nonchalant. Just as it was now . . . as he sat there and warned me. "Peace may be all very well, my dear Stuart, but sometimes that condition of peace has to be purchased at the price of war. And we are prepared thus to purchase it."

I argued with him. "But you can't with certainty go all the way even then."

His eyes were insolent as he looked me over. "I don't know that I quite understand you, Stuart. Explain—please."

"You spoke of war as the purchasing price of peace. But war means combat. Combat means combatants. And it isn't always the expected one that wins. The dark horse has been known to triumph before now. You must have heard of the insiders' club." I gave him back insolence for insolence, arrogance for arrogance, look for look. I saw Madeleine flinch at my words. Almost as though she feared a blow. Or sensed that violence was unpleasantly near. But Rupert Halmar was unmoved. He knew that he and I had started level at the beginning, which fact I think gave him a certain confidence.

"At any rate, Stuart, you and I will soon know exactly how we stand. Which will be all to the good from the point of view of each of us. Thank you, Madeleine." He acknowledged something that she passed to him and his white teeth showed as he spoke. From that moment the tension eased a little and I kept myself well in hand. The conversation became commonplace. But I knew that it could only be the lull before the storm that was bound to break before very long. After a time, when tea was over, Rupert began to talk again in terms of "we" and "us". He referred more than once to an "organization" and "the Service generally". I began to understand him. But, although all these remarks were directed against me as a warning, I was resolved to go through with my plan. When he rose, about a quarter to seven, to make his departure, I left him alone with my wife for a matter of five to ten minutes. There was something I felt that I must do. Something which I could not leave for another moment before testing.

I went to my bedroom and opened my private drawer. It was my habit to keep certain letters and papers in there . . . and I was soon able to see that they had been recently disturbed. I took my wallet from the breast pocket of the coat which I was wearing. The two sheets of paper about which I had been feeling the most acute concern were still in there! Madeleine had not found these. She had been under the impression, evidently, that *all* the documents were in the drawer. So they might have been—but for Armitage's message. I smiled grimly to myself and put a revolver in my side pocket. As I walked back to the room where I had left Madeleine and Rupert I wondered if any man had ever been called upon to face such an issue as that which confronted me. I heard her say: "I can't—before surgery is over. I must have time to do certain things. Besides, Stuart won't be able to—" She ceased speaking abruptly as I entered and Rupert began to brush his hat with the back of his sleeve. Curious how one recollects trivialities like this. He had his overcoat on as he stood there. "What sort of a night, is it, Stuart?" he asked me unconcernedly.

"Pretty foul," I answered. "Very dark . . . and looks like rain. Shouldn't waste any time in getting home if I were you."

His dark eyes mocked me and with his long, thin, clean-shaven, sharp-featured face he seemed more gaunt than ever. I knew that Rupert Halmar, when the time came, would look death in the face with no qualms—for nothing had any terrors for him. I was not so sure of Madeleine, and the thought troubled me. I saw that Rupert was holding out his hand to me. Madeleine had made her case good. He had read all that she had showed him. Except those two sheets that I had so luckily placed in my pocket-book. . . . I took his hand and I know that he read the challenge in my eyes.

"Well, good-bye, Stuart. Pleased to have seen you once more. It won't be so long in between when I see you again."

"That's good news," I countered. "Next time you come perhaps I shall be here to receive you, instead of Madeleine."

"Ah—that's an idea," he responded with a drawl in his voice. "Thanks a million. But don't forget one thing, Stuart. The next time I come here I shall probably bring one or two others with me."

"Really. Thanks for the warning, Rupert."

"I trust that they will be welcome. As the—er—flowers in May."

"Not that," I replied to him. "Say—just as welcome as you yourself will be." His eyes glinted as he turned away from me.

"Are you going straight into the surgery, Stuart?" asked Madeleine.

"Yes, I'll see you afterwards."

"Good-bye, then, Rupert," she said calmly, but if she thought that she concealed from me the relief that was on her face she was mistaken. And I knew that when my surgery was finished, in a couple of hours' time, the documents that she had taken from the private drawer in my bedroom would be replaced.

"Right-o," I said, "I'll see you later."

I went out of the room quietly.

Rupert was close on my heels as I descended the stairs.

I interviewed my various patients that evening almost mechanically. My manner must have seemed extraordinary, for more than once I caught a patient glancing curiously at me. However, the hands of the clock crept on and eventually showed nine. I closed the surgery door behind me and went straight upstairs to my bedroom. A quick glance at my drawer told me the instantaneous truth. The papers had been replaced. Madeleine had acted exactly as I had anticipated. I put the letters and the other documents carefully into my pocket-book and went straight down to the lounge. Madeleine was there. She was white-faced but otherwise cool and collected.

"I want to speak to you for a moment," I said.

"What is it, Stuart?" she asked.

"When are you going to Rupert?"

The question stung her. A pink flush showed in her cheeks.

"What do you mean, Stuart? I demand to—"

"You know very well what I mean."

"I assure you that I—"

I cut into her words. "Your assurances, no matter what they are going to be, are useless. I may have been blind for a long time, Madeleine, but my blindness has passed. You have betrayed me. Deliberately, and, I very much fear, without a qualm of conscience."

She sprang to her feet, her hand to her throat. "Stuart! You too have had no thought for me. I've long felt it. More recently I have come to know it. How can you accuse—"

"Never mind that. I'm dealing with this matter of you and Rupert. And I have made my decision! Today! Do you want to know what it is? Or aren't you sufficiently interested?"

My eyes must have told her that I was deadly serious, for she shrank from me a little and took her hand from her throat.

"What are you going to do?" she whispered.

I took my revolver from my pocket and showed it to her. Her eyes opened wide as she looked at the revolver. She seemed to be fascinated at the sight of it.

"An hour ago, Madeleine," I answered quietly, "I had made up my mind to shoot you. I consider that I have every justification. I will not weary you with platitudes concerning the unwritten law and the man's right to take certain personal matters requiring redress and adjustment into his own hands. I have realized however that this trouble that has come to us goes back to a question of loyalties. You would argue, doubtless, were you faced with the question, that you have a duty to Rupert because of what he represents to you."

"I have! I have!" she cried. She was deathly pale now.

"I will admit it then. A man's wife . . . and a man's patriotism . . . they are such tremendous issues as to be outside ordinary laws and conventions. As I say, I have realized it. And because I have realized it I have changed my mind."

"You have changed your mind," she repeated after me in a whisper.

"To this extent. I shall not shoot you in what would have been perilously close to cold blood."

The colour began to ebb slowly back to her face. "What do you mean?" she asked, her voice broken with fear.

"I am going to do what few men in my position would do. Because you are my wife . . . no . . . because you have been my wife, I am going to give you a chance of living. An equal chance with me." I laid the revolver on the little table at the side of the divan. "The revolver is loaded," I proceeded calmly, "and in this drawer is a pack of cards. That is where you are going to get your equal chance." I opened the drawer and took out the playing-cards, leaving the outside case in the drawer. "We will cut the cards," I said, "ace counts low. And as we are each in one another's way the winner of the cut may . . . take and use the revolver. I assure you, Madeleine, that should I be unlucky enough to lose, I shall offer no resistance. The revolver will be yours. When you have executed the necessary sentence of death . . . put the revolver in my dead hands . . . everybody will say that it was an undoubted case of suicide . . . and you can join forces with Rupert. If I win . . . well . . . *you* will have committed suicide in that case."

She stared at me incredulously, but presently the truth sank in and she knew that I meant every word of what I had just said and would most assuredly keep that word. She slowly clenched and unclenched her fists and twice her right hand went upwards to her breast.

"The revolver is between us," I continued. "I will shuffle the cards."

She still stared at me. Her eyes did not leave me all the time that I manipulated the cards. I shuffled the pack once, twice, three times. Then I placed the pack neatly stacked on the little table in front of her. My brain seemed packed in ice, so coolly and methodically did I go about the entire procedure. "Cut," I said curtly.

Her hand went towards the stack of cards waveringly before she withdrew it. "I can't," she said. "I don't agree—it's awful . . . it's nothing more nor less than murder."

"It's not," I answered fiercely; "no more than a duel is. One of us must go. Even you wouldn't deny the truth of that! The chances are equal." I towered over her. "Cut!" I cried again.

As one in a trance, Madeleine cut the cards. She showed the card to me face upwards. "Queen of spades."

"The death card," I muttered; "the dice are loaded against me. I will trust you to make a clean job of it." I cut the pack. "Queen of diamonds. Blondes were always lucky for me . . . except in your own case, Madeleine. Will you cut again, please?"

She obeyed mechanically. "Nine of diamonds." I turned up my second card. "Ten of diamonds. That decides it," I said quietly. "Rupert must mourn as well as I." I stretched out my hand for the revolver and as I did so a feeling of compassion came over me. She had been a tool in Halmar's hands, no doubt, and there were all the years of her life before she had met me. I suppose that my thoughts strayed and enticed me from my guard. For in the next moment I saw Madeleine snatch a revolver from the top part of her dress and aim straight at me. I dropped to the floor, and either she failed to pull the trigger or I beat her shot by a split second. As I fell I caught the legs of the small table. The cards fell on to the carpet and my own revolver clattered to the ground. As I grasped it she bent over me, her finger on the trigger for a second shot. The two weapons spoke almost simultaneously. Her bullet furrowed the back of my hand. Mine must have gone clean through her heart, for she swayed, sagged and fell. As she died there at my side the blood stained her dress a dark crimson.

CHAPTER III
I GO INTO MOURNING

(Dr. Traquair's Narrative—continued)

I STUMBLED to my knees and then picked up the overturned table. After the first shock had subsided a wave of relief came over me. I had killed her as I had known I was going to, but I had done it in self-defence and to feel that was much more satisfactory. And when I thought of everything I had few regrets. My hand was bleeding, the back of it, but for the moment I paid no heed to it. I know that I sat down on the divan and tried to think things out. As I saw them, I should have to cut and run for it. That had been my original intention, if matters had gone along the lines of my first plan. My wife lay there dead and there was a bullet from my revolver in her heart. The only defence that I had, my inherent justification, I could not put forward. It would be too dangerous and would bring to light matters about which I must not speak yet awhile. As I sat and thought, the ideas in my brain racing backwards and forwards perilously, I heard a slight sound which seemed to come from just behind me. I turned towards it and suddenly a torrent of abusive words was hurled at me. They were spoken by Rupert Halmar . . . for it was Rupert Halmar who was standing just by the door of the room.

"So you've killed her, Traquair—eh? Murdered her? I should have known. I should never have left her. Well . . . I promise you, Traquair—you will pay! My God—how you'll pay! How I'll make you pay, I and my . . . the others."

I smiled at him. For I knew that I had a revolver close to my hand . . . and I felt pretty certain that he had none. The best thing that I could do from all points of view was to send him to join his beloved Madeleine. I raised the revolver without saying a word. And at that moment a cold fear clutched at my heart. I remembered that it had been loaded in but one chamber, and that knowledge so paralysed my brain that I gave not a thought to the other weapon with which my wife had attempted to shoot me. There was another thing, though—Halmar wasn't to know what I knew.

"Halmar," I said, "I'm top dog at the moment—and you know it. You dare not send for the Police . . . yet! You know why. There's a lot that you would like to do before that happens. And if I should hang—for one or for both of you—"

He cut in on me in a cold fury. "You'll never hang, Traquair! Don't you worry over a little thing like that. You'll never hang . . . because you'll never leave this house alive! That has already been attended to." He stopped and I cursed the fact that my revolver was empty. Then he began to speak again:

"Before you die, Traquair, you'll wish many times that you had been kept for hanging. *Au 'voir!*" Halmar turned quickly on his heels and disappeared. I put down the revolver and thought hard. He must have a key . . . had obtained it from Madeleine doubtless. For Phoebe the maid had gone out at eight o'clock, as was her habit on this evening of the week, and would not return until half past ten. Where had Halmar gone and what had he meant exactly by his phrase "that has already been attended to"? I paced the room and then I realized that my hand was bleeding. I went to the bathroom, washed the wound carefully, used an antiseptic on it and bandaged it. Then I looked at my watch. Eight minutes to ten. A thought struck me. I walked to the front of the house and looked through the curtains. It was a dark night but there was a street lamp just in front of my premises, on the same side of the road, and there was a second lamp on the other side of the street at a distance of about fifty yards. I stood at the curtains and watched. I soon saw that the suspicion which I had just formed was amply justified. There was a man standing close to each lamp, watching the house. The one nearer to me I fancied I recognized. I had met him once at Rupert's house a year or so before. His name was Muller or something like that. He was a stout burly fellow who looked like what a butcher should look like. The man farther away appeared to be a tall spare man, from what I could see of him from behind my curtains, and I had already seen sufficient to tell me that Halmar's words had not been altogether an idle boast. I thought hard for a moment.

Leaving the light in the room still burning, I went quickly to the back of the house. It must be remembered that my time for necessary action was all too short. At the most liberal estimate a short half-hour. As I have already said, Phoebe was due back at half past ten. I went to the bathroom, which commanded a view of the passage or mews which ran along the back of eight establishments. Mine was the fourth counting from the corner of East Street where it met the High Road. I switched on the light in here. From this window, which was of ordinary glass and net-curtained, you could see a fairish distance to either side of the narrow passageway which I have just described. But now it was dark and the only illumination came from the backs of the houses on the farther side of East Street. I stood at the window for a few minutes and again my fears were vindicated. I saw after a time, when my eyes had grown accustomed to the conditions, dark moving shadows coming from both sides of the mews beyond my back gate, and I knew that Halmar's men were also posted there. Escape that way, for which I had hoped, would be difficult!

I looked at my watch again. It was now five minutes past ten. I had about twenty-five minutes—no more. I came away from the bathroom but was careful to leave the light still burning in there. For my mind had begun to toy with a plan of campaign. I ran quickly downstairs to the surgery and collared the clothes of the poor devil who had come to grief in the morning. Black top hat, black tie, black coat, black suit and trousers, white shirt—all the funereal trappings of the assistant undertaker's. I tried the hat on first, but it was sizes too big. I dashed upstairs again to the bedroom, changed down to my vest into the black apparel and its attachments—luckily the suit and the outside coat weren't too impossible a fit—took my own silk hat from the hat box, replaced the other in the same box and then looked round at my own suit of clothes and shirt, etc., just discarded, and lying in a heap on the bedroom floor.

It would never do to leave them there like that. I took out the papers and everything else that I needed from the various pockets. Then I found some string and brown paper, made a neat parcel of the clothes and deposited the package at the bottom of my wardrobe in the bedroom. Here it would attract no special attention for some time at least. My brown shoes that I had taken off I put on to a spare pair of trees. I was determined to avoid the usual vital mistake that murderers are commonly supposed always to make. Gloves and socks! The socks were simple and I needed black gloves. I had a pair—I used them for funerals. I knew where they were and it was the work of but a moment to get them. What else? Money. My fountain-pen, a knife. The letters and papers from my private drawer in the bedroom. And an electric torch. I saw to all these. I had about twenty-two pounds in the house, I knew, and I took it all. Anything else? The two revolvers. I meant to take them with me for a definite purpose.

I went back to the lounge and got them. That should be all. No—I must have luggage of a kind. It were far better to have it.

The mere possession of luggage avoided awkward questions. So I procured a small suit-case and put into it a razor—not the one I had been recently using—pyjamas, a clean pair which I took from the ironing cupboard, a clean collar and a toothbrush, a pair of horn-rimmed spectacles that I seldom if ever wore, and my make-up box, the relic of the days when I had played for my Hospital Dramatic Society. Again I looked at my watch. I still had something like five minutes. I would leave all the lights burning in the rooms where I had been, except the kitchen. It might make the watchers think that I was still moving about the house. I was ready. I brushed the old silk hat . . . that hat I had worn the day I married Madeleine . . . with my sleeve. "Look at their top hats," I muttered to myself crazily . . . "polished with Guinness."

CHAPTER IV
OUTWIT THE WATCHERS

(Dr. Traquair's Narrative—continued)

PHOEBE might be back any time now, so that I literally hadn't a second to lose. But even then, at that eleventh hour as it were, I resolved to take one more precaution. When she did return, she would come in by the side entrance on the East Street side of the surgery and enter the house by the back door; that is to say the door by which I intended to go out within the next few moments. So I hastily penned a note and left it on the kitchen table, from which position she couldn't miss seeing it. There was nothing unusual about this procedure because Madeleine occasionally left messages concerning domestic matters for her to see in exactly the same way. The message which I wrote ran as follows:

The mistress has gone to bed. She isn't feeling too well. Don't trouble to get anything for supper as I may be rather late.

I didn't sign it, but there was no need, as Phoebe knew my writing well enough and would go to bed herself directly she knew that there were no more duties for her that night. Now for it! I had written the note in the hall, so that I need show no light in the kitchen, as it was through the kitchen that I must pass in order to reach the back door. The kitchen therefore must be in absolute darkness. Gripping my small suitcase, and with the silk hat jammed tightly over my forehead, I opened the back door noiselessly and slipped out. Then I closed the door just as noiselessly behind me. For a moment I stood there on the narrow cement path fervently praying that Phoebe would not come round through the side entrance before I had taken my next step. As far as I could judge, it must be just about the normal time for her returning. There were lights showing from the backs of the places on each side of mine and it was imperative that I should keep out of the patches which they partly illuminated.

I had to move towards my left and at the same time keep away from the middle of the garden because of the men whom I had spotted in the mews at the back. Those men were now but a matter of fifty yards away from me. But I had a plan to outwit them already working in my mind. In the ordinary way, it was pretty quiet out at the back here at this time of night, and the wooden fences which separated the adjoining properties were not unnaturally high. After thinking it over, I assessed them at about five feet. I have already stated that my place was the fourth of the block counting from East Street. This meant that I had three fences and a wall to negotiate . . . the wall that was in East Street itself. As I remembered it, this wall was about nine feet in height.

This was my plan. I was going to keep along the tops of the gardens, thereby avoiding the parts of them that abutted on the mews, and climb the barriers between until I came to the wall that separated me from East Street. My hope was that all Halmar's men posted to watch the back of my house would be *along the mews itself* and none of them actually *in* East Street. So I stealthily crept along to the first fence, the one that separated my place from the next, and took a look at it. It wasn't too bad. I'm an active man—strong and muscular—and had "hooked" for the Hospital in my Rugger days. I put on my black gloves for comfort and convenience and reached, with hands outstretched, for the top of the fence. Then I thought of my suit-case. I couldn't hold it whilst climbing—that was certain—and I dared not throw it over the fence in advance of my own coming, because of the noise that it must make as it struck the ground on the other side.

Suddenly I thought I saw how I could make the trick.

Holding my suit-case tightly between my knees I drew myself up with scarcely a sound until I sat on the top of the fence. It was very dark here, and I listened. Yes . . . I heard a low cough come from one of the watchers in the passageway those uncomfortably few yards off. I now reached down and let the suit-case drop lightly on to the bed of earth below, dropping my body, as lightly as I knew how, after it. Crouching in the dark shadow of this fence in the garden of my next-door neighbour, I drew a deep breath and waited. There wasn't a sound. Truly, I thought, "the dead of night".

Well, so far was so good, and the first obstacle to my escape had been safely negotiated. I stayed absolutely still for a matter of what must have been minutes. All the time not a sound came to break the stillness of the night except the subdued hum from the High Road. Eventually I decided to make my next move, so I cut quickly across the intervening garden space and made for my second fence. But I must have made a noise over the journey, as when I came to it I heard low voices from the passageway. I crouched there in the darkness with my heart in my mouth and the blood throbbing in my temples.

Suddenly I heard a swishing noise in the air and a great clod of earth came hurtling against the fence with a thud loud enough to wake the dead. I heard a voice say "Cats", and simultaneously all the dogs in the neighbourhood bayed the moon in an unharmonious chorus. "This is the genuine lid on it," I thought to myself, but I kept perfectly still and suddenly all was quiet again, as suddenly quiet as it had been suddenly disturbed. When I judged it comparatively safe, I went up fence number two in exactly the same way as I had fence number one. My luck still held. The dogs kept quiet and no more earthy reminders came in my direction. I felt now that I must finish the job as quickly as I possibly could. That is to say, to the point of my original intention. I was no sooner in the next garden, therefore, than I ran rapidly across to the third fence, pulled myself up as I had done twice before with my suit-case held between my knees, and dropped into the last space, which meant that I had now only the wall of this last garden between me and East Street itself. Now I will tell you what my intentions were. I had to climb a nine-foot brick wall skirting a road which a fairish number of people used. A road which, it must be remembered, led out to the High Road. The time now was about a quarter to eleven, and I was resolved to stay in this garden for at least another hour. It was very dark against the wall and the premises were used as a restaurant. They closed about midnight.

Just before they closed I would make my next move on the darkest part of the wall which I could then find. There were numerous boxes and crates lying about in the yard, so I snuggled myself between two of the highest I could find and, on the whole, wasn't too uncomfortable. By this time Phoebe would be well on the way to bed. Certain lights in my establishment would still be burning, and Halmar's posse of men were still waiting for me both at the back of my house and at the front. I calculated that they would wait until at least two o'clock in the morning before they closed in and entered the house. It would be scarcely safe for them to move in that manner before that time.

So here in the yard of Fox's restaurant I lay, looking every now and then at my wrist-watch, and almost praying for a quicker passage of time. Slowly and tantalizingly the hands crept round until a quarter to twelve, and then Providence threw me the ace of trumps. A man wearing an apron came through the back door and marched down the path towards the mews, carrying a garbage bin. I acted quickly. I scrambled up, put on my hat, seized my suit-case, darted through the premises like lightning and found myself in the passage that led to the kitchens. A man came towards me eyeing me askance. "Gents' lavatory?" I said innocently in a hoarse voice. "Have I come wrong?"

"You have, mate," he said uncompromisingly—"back to the tea-room and then down the end on the left."

"I must 'ave missed the door," I replied; "sorry, guv'nor."

"O.K.," he remarked, "I'll show you the way." He led me into the tea-room, pointed vaguely, and then, directly his back was turned, I sank into a chair at a marble-topped table and heaved a sigh of relief.

"Your order, please," said a waitress who appeared in front of me with amazing celerity, "we're closing in a few minutes."

I understood and ordered a coffee. As she disappeared to execute the order, I ventured to look round and take stock of the people who were in the tea-room. Despite the lateness of the hour, there was still a considerable number. I counted over sixty. I was pleased at this. The bigger the crowd on the pavement when the establishment closed, the better for me. I pulled the silk hat well down to the eyebrows and put my hand to my face. In case! I couldn't see everybody's face and I couldn't afford to take any risks. The girl brought me my coffee and scribbled the bill, which she slapped on to the table in front of me. Then I looked across the room again and my heart sank into my boots, for there, almost exactly opposite to me, sat Rupert Halmar!

CHAPTER V
I SET THE PACE

(Dr. Traquair's Narrative—continued)

I THANKED my lucky stars that I had kept my hat on when I had entered the tea-room. Would this, plus my generally sombre trappings, be enough to defeat my adversary? I counted the tables that separated us. There were five of them. Luckily he didn't seem to be looking in my direction, and it was obvious to me as I glanced at him that his thoughts were elsewhere. I had no doubt that directly the restaurant emptied Halmar would join forces with his men and take the reports that they had for him. I decided to wait for closing-time and then make my way out in the wake of the crowd of customers that must stream towards the doorway. Between that time and now, a mere five minutes, salvation would lie for me in the astute use of my coffee-cup. As I was thinking this, Halmar's eyes came right across the space between the tables and fixed themselves upon me. I knew this, rather than actually saw it, and in trepidation raised the cup to my lips and almost buried my face in it.

I knew then that he had not recognized me. For, of course, I was the last person in the world he could have expected to see in there. Then, to my exquisite relief, he glanced at his watch, picked up his bill and sauntered towards the cashier's desk. I was safe—for the time, that is! A few minutes later I was following the crowd to the same pay-desk and out into the friendly street. Its friendliness lay in its size, its bustle, and its suggestion of spaciousness. Again I had my plan worked out. There was a trolley-bus stopping-point at the corner of East Street on the other side of the High Road and I made for this point immediately. Some of the crowd came with me, but there was no sign of Halmar. I knew well enough where he had gone. To the men under the lamp-posts who were keeping the front part of the surgery under observation.

I waited, I suppose, about five minutes before my 'bus came up. The crowd around me grew bigger every moment, but I was undisturbed at this. In fact, it pleased me rather than otherwise, because I was well in the middle of a mass of people and therefore more or less shrouded from other observation. When the 'bus did arrive, the crowd surged forward and I with them. I got on and went to the top deck. There was a vacant seat, right at the back, and I took it. Again I knew where I was going and had a definite plan all ready. When the conductor came upstairs to collect the fares I booked to the docks. Now, the great Commonwealth dock lay right at the south end of the town, and I knew that all round it there were lodging-houses and establishments used by sailors and Lascar firemen where I should experience no difficulty at all in obtaining a room for the night without exciting any curiosity worth mentioning.

The 'bus travelled smoothly and quickly and within twenty minutes I came to my destination. We had stopped outside a garish-looking public-house which I knew of repute, and I descended the staircase with my suit-case gripped tightly in my hand. I walked in the direction that I judged best—that is, towards the docks. Soon I came to a street which I knew must contain dwelling-houses of the kind that I was seeking. I hadn't very far to walk. About a third of the way down the street, which was dark and cheerless, I found a house that exhibited within its front window a notice that read laconically—"Beds". This place would suit my purpose admirably. So I pushed open the gate and walked up to the front door and knocked. A slatternly woman came to the door and betrayed no surprise at seeing me there. I told her what I wanted and she immediately beckoned me into the house.

"Off one of the boats," she said in a tone of voice that asks a question and at the same time knows the answer to it.

"Yes," I said simply.

The woman asked me no more, and there I was in the room that was to

be my bedroom for that night and, as I feverishly hoped, for that night only. It was very dark in the passage of the sordid house and the woman's features were almost indiscernible. I was glad that these conditions existed. For I had two jobs at least to do before I went to bed that night. One was to make use of my make-up box and the second was to consider my best method of getting away from the town. I had calculated that Halmar and his men would close in on my house in the region of two o'clock. They would search the place but they would not find either me or what they sought. I had already seen to that. I did not think that Halmar would go any farther than that at the moment. He would call off his men and leave the rest to natural consequences. Phoebe would find Madeleine's body about seven in the morning, I reckoned. Unless Halmar's activities aroused her before that. But I knew the normal thoroughness of his methods and the precautions that he always took with regard to everything, and I considered this possibility unlikely.

If I were right in these calculations, the Police would be on the spot about half past seven. Soon after that the hunt would be up! The hunt for Stuart Traquair. I smiled to myself. The handcuffs weren't on me yet. My first task was going to be the changing of my appearance. I was not going to attempt too much. That was where most criminals went wrong. Criminals! There was a sting in the word. I "greyed" my hair round the temples with a "white liner", took a pair of "plumpers" from my box to fill out my mouth when I went down in the morning, and prepared from some strands of hair a small short-clipped grey moustache for my top lip—also for use in the morning. Then I undressed, slowly got into bed, and thought things out. I knew that the railway stations and all the ordinary modes of transport would be well watched to-morrow morning—if not before.

How was I going to get away from the town? The possibility of disguise would undoubtedly occur to the Police authorities, and there was no doubt that everybody travelling would be most carefully scrutinized. But I already had, remember, a trick up my sleeve with regard to that. My description would be in the terms of the suit that I had taken off and most carefully stowed away. Still—all the same—I was taking no risks. And as I thought matters over I smiled to myself. For I thought I knew how I could get away from the town! I would present myself at Morleys', the undertakers', as an "extra hand". I would ride right through the ranks of the enemy, and if my appointed destination happened to be the cemetery of St. Clement's—and a hundred to one it would be—once again I should be well on the road to Grantley—and 'buses and coaches run from Grantley to many other places. At one of these places I would go into hiding. I dared not communicate with Armitage yet and I knew that for a time at least I had to play it all through off my own bat. Never mind—sufficient for the night was the evil thereof! I turned out the gas-light; got into bed, turned over twice, and went to sleep. I went to sleep for the reason that I was both mentally and physically exhausted.

CHAPTER VI
I RIDE BEHIND A HEARSE

(*Dr. Traquair's Narrative*—continued)

I WOKE at a quarter to seven. Almost my usual time to the minute. There was hot water outside the door. I shaved, washed, and completed my make-up. Then I took the bandage that I had removed from my hand and burnt it. The wound was going on nicely. Luckily my spirit gum had been well stoppered when last put away and proved quite effective. I fixed the "plumpers" and looked at myself in the dirty little looking-glass that stood on the ramshackle chest of drawers. With what I saw I was more than satisfied. I paid the woman for my night's lodgings and emerged from the front door into the street. The morning air was sharp and very soon I was hungry for my breakfast. There were any number of coffee-houses within the docks area, and selecting one that was comparatively empty I slipped in and ordered a "rasher and two".

The food was quickly brought and quickly eaten, and I noticed that the two men who were already eating a meal in there accepted my appearance as the badge of my unpopular but inevitable trade, and after the first natural glances in my direction evinced no further curiosity with regard to my presence within the establishment. I drank a couple of cups of coffee, paid my bill, and cleared out. The time was now close on nine o'clock. If my calculations of the evening previously were anything like right, the hunt by now was well up. In that case, I decided to get away from the dock surroundings. At any moment now I considered the Police might give it the "once-over". I would walk in the direction of Morleys' and I reckoned that the journey would take me at least an hour.

I walked along, therefore, at an even pace, neither hurrying nor loitering, and I gradually drew away from the docks and came to the heart of the town.

The police-station was almost opposite the Town Hall and marked just about a half-way point of the route that I had to travel. I crossed over to the station side of the road and reflected comfortably that my walk had no striking peculiarities. It couldn't have—for the casual observer. For the reason that I seldom walked anywhere. I almost invariably went by car. As I drew near to the Police headquarters I could tell that the news had reached them. A car drew up outside. Two cars dashed off in the direction of my surgery and three uniformed men came down the steps and hurried off in the same direction. I showed no interest in the proceedings and walked stolidly on my way down the High Road.

It was ten minutes past ten when I reached the premises of Morley & Son—those gentlemen of the final ceremonials. I walked straight into the shop and asked to see "Mr. Morley senior". I had seen him before and he must have actually met me at least once or twice at some mutual conduct of duties, but his eyes betrayed no recognition when we faced each other in these surroundings of coffins and brass plates. He was a stout ruddy-faced man, totally unlike the usual conception of an undertaker.

"Mr. Morley?" I opened on a note of inquiry.

"That's me, chum," he answered. "What can I do for you?"

"I've come from Fred Curtis. He's had an accident—pretty bad, too, and been taken to hospital. You had a job for him this morning, so rather than let you down he's asked me to come along in his place."

"Oh-ah! Fred Curtis, eh? That's bad news. I'm sorry. But let me have a squint at my book." He opened a long narrow book that lay on a sort of counter. He then put on a pair of old-fashioned spectacles, held the book at arm's-length, and peered down the page to which he had turned. "Yes," he remarked at length. "Yes—Fred Curtis. That's right. We've got a job down the High Road here, and I've got him booked for that. At the hairdresser's—Plummer's—by the rail-way bridge. The old lady—Mrs. Plummer's mother. We've got seven jobs to do this morning—trade's fair humming—that's why I had to fix up with Fred Curtis."

Plummer's! I felt by no means too happy about that. The shop was almost opposite my own surgery. No word had come to me with regard to a death there. I think that I must have been too amazed to speak, for I just nodded to him weakly and waited for him to continue. "The funeral's at a quarter to eleven from the 'ouse. Half past eleven at the cemetery."

"Which one?" I asked as nonchalantly as I could.

"St. Clement's," he replied. "I expect you know it if you're used to working round here. Well away on the Grantley road."

Again I nodded. "When do we start?" I queried.

"In about ten minutes from now. The 'cortigy''ll be here in front of the shop in a few minutes. As a matter of fact, I was wonderin' what had happened to Curtis when you stepped in just now. By the way—what's your moniker?"

The question startled me, although I admit that it shouldn't have done. I gave the first name which came into my head. "Er—Miller—Jack Miller."

"Right-o! I'll make a note of it. And the address—in case I should want you again."

I thought of a street in the dock area where I had spent the night.

"Twenty-two Corunna Street," I answered.

"I pay five bob a day," said old Morley, "for extra-hand work. And it's not bad pay either. You don't 'ave to work too hard and it's pleasant and clean, to say nothing of the sacred atmosphere. My men always strive to get that at once, and having got it, to keep it. You might remember that in respect of control of the features. What will you do with your case, Miller, leave it 'ere or shove it under the driver's seat in the front of the 'earse?"

You can bet I chose the latter alternative, and old man Morley nodded his cheery head with signs of satisfaction. "My son, Mr. Leslie Morley, is in charge of your job. Take your orders from 'im and call back 'ere to-morrow. I'll either 'and over your dough then or engage you for another day, providin' Leslie gives me a good report of you. Bring your insurance cards with you. 'Ow long do you think Curtis'll be away?"

"Some time, I should say, Mr. Morley. From what I can hear the poor fellow's pretty bad."

He looked up. "'Ere they are. Leslie'll tell you where to get up. You've a good figure—you'd look well behind the 'earse." I heard the clop of horses' feet outside as he urged me to the door of the shop. His next words, though, made me steel my nerves. "Shouldn't be surprised if you don't run into a spot of bother when you get over the bridge." He dropped his voice. "There's a terrible thing 'appened in the night. Down at Dr. Traquair's. I don't suppose you know him. Murder! It's his missus. I 'aven't 'eard the rights of it yet, but they tell me that she's dead and 'e's gone. Some say that 'e's been done in as well—there's blood in one of the rooms, but I expect the local rag'll be out before long and then we shall know more about it. Garstly—ain't it? Decent bloke he was, too. P'raps I shall execute the order. 'Ope I do. Bit o' publicity does you no 'arm.

"Leslie! Fred Curtis has 'ad an accident. Had to go to 'ospital. This man's taken his place. His name's Miller. Take 'im with you to Plummer's." The younger Morley nodded to me. "I'm ready," he said. "Come with me." He pointed to the hearse itself. I could see that they were all ready to go. I went to the front of the hearse and, as the driver had descended for a moment, pushed my suit-case under his seat. Then I joined Morley junior and stepped up with him to stand on either side at the rear of the hearse. It was an old-fashioned town where I lived, in many ways, and the manner of the old-fashioned funeral died hard.

Thus our procession started on its way to collect the mortal remains of Plummer's wife's mother. As I stood there the thought came to me that she must have been sick of a fever and died. We trotted slowly along up the station bridge approach and down the other side. I stood solemnly upright and for a time looked straight ahead of me. I wasn't desirous of Leslie Morley scrutinizing my features any too closely. The streets were absolutely thronged and I could see many people moving in a mass towards my surgery. Knots of men stood at the corners of streets with much head-nodding and shoulder-shrugging. Women, too, were in full force, many bare-headed and all persistently talkative. Our solemn retinue trotted on its way.

As we came nearer to the surgery there were large groups of people gathered on the pavement. But I stood in my position impassively and continued to fix my gaze straight in front of me. Just opposite to my place I sustained a shock. For there, staring as I imagined straight into my eyes, stood Rupert Halmar again. He seemed to me to hold my eyes with his as our procession passed by him, but it must have been, as I said, pure imagination on my part, because his eyes showed no sign of recognition as the hearse and the carriages swept by him. His eyes were hard and steely . . . they held smouldering rage . . . and because of this I felt a thrill of triumph. I had cried "check" to him and for the moment he and his henchmen were nonplussed. There were uniformed police everywhere here, and a subdued hum of excitement. A hundred yards or so up the road, Morleys' horses halted before a shuttered shop. We had come to Plummer's. I stepped down from the hearse with Leslie Morley. Two black-coated men joined us; the door opened almost magically to Morley's ring, and with the others I stepped into the shop.

Morley made a quiet sign to us and we quickly followed him upstairs to the room that held the coffin. I watched the others closely, and after Morley had effected certain preliminaries with the many wreaths that were there I moved forward again and placed one of my shoulders under the coffin. Thus we came downstairs again and carried our burden to the hearse. The usual curious crowd were now assembled outside. I helped to collect the flowers and to arrange them, my eyes and ears alert for any remark that would put me on my guard. I heard nothing.

I concluded that I must look the part well enough and was passing muster. Leslie Morley assembled the mourners. They took their appropriate places. I walked along at the side of the hearse with young Morley and the cortège started off again for the cemetery dedicated to St. Clement on the Grantley road. As we moved off I heaved a sigh of relief! Every step now took me away from the place of most danger. By the afternoon I should be in Grantley itself whilst the Police would be watching for me round home. I thought of what old man Morley had told me. I was puzzled. Whose blood was it that had been found in one of the other rooms? Were the Fates conspiring to my advantage? Then young Morley motioned to me. The procession stopped. I swung up again at the back of the hearse. Our horses broke into a trot and shook me sharply from my reverie.

Their pace gradually increased and we bowled along until we came to the hill at the summit of which stood St. Clement's cemetery. Here the horses slowed down again to the conventional walk and the tolling bell greeted us as our mournful procession passed through the big gates of the cemetery. I kept my eyes glued on the other men. What they did I did, and we had the coffin on its trestles in the little church without the slightest hitch or hindrance. I took my place with the others at the back of the church until the service was over, and then carried the coffin back to the hearse for the committal. The grave, evidently, was a long distance away. St. Clement's is a big cemetery and the distance to the grave too far for the men to carry the coffin. We came to the path nearest to the grave. Again I put a shoulder under the coffin and we carried it to the mound of new earth, where the yawning hole waited for its burden. As I reached it—I was walking at the rear—I ran into another shock. For there, standing at the side of the grave in the company of mourners, was Capworth the draper, to whom belonged the shop next to my surgery. But my head was tucked well down at the side of the coffin and he betrayed not the slightest interest in me.

I was determined now, however, to get away from all this at the first opportunity. I helped the grave-diggers with the ropes as we suspended the coffin over the grave and then helped to lower it to the depths. We pulled the ropes away and the crowd of mourners surged round the clergyman for the last offices. I heard the earth rattle on the coffin and at that moment I began to stroll away. After retrieving my suit-case from the driver's seat of the hearse I made for the west gate of the cemetery, which was right on the opposite corner to the gate by which we had entered. A quick detour from here would put me on the main Grantley road, and that was my clear objective, for 'buses run along it, and to hail one near the cemetery would be all in the order of things. Clad as I was, I walked quickly down path after path until I came to the west gate. This gate wasn't used very much—almost exclusively for exits in respect of funerals returning to Grantley—and as I passed through it there wasn't a soul in sight. I cut across the road and within five minutes had made the main Grantley road.

To my intense satisfaction, a 'bus was coming in my direction. I waited for it to come up, with the feeling that things were going well for me. I hailed it. It stopped. I swung myself aboard. The conductor paid me no special attention as he collected my fare. Within half an hour I got off in the market square of Grantley.

CHAPTER VII

I REMEMBER HELEN TREVOR

(Dr. Traquair's Narrative—continued)

IT WAS my intention to leave Grantley at the first convenient moment. For one thing it was too near to my home town for me to feel absolutely comfortable there. But it was a well-known marketing centre for the surrounding district, and, as I have previously stated, coaches and 'buses ran from it, not only to outlying villages but also to good-sized towns, and it was to one of these latter that I meant to make my way. So I stood there in the market square, where I had alighted from the 'bus that had brought me, and scanned the destination indicators of the many vehicles that were parked in the square, preparatory to departure. Suddenly the name on one of them caught my eye and my heart gave a quick leap, because

I remembered something. The name on the long raking coach at which I looked was "Lifford", and it was this name which caused me to remember the "something" to which I have just alluded. For at Lifford there resided the girl whom I had known years ago as Helen Trevor.

I will explain what this memory of Helen Trevor meant to me. About eight years previously, before I had taken my present practice, I had secured an appointment as Lecturer on medical science at one of the London institutes, and during that time Helen Trevor had been one of my keenest and most intelligent students. I suppose that a man generally knows when a girl is in love with him. It was so in this case. Helen Trevor had a wistful charm, and seemed to sit at my feet with regard to most things.

After a time, during which, I must confess, I had been oblivious with regard to this fact, my leg began to be pulled about "my charming conquest". This good-natured banter drew my attention to the girl and I soon realized that I had in her a most loyal and faithful adherent. I felt in my bones that at one sign or overture from me this loyalty would give way to an even deeper feeling. In fact, I was dismissing the students one night after my lecture, when Helen was left behind and for a few seconds we were alone together in the lecture hall. Her eyes shone like stars as she looked at me, and suddenly she said, to my surprise and embarrassment:

"If I ever marry and have a son I've chosen his name already. I shall call him 'Stuart'."

I never gave that sign to her, however, and eventually I lost sight of her. My course of lectures finished, the students dispersed, and I qualified and married Madeleine. Thus the position had remained until about a year ago. One morning I had received a letter that bore the Lifford postmark. I had opened it in some surprise, wondering who my correspondent could be. It was from Helen Trevor, or, as she now was, Helen Eversley. She had married a licensed victualler, so she wrote, and they had taken an hotel at Lifford. She thought "that I would not have forgotten *her* because *she* would never be able to forget *me*". And I had read between the lines of that letter, before putting it away in my drawer, and the thought had come to me, had come to me intensively, that the banter which had been directed against me concerning Helen might have been based upon a much more solid foundation than I had anticipated.

Anyhow, I have explained enough to show why the destination of "Lifford" on the motor-coach in the market square of Grantley interested me so tremendously. I wondered next what time the coach would start, as I had no desire to hang about where I was for a long spell. I didn't want to inquire as to the time of starting, so I scouted round for a time-table. I guessed there would be one posted up close at hand, and I guessed right. About three shops up the road, from the point where the coaches were standing, stood the post office, and on the wall, just at the side of it, I found a time-table enclosed within a glass case. I found the Grantley-Lifford section and saw that the time between the towns was 144 minutes according to the schedule and that a coach was due to start from the market square at Grantley in a matter of eight minutes. So I walked straight back to the waiting vehicle and slipped quietly and unobtrusively into a seat right at the back. The coach was about half full when I entered, but by the time it started there were only about three seats available. I booked to Lifford and tendered six shillings to the conductor. I had seen that this was the amount of the single fare from the glance which I had taken at the time-table outside the post-office. He was a surly-looking customer, this conductor, who, from the expression on his face as he took my money, seemed to have a grudge against the world in general and against me in particular.

In a short time we had left the town behind us and were running through open country. I saw the name of a little village through which we passed—Craze—and as I saw it, for the first time since I had looked at Madeleine lying dead on the floor just in front of me, something like a condition of tranquillity came to me. For a couple of hours, at least, I thought that I could safely count upon being unmolested. I considered that I had broken through the cordon that Halmar had thrown round me on the night previously, and that I had got away, too, before the ring which the Police would use could be made anything like effective. With that temporarily comforting thought in my mind, I put my head back into the upholstery of the seat and went to sleep, secure in the knowledge that Lifford was the destination of the coach as it was also mine. I must have slept, I suppose, for about an hour and a half, for when I awakened I looked at my watch and I saw that according to the information on the time-table we were within a short twenty minutes of reaching Lifford.

My mind was now made up as to what my next step was going to be. I would endeavour to find Helen Eversley as soon as I reached Lifford, in the hope that in someway I might be able to find at least a temporary salvation. The next twenty minutes passed seemingly quickly and we ran into Lifford swiftly and smoothly, to pull up in front of an honest-looking hostelry which bore the name of "The Unicorn". I got out with little fuss, collared hold of my suit-case and looked at the name of the licensee on the front door' of "The Unicorn". It was not the name which I was seeking, but "Robin Grade". Then I realized something which I should have thought before. That the pubs wouldn't be open for another hour and a half yet and that during that time I must either walk about aimlessly in Lifford or find something there with which to amuse myself. I smiled ruefully to myself as the thought sank home.

Then I thought of something else and immediately felt a little better. There was certainly one important task that I could set myself and one which, conceivably, might take up a great deal of the time which it was necessary for me to cut to waste. I had to find out where Helen lived! It might take me five minutes. On the other hand, it might take me an hour—but whichever would eventually prove to be the case it was a job that I must tackle as soon as I could. So I picked up my suit-case again and marched off up the High Street of Lifford looking for the name of Eversley. It was at that moment that I saw the newspaper boy. To be strictly correct I heard him some little time before I saw him. He was shouting "Horrible murder at Brooke. 'Tragidy' in doctor's surgery", and many people were stopping him to buy copies of his papers. In front of him he showed a yellow placard with the words printed in black:

BROOKE MURDER. FULL DETAILS

I waited for him to reach me and, like the others who surged round me, purchased a paper. I put my suit-case down on the pavement so that I could read the first published account of what had happened in the drama of the previous night in which I had played the leading part. This is what I read:

Early this morning the Police were called to the surgery of Dr. Stuart Traquair, in High Road, Brooke. The information was given by Phoebe Hubbard, a maid in the doctor's employ. As a result of this information it was discovered that Mrs. Traquair had been murdered in the night, having been shot through the heart. Dr. Traquair is missing, and the Police fear that he may also be dead. Early and sensational developments may be expected and a description of the missing man is being prepared by the authorities for early circulation. For further details see our later editions.

I folded the paper and tucked it under my arm. So far so good again. The start that I had obtained, and upon which I had calculated I should gain, was still standing me in good stead. So I picked up my suit-case from the pavement where I had placed it and started off again to look for the name of Eversley. It took me about half an hour to find it. Fortunately I stumbled across it in a turning off the High Street called Chandos Street. A prosperous-looking public-house, under the sign of the "Nell Gwynne", also showed upon its doors the name of the licensee . . . "Donald Eversley". But it looked so obviously and emphatically closed for the afternoon that I hesitated about applying there and then. Far better, I thought, to wait until the time came for opening and slip in as a customer. Once in, in that way I could inquire as to the whereabouts of Helen, or, better still, if the coast seemed moderately clear, ask if . . .

My thoughts were suddenly cut off at the main, as it were, for as I stood on the opposite side of the street, weighing matters up, the private door of the "Nell Gwynne" opened and out came the girl whom I had once known as Helen Trevor.

CHAPTER VIII
I FIND SANCTUARY

(Dr. Traquair's Narrative—continued)

TO MY eye she had changed but little, if anything at all. She had pale gold hair, and eyes so blue a shade that I had always called her (to myself in contemplation) a "wraith of the moon". She was slim too, of medium height and with the most charming voice, I think, that I have ever heard. When I had been lecturing, as I have so recently described, it had been no uncommon thing for me to refer to her, if I called upon her for any answering, as "Miss Trevor, the silver-tongued".

She crossed the street and came towards me. Passed me by and then turned down another side street. I resolved to follow her at a discreet distance. I waited until I considered that she was far enough away from me. Then I took the turning that she had taken. No sooner had I done so than I saw a notice on the wall at the corner of the street which pleased me. "To the River and Holme Park". One of these, doubtless, was her destination. And if she were on her way to the park it might well be that I should get an opportunity of speaking to her under extremely favourable conditions.

Straightway she went, with me in her wake, and within five minutes I could see the waters of the Liffe and the railings of the park just beyond. Helen tripped quickly up steps and across a rustic bridge to disappear within Holme Park. I quickened my pace and made up some of the leeway. I did not want to lose sight of her altogether when she was inside the park. My luck still held, for I had scarcely passed between the gates when I saw her seated facing a bed of most beautiful flowers. I walked slowly up to her. Then I thought of my unusual appearance. Would her quick eye and alert intelligence penetrate my disguise? I took off the horn-rimmed spectacles as I came alongside her. I then removed my atrocious hat.

"Don't be alarmed . . . I want to speak to you." That was all I could think of to say to her. The violet eyes looked startled for a second before they regarded me with a strange curiosity in which there were the signs of dawning understanding.

"Your voice," she said softly. "It's your voice . . . and yet it can't be."

"Miss Trevor," I said . . . "I must call you that first of all—don't be surprised and don't let me disturb you at all . . . but I'm Stuart Traquair."

She put a hand to her lips. "Yes, yes . . . yes . . . but why? I don't understand."

"May I sit down a moment?"

"Of course. But tell me please—"

I put the newspaper quickly in her hand. "Please read that. Then you will understand . . . part of the story . . . at least." I sat down at her side and showed her the paragraph. A look of horror came into her face as she read it. "Let me explain to you," I said quietly.

She shook her head. "Don't, I would rather not know anything. All that I want to know—that I need know—I already know. That you are no murderer by design or intent. As anybody would know who really knows you." She handed the newspaper back to me and I could see that she was thinking hard. "Tell me, Doctor Traquair . . . are you here in Lifford by chance . . . or accident—or have you come deliberately?"

"I chose the place, Helen, because I knew that you were here and hoped that I might find you."

She blushed at my use of her Christian name. "You want help, of course?"

I told her of what I had done since I left the surgery but I made no mention of either Madeleine or Halmar.

"I should never have known you," she said simply, "from your appearance. But I knew your voice directly you spoke to me." She smiled. "I should do! Considering the times I've listened to it and thought it the—" She broke off suddenly. "Fancy you remembering that I lived down here. It's ages since I sent you that silly letter. Still, I'm glad. Because it means that I have the chance to help you. If I hadn't sent it you wouldn't have known where to find me." She folded her hands in her lap and turned towards me with her eyes shining.

"You are pleased at that—really pleased?"

"I should just think I am."

"That's lovely of you," I replied.

"Tell me," she said, "what have you done to yourself to make you look so different?"

I explained to her the steps that I had taken in the matter of my disguise and she nodded various times in sympathy. When I had finished, I became severely practical again. "You are sure that you *can* help me, Helen?"

"I *must*."

"But can you? It's not a question of helping me with money," I went on awkwardly. "I have plenty of spare cash with me. The help must come in another way."

She looked at me steadily. "In what way do you mean?"

"Could you hide me anywhere? Find me a place where I could get a hide-up? Is it possible?"

She didn't answer me, but sat there staring in front of her. "What about Eversley?" I asked her—"your husband? He'll have to be considered."

Her face hardened. "My husband," she said a trifle bitterly. "Yes, you're right, he always has to be considered." I wondered what she meant exactly, but didn't press her for details. The park was almost deserted at this time of the afternoon and as I looked round she must have sensed my thoughts. "It's beautifully quiet, isn't it? That's why I come here. I come here nearly every afternoon. It helps me to—" Again she broke off. I sat there in silence.

"I'm thinking," she said. "I must think. What is the best plan that I can adopt?"

A thought occurred to me. After all, it might have a bearing upon whatever we decided. "I have never heard," I said—"have you any children?"

"No," she answered almost fiercely, and the word had scarcely left her lips when she crimsoned and turned her head away from me.

"I am glad," I said; "that will make it easier."

"Not so glad as I am." The words were almost whispered, but I heard them plainly. She clasped and unclasped her hands on her lap.

"Tell me about Eversley," I said.

She shook her head. "I would rather not. You may meet him yourself . . . then you will be able to judge."

"He treats you well?" I asked diffidently.

"Treats me well?" she replied—"he worships the ground I tread on."

I refrained from making further comment because, suddenly, I seemed to see the solution in a new light. "Look here, Helen," I said impulsively, "don't trouble about me any more. I'll clear out and take my chance over everything. It is not sporting of me to inflict my dirt on you. It's rotten of me. I should have thought before I came. But before I go—let me thank—"

I half rose. She put her fingers on my arm and urged me down again. "Don't," she said. "There is no need. Of course I am going to help you. At the moment, if you want to know, I'm thanking God for the chance. And—what is more—I think that I've found a way." Her dark-blue eyes were dancing now with eager enthusiasm and I wondered what idea had come to her. "It all depends on one thing," she said, "and I think that that one thing is all right. What is the exact time?"

I looked at my watch and told her. She nodded as though satisfied. "Yes, I think that I shall be able to manage it. Dr. Traquair, can you play billiards? And snooker?"

I looked at her in some amazement. "Of course I can."

"Well? Play well, I mean?"

"Depends on what sort of standard you set, Helen. I suppose I'm a good deal above the average. But you see in billiards that isn't saying very much. There's such an enormous gulf between the pro. and the decent amateur."

"What break can you make? Tell me—because it's very important."

I considered the question. "I can do a fifty now and then. Fairly regularly. I might even do better than that if I got more practice. But that's the usual rotten billiard-player's cry."

"Fifty." She nodded her head again as she spoke. Quickly this time. "Now tell me something else. Snooker! What's your form at snooker?"

"Much of a muchness with my billiards, I should say. Pretty decent. But why this catechism?"

"Listen," she said.

"I am listening."

"Donald, my husband, is in town. He will be back this evening—about seven o'clock. When we open—that will be at six o'clock—come into the saloon and ask for me. You are the new marker. We have a vacancy for one. It came to me as a brain-wave just now. Our marker left at the end of last week. Now listen again. You first called this morning. I examined your references—don't forget that bit. It matters a lot. I engaged you and told you to come back when we opened in the evening. Have you got all that?"

"Where do I sleep?"

"At the house. All the staff sleep in. That's one of the facts that makes it such a splendid idea."

"Clothes. I can hardly—" I looked down at my clothes ruefully.

She regarded them intently. "As a matter of fact, they're not too bad. They'll do for to-night at least. When you start work, take your jacket off and roll your shirt-sleeves up." Two brown dogs came up and sniffed at us in friendliness.

I patted the larger on the head. Helen rose from the seat. "I'm going now, Doctor. Now that we've arranged this, we mustn't be seen together. Stay here until about a quarter to six and then come straight to the 'Nell Gwynne' and do as we've said. We'll win through yet."

She held out her hand to me. My gratitude to her showed in my eyes, I know, for she dropped hers from mine and blushed deliciously. Then I remembered something. Something which up to now both she and I had forgotten. "Just a moment, Helen," I said to her, "before you go. What's my name? We'd better settle that before we part company now."

She crinkled her nose at me and I saw her then, for the first time that afternoon, as I had seen her years before in my company of students. "Have you any special fancies?" she asked me.

I shook my head. Then I thought of the name of the man whose place I had taken on the staff of Morleys'—the man who had lain injured on the couch in my surgery. "I'll be Curtis," I said to Helen Eversley. "Call me Curtis. Say that I'm from Canterbury. That's a cathedral city for which I have a warm corner in my heart."

She repeated the name after me. "Good! Now the rest is up to you."

"No," I replied, "up to us."

She blushed again. "All right. I like the sound of it better when you put it like that. See you soon after sue o'clock. *Au 'voir.*" She turned in a flash and flitted across the grass. I stood there and watched her. The hunt might be up, but I still had my start of the hounds . . . and they wouldn't take me without a struggle!

CHAPTER IX
I TAKE MY CUE

(*Dr. Traquair's Narrative*—continued)

AT A few minutes past six I marched into the "Nell Gwynne" and asked for the "Missus". There was a snack-bar at the end of the counter nearest to the door marked "saloon" and the white-capped chef looked at me with a cunning mixture of indifference and supreme contempt. "What's your business?"

"I'll tell her," I said, "so there's no need to trouble you with it."

His nose lengthened. He turned to an auburn-haired girl who stood a short distance away from him lazily wiping a glass. "Rose! 'Ere's a chap wants the missus. Tell 'er, will you, Rose? Then I can wash my 'ands of the 'ole affair."

Rose tossed her head, either at the remark or at me, and rather sulkily set off on her quest for Helen. I put down my suit-case and lolled up against the bar in what I regarded would be the authentic manner. The place was almost empty—just two or three people in odd corners. Then I heard the sound of approaching voices and Helen's was one of them. I saw her coming towards the counter where I was standing. I raised my hat deferentially. I flatter myself that I did it well. "Good evening, ma'am. I'm reporting for duty as per instructions." I've always noticed that people of the kind I was representing myself to be invariably say "as per". Helen looked at me sternly.

"Oh—is that you, Curtis? Come this way with me, will you?" The barmaid who had been addressed as Rose opened a flap in the counter for her. She came through and beckoned to me to follow her. I adopted an air of humility and did so . . . at what I imagined was a commendably proper distance, with my case in my hand. I followed Helen up a broad staircase, at the same time watching her closely for any sign that she might think fit to make me. At the head of the staircase was a door that showed a notice—"Billiard Room".

"We have three full-size tables, Curtis," she said rather loudly as she opened the door and went into the room.

"Yes, ma'am," I said dutifully. To my relief, I saw upon my own entrance that the billiard-room was unoccupied. Helen dropped the mask for a moment. "I wasn't sure if there was anybody about . . . and we must be careful."

"Of course," I answered. "I understand."

"Everybody's talking about the murder. At least, that's how they describe it. I'm listening best part of the time and saying little myself. I'll keep you posted. For heaven's sake be careful, Doctor. You will, won't you, for all our sakes!"

I nodded. She went on hastily: "Donald—my husband—will come up to you almost as soon as he comes in. I'll try to give you warning of his coming if I possibly can. Be on your guard. He's—" She paused rather abruptly.

"Yes?" I queried. "He's what?"

"Well, just a little overbearing at times. Now I'll leave you. There'll be people coming up soon, I expect. Both tables will be going before long . . . at any rate, they are usually. Pick a cue from the stand there and knock the balls about a bit and get the pace of the table. Otherwise you'll be losing too much money. Now I must see about your sleeping arrangements. Let me take your suit-case. It's lucky there are no initials on it." She gave me the flash of a smile which reminded me of the old days and was gone through the door before I had realized that she was leaving me. Well—her advice was pretty sound, so I dropped my jacket, turned up my shirt-sleeves and selected a nice shortish cue, put the balls on the middle table and practised a few of the strokes that in the ordinary course of events I could manage best. After that I took a hand with a set of snooker balls, and was feeling quite satisfied, considering everything, when a couple of young fellows came in for a hundred up. I got them going and I must admit that I was surprised at the high standard of skill which each showed. Gradually the room filled up and all the tables were in play. I waited, fetched trays of drinks, took orders for snacks and sandwiches and generally went through a pretty strenuous time. This pleased me, because it took my mind off the contemplation of other things. I was standing at the snack-bar waiting for a "Welsh Rarebit" to be prepared when I heard Helen's voice calling to me.

"Curtis. Just a minute." I went along the bar to where she was standing. "The Guv'nor wants to see you. He'll be coming upstairs in about five minutes. You understand?"

"Very good, ma'am," I replied. She dismissed me with a quick nod of the head, so I picked up my order and went up the staircase again to the billiard-room, bracing myself for the ordeal that I now knew was at hand. Billiards and snooker were now in full swing. I began to dodge about again when the door opened and I knew that the man who entered was Donald Eversley. He was a powerfully built man of middle height with jet-black hair, a fleshy nose and a bull neck. "Hyperpiesis," I thought, the moment I set eyes on him. He was well dressed and carried himself well, but there was a definite suggestion of arrogance in his manner, and I felt instinctively that he and I weren't going to like each other overmuch. He came straight over to me and looked me up and down rather discourteously. "My wife tells me that she's given you the job of marker here."

"Yes, sir," I answered, very much against the grain, let it be said.

"You don't look much as far as I can see," he added, "but I suppose that she's engaged you and there the matter must stand for the present."

"I hope that I shall be able to give you satisfaction, sir," I contributed.

"I'll be the judge of that. And I don't put up with any sort of thing, I can tell you. Or any back-chat. You may as well be told that at the beginning of your service here as at the end. Let's see, what's your name?"

"Curtis, sir. Fred Curtis."

"H'm . . ." he said. "Wish I'd been here when you walked in. What brought you along?"

Here was danger for me at once. I hesitated on the answer, but knew that I must take a chance. "I saw your advertisement, Mr. Eversley."

"Where?"

"In the paper, sir."

"What paper?" His dark eyes stared out more relentlessly. I knew that any attempt on my part to evade the issue would be certain to bring disaster on my head.

I thought for a moment and then took my second chance. "In the *Morning Advertiser*, sir."

Directly I had answered I knew that I had brought it off. He nodded. "I see. Well, we'll see how you go. How old are you?"

"Forty-three, sir," I answered mendaciously. "In June, my birthday, June the second—"

"I don't care when your damned birthday is," was his last remark as he turned on his heel and left me. I went back to the tables . . . marvelling! So this was the husband of the Helen to whom I had lectured on medicine but a few years before! The ways of men and women are indeed strange.

On one of my journeys down to the saloon I had learned from Rose, the barmaid whom I had previously seen down there, that closing-hour was half past ten, and from the moment of Eversley's departure time passed for me on leaden wings. When the time for packing up did eventually arrive I was profoundly grateful and inexpressibly relieved. I started to put the cues in the racks and the various appointments away in their respective places before covering up the tables. On the point of finishing off the job for the night I saw a head poked round the corner of the door and heard a voice say: "Hi, mate, you'll find a bit o' supper laid for you in the staff-room. That's down at the end of the landing." I signified my understanding of the message and thanked the giver of it suitably.

Two or three minutes later I drifted along to the staff-room, as I had been directed, and found three of the male staff already in there. I soon learned that two were waiters attached to the lounge and the other the "crate and bottle" hand. It was his job every day to collect the empty bottles, according to their capsules, and stack them in the proper crates, for return to the various brewers, etc., who had supplied them. He was addressed as "Bernard". The other two were "Alf" and "Bert" respectively. The latter soon informed me that Bernard was "fair daft", but I never learned the justification of this piece of trenchant criticism.

Supper consisted of a plate of cold beef and pickles. I was hungry. I had tasted nothing since breakfast that morning, and I did ample justice to the fare that had been provided. Since breakfast that morning! About fifteen hours! To me it seemed much more like fifteen days. Suddenly, to my dismay, the conversation of my three companions switched on to the murder. To my utter amazement, I heard the man whom I had come to know as "Bert" say, "I knew that carmine doctor! Knew the unspeakable well! And I'll tell you fellows something—I always thought there was something peculiar about him! I'm not trying to be a wise guy after the event—it's the truth I'm telling you, and that's an unmentionable fact!" Now, I had not seen Bert before at any time in my life! Of that I was as certain as I was of my own name, so I waited rather interestedly to hear what was coming. I reckoned that Bert belonged to that extraordinary class of people who have always "known" a notoriety, and who weave highly coloured pictures, all purely imaginative, covering their association with such. Alf invited further particulars of so fascinating a subject, and Bert, encouraged at the outset, proceeded to make hay while the sun shone.

"I'll tell you," proceeded Bert, "how I first come into contact with this 'ere Trakware." I noticed the pronunciation that he gave to my name. It only confirmed what I knew—that I had never seen him before. "My people," announced Bert, "used to live near this 'ere doctor chap, and one summer the old man had a carbuncle come on his neck."

"There's worse places than that," murmured Alf, in a tone doubtless intended to be sympathetic, "still—go on."

"Well, Dr. Trakware was called in to him and one day I 'appened to be at the old people's place when he arrived. He wouldn't lance the carbuncle. Was all for 'ot water fomentations. I argued it out with 'im and put 'im in his place a bit. Very ''otsy-totsy', I can tell you. Blimey—the old man was bad for weeks with it! In the end, of course, they got it away . . . 'oo wouldn't 'ave done? Little Bertie

Higgins, 'im they called the 'twopenny doctor', come and squeezed it. Struth, you should ha' seen the core!"

Bernard gazed at him open-mouthed. "Big?" he muttered with a note of incredulity.

"Big!" repeated the imaginative Bert, scornfully contemptuous. "Take it from me, Bernard, my son, 'big' ain't the word."

"What would be the word?" quavered Bernard.

"Enormous," retaliated Bert on a note of complete stupefaction. "You'd 'ave to see it to believe it. The core was the size of an 'Oxford'. Without the word of a lie, I never see a core like it either before or since and I don't know as 'ow I wants to. When little Bertie busted it with 'is own special grip it was on a Whit Sunday afternoon. I remember it well, it fair turned me up for the rest of the day . . . and I don't wonder."

"All right," said Bernard uneasily, "don't forget I'm trying to eat my supper . . . and it's mustard pickles too. I 'aven't got the strong stomach you seem to 'ave. That's the worst of you, Bert, when you tell a yarn you always give too many details, and it's not everybody what can stand them."

I looked across at Bernard and I saw that the man was looking unmistakably queasy. But Bert had had his narrative triumph and he glanced towards me to see, I think, the effect that his story had produced as far as I was concerned. I smiled to him cordially. "Don't mind him," I remarked jocularly, indicating Bernard with a jerk of my head, "he can't take it. But fancy you knowing that there doctor." I inserted a tinge of admiration in my voice, which Bert accepted with obvious relish.

"I knew him all right and I'll tell you now what I said to the old pot and pan when he was convalescent." Bert pointed the prongs of his fork at me, almost belligerently. "About Trakware I mean! I said, 'Whenever I look at your medical adviser, Dad' (I can describe a man, you know, when I get the chance, in just the correct terms— and that's what I called 'im) 'I always think of Crippen and Buck Ruxton.' That's what I said. I can remember it as though it was yesterday."

"Good for you," I said to him, chiefly, I think, for the lack of anything else to say. "Your words have come true if what you say is right."

Bert looked at me with a sort of scornful truculence. "What d'yer mean? 'If what I say is right'. You've seen the papers, 'aven't you?"

"Well, as a matter of fact, chum, I've not. All that I've heard so far has been people talking."

Bert stopped in the act of conveying his knife to his mouth and delivered himself of his opinion. "You've got a proper Oxford accent, and no mistake. 'I say, you cads'—and all that. Where'd yer pick it up?"

I shook my head in an attempt to suggest a touch of personal shame and contrition. "I've come down in the world, Bert. I'm ashamed to say it, but I can't deny it. The old dad gave me a good education, went without himself so as to afford the cash for it, but I was a young fool and squandered the chances he gave me. I didn't realize what I was doing . . . playing the giddy ox like I did, and when I woke up and pulled myself together it was too late." I shook my head again sorrowfully. "He told me I'd live to regret my folly and his words have come true. Many's the time that's come home to me."

"Why, did yer go off 'the straight and narrer'?"

I conveyed the affirmative by a suggestive nod.

"Did they give yer 'stir' for it?"

Again I nodded.

"Blimey," said Bert almost in admiration. "'Ow long ago was this?"

"Oh, a long time," I answered curtly; "don't remind me of it. I try to think that it's all past and forgotten."

"I wouldn't rub it in, cocky, don't you think that. And you ain't on your ticket now. Nor would Alf here, would you, Alf, mate?"

"'Course not," said Alf stoutly. "The man what never made a mistake never made nothink. That's what I always say."

I secretly hoped that this statement was too sweeping. "And what Bert and Alf says goes for me," said Bernard. "I ain't one to kick a bloke when he's down."

"Thank you," I returned, "one and all. That's very sporting of you." I finished up my plate of grub. Bert looked across at me.

"Just a word of advice . . . Fred . . . ain't it?"

I nodded.

"Only too pleased to take it, Bert. You've been here longer than I have. What is it?"

"Keep it dark from the Guv'nor. He ain't everybody's money, believe me, and 'e mightn't be too pleased—you never know. Mum's the word with me and with Alf and Bernard, so let it be the same with yourself. That's the word of advice that I'm giving to you. No offence, I hope."

I smiled at him reassuringly. "That's all right, Bert. No offence, of course. I appreciate your good intentions and I'll keep my own counsel as you've advised me." I pushed back my plate and rose from the table. "Where do I sleep? Could you direct me? I've had a long day to-day and I'm a bit tired."

Bert shook his head. "Couldn't say, Fred. Alf and I are together in the double room, but Bernard's alone. Maybe they'll shove you in the spare bedroom. That's next to Bernard's. Didn't the Guv'nor tell you nothing?"

"He didn't mention my sleeping arrangements. He probably wasn't as interested in them as I am." I heard a step behind me and turned to see who it was that approached.

"Here's Rose," said Bernard; "maybe she's come to tell you."

He was right in his surmise, for Rose came straight up to me and spoke at once. "The mistress says will you please sleep in the spare bedroom. That's the room next to Bernard's. I'll take you along and show you the room if you'll come now." She tossed a tawny head at me.

"Thank you," I said simply, and I think that the reply surprised her, for her manner changed as she led the way to the bedroom that was to be mine.

"Here you are," she said. "Good night, Fred."

"Good night, Rose," I returned. "Thank you."

It was a pleasant room and looked comfortable enough. I undressed quickly and got into bed. One day had passed since I had slept near the docks. One day . . . and with that thought dominant in my mind I fell asleep.

CHAPTER X
I Face Danger

(Dr. Traquair's narrative—continued)

I saw nothing of Helen all the next day. Eversley sought me out during the morning. I was helping to clean out the various bars when he came up to me."

"Oh, Curtis," he said with his customary peremptoriness. "You're free in the afternoons from 2.30 until 5.30. You can stay in or go out just as you please. And you get one half-day each week. I'll let you know later which day you can take yours. Oh—and pay day is Monday. *Midday* Monday. You understand?"

"Yes, sir," I replied. "Thank you, sir."

When we closed for the afternoon I waited to see if any sign were forthcoming from Helen, but none came. So I decided to go out. I felt pretty safe and I wanted to get hold of certain vital information. There was always the park where I could go, for my previous experience of it, when I had been there with Helen Eversley, had taught me that it was an easy matter to obtain certain privacies in there. At 2.30, therefore, I went out, straight into the High Street, and bought the latest newspaper that I could find available. I pushed the paper into my pocket and at once made my way to the park by the same route that I had travelled before. I walked to the same seat, half hoping that Helen would be there already in advance of me. But I was to be disappointed, as the seat was unoccupied. I sat down and opened the paper, searching eagerly for the item of news that I wanted to see. It was on the front page below heavy, sensational headlines.

DOCTOR'S WIFE MURDERED. HUSBAND MISSING.
SERVANT MAID'S DRAMATIC DISCLOSURES.

I proceeded to read the report proper.

Following upon the report which appeared in our earlier Editions, we are now able to give our readers a more detailed account of the tragedy that came to the home of Dr. and Mrs. Traquair some

time between the evening of the day before yesterday and yesterday morning. It will be remembered that the Police were called
to Dr. Traquair's surgery in High Road, Brooke, by a maid of the
name of Phoebe Hubbard, who telephoned to them early yesterday morning. When the Police arrived at the surgery in answer to
her summons the dead body of Mrs. Traquair was discovered lying
full-length on the floor of the lounge, shot through the heart. Dr.
Stuart Traquair himself was missing, and at the moment the Police
have been unable to determine satisfactorily when and where the
doctor was last seen. Inquiries in this direction are pending and
results are anticipated almost immediately. It is, however, from
the statement made by Phoebe Hubbard that the case assumes its
most sensational aspects.

The girl states that when she returned to the home of the
Traquairs on the evening before last, about twenty-five minutes to
eleven, she was surprised to discover that a note had been left for
her by Dr. Traquair himself. The note stated, she says, that Mrs.
Traquair had gone to bed and that Dr. Traquair himself would not
be in until later. She obeyed the instructions that the note contained
concerning her own movements and went to bed shortly after finding it. She has been questioned on the point and is certain that this
note was written by Dr. Traquair. She did not hear the doctor return
to the house and was very soon asleep. But, and here the girl's story
takes a most sensational turn, she declares that she was awakened
in the early hours of the morning by hearing strange voices coming
from various parts of the house. She was very frightened, she says,
and did not leave her bed for some considerable time.

When she eventually did pluck up sufficient courage to do so
she heard more noises which intimated to her that a number of
people were rummaging up and down the stairs and also going to
and from the rooms. This prompted her to bolt herself within her
bedroom, where she remained for the next two hours. These noises,
she says, and the general disturbances, continued until dawn, when
gradually the house became quiet again. At last Phoebe Hubbard
summoned all her resources, put on a few articles of clothing and
decided to go round the house on a tour of inspection. In the lounge
the terrified girl came upon the dead body of her mistress, as has

already been described, but nowhere, either in the house or garden, was she able to find any traces of Dr. Traquair.

It must be noted, in these last connections, that Phoebe Hubbard is certain that she heard no sound of a shot being fired. She has been in the service of the Traquairs over two years, and from her own experiences in their service can advance no theory as to the cause of the trouble. In an interview given to our special representative Miss Hubbard stated her belief that Dr. Traquair had been captured by these "midnight marauders", as she describes them, and gives convincing reasons for such belief, but we understand that the Police authorities themselves attach little or no importance to Miss Hubbard's theory.

The following description of the missing Dr. Traquair, together with other relevant particulars, has been issued by the Police:

Wanted in connection with murder at High Road, Brooke, man known as Dr. Stuart Traquair. About 33 years of age. Height, 5ft. 11ins. Hair, black. Eyes, dark. Rather high cheek-bones. Weight, 12 stone 5 lbs. Teeth regular. Dressed in brown tweed suit, brown soft felt hat, brown shirt with soft collar to match, brown tie, brown shoes, brown socks. Walks with a swinging stride and in most matters suggests the athlete. Ready-made tailors and outfitters are requested to keep a sharp look-out for the missing person, as it is confidently expected that he will try to effect a change of clothing as quickly as possible, and all people who let lodgings or have rooms to spare are asked to co-operate in this matter and to inform the Police immediately they come in contact with anything of a suspicious nature that may seem to have a bearing upon the case.

The affair has been placed in the capable hands of Inspector Rudge, who, it will be remembered, was recently instrumental in bringing the Scudamore Poisoning Case to a successful conclusion.

As I put the paper down I smiled to myself, at more than one of the given particulars. If the Police were waiting for information to trickle through to them from outfitters' shops and the keepers of "doss-houses", they were going to wait a hell of a long time. I was "two up" on them as far as these factors were concerned. Not so bad for a comparative novice in the fine art of Police evasion. My main problem now was my own occupation of the "Nell Gwynne". How long could I remain there entirely unchallenged and unsuspected? One of my difficulties was my suit-case. When I had left the surgery at Brooke on the night of the disaster I had omitted to bring the key with me, so that I was unable to lock it, which meant that when I was away from the hotel my suit-case was in my bedroom . . . and there were one or two articles in that suit-case which I would prefer alien eyes not to see. You never knew, I considered, in an establishment like the "Nell Gwynne". I was not certain that even the ordinarily accepted conditions of personal etiquette would be regarded. The Police net would be cast and Lifford eventually would be within the arena of that casting. Could I escape its toils? My appearance was considerably changed, it is true, and also the clothes that I was wearing—but—! Whichever way I looked at the problem that "but" always reared its ugly head to worry me. I had not travelled far enough away from Brooke to feel even moderately comfortable. The more I thought about it, the more I realized the truth of this. The best thing I could do would be to lie "doggo" here for as long as possible and then, when the hue and cry had died down a bit, make a cut-away somewhere else. For there was still my particular job of work to be done, no matter what the immediate future might bring forth.

Towards opening-time I strolled quietly back to the "Nell Gwynne". I hadn't been there for more than a quarter of an hour or so when I was destined to receive my first disquieting shock. For who should come striding up to me in the billiard-room but Donald Eversley himself.

"Oh—Curtis," he said brusquely, "you might let me have your insurance cards, will you?"

The moment the words had left his lips I knew that I was facing a real danger. What could I do? How could I finesse for time?

"I haven't any," I said.

He frowned heavily. "What the hell do you mean—you haven't any?" he demanded.

"I haven't any cards—either for health or unemployment." I knew the two terms, you see, from my contact with panel patients as medical adviser.

"Why not? How do you make that out? You must have been in a previous job somewhere. Why, I remember, you told Mrs. Eversley when she engaged you that you had come from Canterbury. I remember the name of the town distinctly. Where did you work in Canterbury?"

Canterbury . . . My quick brain showed me a way out of the dilemma even though it might be but temporary. What a lucky touch for me that, almost unthinkingly, I had nominated Canterbury! I kept my head, my features composed, and even smiled at him.

"Quite right, sir," I answered. "But I think, sir, that you're possibly confusing two towns of the same name. Quite understandable. The place I came from is Canterbury in New Zealand. Not our cathedral town in Kent, sir." He looked at me suspiciously. I proceeded to follow up the semblance of the advantage that I had just established over him. "I wasn't in work down under, sir. To tell the truth—I've seen better days." The suspicion still showed in his eyes.

"Go on," he said in a harsh voice. "I find this extremely interesting."

"Not so good," I thought, but I accepted his invitation and kept at it. "Yes, sir. My people had money and I was more or less independent. But there was a crash and the old Dad was unlucky enough to be heavily involved. The shock killed him. I had to turn to and find a job. So I came over to the Old Country. There is always a soft spot—"

"Don't give me the 'Land of Hope and Glory' stuff," he snarled, "because I can't stand it. I suppose that, if the truth's known, all you could do was to play a decent game of snooker and billiards and you hoped that particular ability might bring you your bread and butter. Come, now—that's so, isn't it?"

"Partly, sir," I replied hopefully.

"H'm," he grunted. "Well, I shall have to have cards, and it's up to you to get them from somewhere." He turned as though about to go, and then suddenly swung back again on his heel. "What boat did you come over on?"

"The *Ormarna*," I answered promptly.

"When?" he demanded again.

"About two months ago, sir."

"Where have you been in between then and now?"

"Up in London, sir." I thought London was the best place that I could possibly pick.

"What have you been doing up there all that time, then?"

"Nothing, sir—if you mean by way of employment. I had a bit of money by me—saved from the wreck, as you might say—and while that lasted I was all right and didn't have to worry. When that went—well, I just had to look round for something. You can see how it was."

"And so you came along here. Funny you should have hit on this place."

"I told you how that was, sir. I saw your advertisement in the paper, thought it would just about suit me, and came along to see. Your missus seemed satisfied with me—and fixed me up. I'm sorry about not having the insurance cards—but you see how it is. All clearly explainable."

"Well, I suppose it's all right. You'd better get emergency cards from the Post Office people. They'll do until you get yourself properly fixed up with one of the Approved Societies." With that parting declaration Eversley lurched away. I began to knock the balls about rather aimlessly when he had departed and to wonder, at the same time, how I stood. Whether, in taking stock of my position, I was now in a less favourable light. On the whole I considered that I was. This wretched insurance card business had done me harm. If nothing else, it had caused Eversley to be suspicious of me, which was the last condition that I desired to exist. But I was extremely busy in the billiard-room all that evening, and gradually, under the stress of continued employment, my mind left the contemplation of my chief trouble and I became more equable. I had supper and then went to bed, for if there were anything about this new job that impressed me more than anything else it was that it made you devilishly tired. Due chiefly, I suppose, to the fact that I wasn't used to it. But I hadn't been in bed more than about ten minutes when I heard a light tap on my bedroom door. I raised myself on an elbow and listened. The light tap was repeated. I slipped out of bed and went to the door, which I always kept locked of a night.

"Who is it?" I asked in a low voice.

"It's Helen Eversley," came the reply in almost a whisper. "Will you please let me come in for a moment? It's terribly important."

I hesitated. Then confidence came to me. Helen would not be here at my bedroom door unless she were urged by the best of reasons. I switched on the light. Then I turned the key in the lock and opened the door to her. She was in the room like a flash and at once put her finger to her lips, enjoining my silence. She stood with her back against the wall, just inside the door. "Don't you speak," she whispered. "Your voice carries so. I know it too well of old not to know that. But I've just seen something in to-night's paper—in the final edition—we have one in the saloon bar—that I simply had to come to tell you. The officer that has been placed in charge of the case . . . our case . . . is Detective-Inspector Rudge. And Detective-Inspector Rudge is Donald's brother-in-law. He married Alison Eversley, Donald's sister. Isn't it too-awful luck?"

I nodded. I couldn't have said anything because I couldn't think of anything to say.

"I had to tell you," she repeated—"forewarned is forearmed, they say, and you're better off knowing things than remaining in ignorance of them. We shall have to watch every point. I must go now because it's terribly dangerous my being here—especially—"

I nodded, weakly. She seemed to realize what she had said, because she blushed deliciously as she turned to go. "Good night . . . Dr. Traquair," she whispered.

"Good night, guardian angel," I whispered back as I locked my door again behind her. Then I stood in the darkness again . . . thinking. I could have sworn that it had been on the tip of her tongue to call me "Stuart". I listened carefully for any sound . . . but everything in the "Nell Gwynne" was quiet. I slid into bed again. As I put my head on the pillow I wondered how long that condition would remain. I was soon to know.

PART TWO
The Chase

CHAPTER I
The Annoyance of Sir Austin Kemble

(Told by the Author)

Sir Austin Kemble was both annoyed and impatient. As Commissioner of Police, and head of New Scotland Yard, life for him these days was far from a bed of roses. Chief Inspector Andrew Mac-Morran, seated opposite to him in Sir Austin's private room, was well aware of the mood which dominated his chief at the moment. "What I can't understand, MacMorran," said Sir Austin, pacing the room in front of the Inspector, "what I utterly and entirely fail to understand, is that a man of your experience—I will not employ the word 'ability'—should be *content* to confess that you're at an absolute loss to explain so many features of this Traquair case. Since the Brooke police called for our co-operation what headway have we made? Now, MacMorran, I ask you! What new progress have we made at all?"

MacMorran was disturbed. "Verra little, sir. I am not denying that for a minute. It's no good my arguin' about it. I regret the fact . . . but there it is."

Sir Austin warmed to the attack.

"Well, then! Take the two main lines of the case, MacMorran. Take them separately if you like. First the murder of Mrs. Traquair. And then, as a secondary consideration, the disappearance of Dr. Traquair, the dead woman's husband. If we admit that the first matter contains definite difficulties, the second surely belongs to an entirely different category. A man can't vanish into thin air! Especially under modern conditions. I simply won't have it, MacMorran. It isn't as though this doctor fellow was an ordinary man—a sort of—er—man in the street—as you might say! He's not. On the contrary, he's a well-known general practitioner—been in the place years . . . his appearance must be well-known to thousands, and yet you come here and calmly tell me that you haven't picked up a trace of him anywhere. It won't do, Inspector! It really won't."

The Commissioner, having said his say, slumped into his seat again. For a moment or so MacMorran vouchsafed no reply. Experience had taught him that in this mood the Commissioner must be endured with equal parts of patience and resignation. Instead of speech, he referred to his notebook. "Since I went to Brooke, acting on your instructions, sir, no less than five lines of inquiry respecting Dr. Traquair have been followed up and carefully investigated. Each one of 'em yielded nothing—or next to nothing. Chatterton, Ashcroft, Maynard and I myself have between us been to Southampton, North Woolwich, an obscure village of the name of Pillerton Priors, Lyme Regis and Gravesend. Five different people—so we were informed—had seen and recognized the missing doctor. And every one of those five was wrong! Verra wrong! In three instances the man we trailed was as much like the published descriptions of this Dr. Traquair as I'm like Clark Gable." As he made his point MacMorran's mouth set in hard, fierce lines.

Sir Austin Kemble made a gesture of impatience.

"Don't talk to me of the mistakes that have been made! Good Lord, man, you speak of 'em as though they were feathers in your cap! You're losing your sense of proportion—that's what's the matter with you, MacMorran. Well, if you won't do it—I'll see that every town and village in the country is combed clean."

"And even then you might miss your man. Have you thought of that possibility, Sir Austin?"

"Every seaport has been covered. Every airport has been covered. And were covered within an hour of the doctor's disappearance being known. The Brooke police made no mistake there. I have examined the instructions they gave and the steps they took, very thoroughly. Traquair is still in the country. Of that fact I am absolutely convinced."

"Well then, sir, if that's the case, it all boils down to a question of time. We are bound to get him sooner or later. If he's in the country, as you insist so confidently, he's in hiding, and the day will come when he'll be forced to come from his cover into the open. Even now, I'm expecting any minute to get information from a landlady, or someone like a landlady, that she's been harbouring the man we're all so anxious to interview."

Sir Austin Kemble rose from his seat again and fluttered in excitement. "Leaving the question of Dr. Traquair for the moment, what about the girl Phoebe Hubbard's story? Who searched the Traquair house? After, mind you, Mrs. Traquair was dead and had been dead some hours?"

MacMorran pursed his lips. He answered Sir Austin's last question by the time-honoured method of putting a return question *to* the question. "How do you know that the house was searched? I should like you to answer that, sir."

The Commissioner stared silently at Inspector MacMorran. Eventually he found words. "Phoebe Hubbard? You mean the girl? Why—what are you on to, MacMorran?"

MacMorran shook his head sapiently. "I'm on to nothing, sir. But I'm merely pointing out to you, sir, something that you cannot fail to appreciate as being the truth—that this servant's story is entirely uncorroborated. For all we know, she may have concocted the whole story of these men having been in the house, for reasons of her own. That's my point, sir, in a nutshell."

The Commissioner became verbally caustic. "And for what reasons, MacMorran, may I ask you, would a girl of the lower classes invent a fantastic story of that kind? Is it likely that she would? Why, to me, its very improbability almost vouches for its truth."

"I'm not sure. Some of these modern young ladies are gifted with a rare faculty of invention. But I'll tell you what, sir! How would it do if you got into touch again with—"

"Mr. Bathurst—eh? Is that what you were about to say, Inspector?"

MacMorran smiled genially. "You took the very words from my mouth, sir."

"Well, in that case, you'll be pleased to know that I have already been in touch with him. I felt that it was the best thing that I could do. And I had a chat with Rudge yesterday afternoon, down at Brooke. I told you that I went down there, didn't I?"

MacMorran nodded. "You did. And what had Rudge to say for himself?"

"Very little. Taking his performance as a whole, MacMorran, I should say that it was about on a par with yours."

MacMorran shifted uneasily in his seat. The Commissioner proceeded with his statement. "It was arising out of my interview with Detective-Inspector Rudge that I came to the decision to ask Mr. Bathurst to come along. You'd be the first to admit, MacMorran, that more than once in the past he has proved distinctly useful to us."

MacMorran's passionate sense of justice asserted itself. "I would that, sir. I only wish that I could think we'd returned the compliment."

The Commissioner missed the point. "I knew you would. Well, Mr. Bathurst should be with us within a very few moments. He's due at half past, and according to my watch it's just on that now."

"If he's due at half past then he'll be with us at half past. It's the same thing with Anthony Bathurst. It'll be good to work in double harness with him again." MacMorran looked at his massive silver watch. Sir Austin Kemble crossed to his desk and arranged certain papers. MacMorran waited in patience for developments. Suddenly the comparative silence of the room was shattered by the shrill ring of the telephone. Sir Austin answered it. "Yes . . . yes. I'm waiting up here now. Very good, then." He replaced the receiver and smiled towards Inspector MacMorran. "Mr. Bathurst is here, Inspector. By now he'll be on his way up. He'll probably ask about twenty-two thousand questions—so prepare yourself."

A moment later, Anthony Bathurst had entered the room. Shaking hands cordially with the Commissioner, he seemed more than delighted to see MacMorran sitting there.

"Good morning, sir. How are things? Why—Andrew of all people! Man, but it's good to see you again! Andrew, my priceless treasure, you are to me as the first hint of Spring—the first deep-scented—"

MacMorran, pumping at his hand, interrupted him. "Not so much of it. You'll soon be telling me to get next to myself." The grey eyes of Anthony Bathurst gleamed in a smile. MacMorran went on. "And I'm that pleased to see you again, Mr. Bathurst. I reckon I don't have to tell you of it."

Sir Austin waved Anthony Bathurst to a seat. "Sit down, Bathurst. And when you've made yourself moderately comfortable I'll talk to you."

"What have I done, sir, to merit such a fate? For a moment let me talk to you. Now there's one thing that I can tell you that should please you. That's this. So far, I have an entirely open mind on the Traquair case."

Sir Austin Kemble looked at him in surprise. From Inspector MacMorran there came a low chuckle. The Commissioner translated his surprise into words. "May one inquire as to how you knew it was the Traquair case that caused me to ask you to come along?"

Anthony grinned at him. "Something in my bones. There's not much else in the murder line filling the bill at the moment, is there? If there is, I must confess that I've missed it."

"I suppose there isn't," remarked Sir Austin thoughtfully. "Anyhow, you're right! Have you looked at the case at all?"

Anthony nodded. "Yes. I know the bare facts of it pretty well. What's the particular point about it all that's troubling you?"

"Two features of the affair are distinctly puzzling. The first is the complete disappearance of Dr. Traquair, the dead woman's husband. The second is the sensational story told by Phoebe Hubbard, the maid. Between ourselves, Bathurst, here's MacMorran, by no means sure (although of course he won't admit it) whether Traquair is dead or alive!" Anthony turned towards the Inspector. "Is that a fact, Andrew?"

"The Commissioner says so, Mr. Bathurst."

"Oh! Is that how the land lies, Andrew? I see! Your doubts, I suppose, are based on the maid's story?" Mr. Bathurst whistled. MacMorran shrugged his shoulders. Sir Austin therefore took upon himself the responsibility of answering for him.

"If the house was invaded in the early hours of the morning by these men, in the highly melodramatic manner which the girl Hubbard has so very vividly described, it's possible that Traquair was murdered by them in some way and his body, for a purpose of which at the moment we are ignorant, removed. Taken away by the gang. And the word 'body' that I have used goes for a dead one as well as a live one."

Anthony shook his head as the Commissioner finished his statement. "I don't think so, sir."

"You don't?"

"No, sir. And I'll tell you why. There's a piece of direct evidence already featured in the case which is in complete antagonism to the idea that you've just put forward. And that's the note from Dr. Traquair which the Hubbard girl found when she returned to the Traquair establishment after her evening out. I understand that she is prepared to swear it's authentic. That Dr. Traquair wrote it himself."

MacMorran replied to Anthony Bathurst's question. "Yes. You're right. I have questioned her. She has told me that she has no doubt on the point whatever."

Anthony spread out his hands. "Well—there you are, gentlemen. I know that I'm late on the case, and that you may be holding certain vital facts up your sleeves. But, all things being equal, I should say that Dr. Traquair wrote that note after he had killed his wife in order that the body shouldn't be found until the morning. Or in other words, that he was playing for time."

"I see," remarked Sir Austin Kemble; "go on."

"Well—his plan succeeded. That's all. He got away that night. In my opinion—*before* the sensational visitation."

"So that in your opinion he killed his wife, eh?"

Anthony Bathurst smiled at the directness of the Commissioner's question. "Oh, sir! I have but little data from which to answer that question with definite certainty. Circumstantially, though, I must say that it looks like it. At any rate—the good doctor got away when the going was good. That's as far as I would care to commit myself at the moment."

The Commissioner burnt his boats. "I was going to ask you to come in on the case, if you would, Bathurst. As a personal favour. MacMorran's dying to do another job with you."

Anthony grinned amiably at the Inspector. "Stout fellow, Andrew! Only too delighted." Mr. Bathurst settled himself comfortably in his chair. "Just a minute before you start on me. Check up first on what I already know of the case. The body of Mrs. Traquair was discovered by the maid Phoebe Hubbard in the lounge of the Traquair house early in the morning. She at once 'phoned for the Police. Right?"

"Quite right, Mr. Bathurst." This from Andrew MacMorran.

"When the Police arrived, they found the body as the maid had described, on the floor of the lounge. She had been shot. I think, from memory, that she had been shot through the heart. Am I right?"

"Quite right again, Mr. Bathurst," MacMorran said.

"So far, then, so good! No weapon was found in the room, and I don't think that any weapon has been found since. Dr. Traquair was nowhere on the premises and the bed usually occupied by him had not been slept in during the night. In the opinion of the Police, that is. The only person to give the Police any statement worth much was, of course, Phoebe Hubbard, the maid. The two main points of her story were (a) the doctor's letter, which we have already discussed, and (b) the visit of the strangers who disturbed her from her sleep. Since then, all the efforts of the Police to lay their hands on the missing doctor have failed. All the people who 'had seen him' saw somebody else. And Dr. Traquair remains at large. Well, is there anything that I've missed?"

MacMorran glanced towards Sir Austin Kemble. The latter nodded to the Inspector. "There's nothing that you've missed, Mr. Bathurst. But there's something that the Police know which so far we have not communicated to the general public through the Press."

Anthony regarded him critically. "Oh—well, that's interesting. The case begins to look better. I had no idea that it had such possibilities. I can bear to hear the secret tidings, Andrew."

"All round Mrs. Traquair's body, scattered, as you might say, lay a pack of playing-cards—on the floor."

Anthony furrowed his brows. "Everything in place—eh? No destruction but the cards on the floor! H'm—not so good."

MacMorran came in again. "Now I'll tell you something else. Of course, I've had all this from Rudge of the Brooke Police, who took over when the Hubbard girl 'phoned. Right against the dead woman's hand, clutched almost between the fingers, was one card. That card, Mr. Bathurst, was none other than the nine of diamonds." MacMorran paused to see the effect of his words on Anthony Bathurst.

That gentleman emitted a soft whistle. "The nine of diamonds—eh, Andrew? Or, in other words, 'the Curse of Scotland'? Is that what you're getting at, man?"

"Being a Scotsman, I must confess that it had entered my mind," returned the Inspector.

"May be nothing in it," surmised Anthony. "Just the fall of the cards, Andrew—one card flickered to the floor near the dead lady's hand and it just happened to be the nine of diamonds."

MacMorran shook his head again more slowly even than on the previous occasion. "Traquair is a Scottish name, sir. And when I tell you that the missing doctor's name is Stuart, don't you agree that that makes it all the more so?"

Anthony considered the reply. "H'm. It's certainly a point to you, Andrew. Though I'll admit that I'm far from convinced."

"Seems a bit fantastic to me," contributed Sir Austin Kemble.

Anthony proceeded to develop an idea. "Look here, Andrew. You say that there were no signs of a struggle. No overturned table. No chairs knocked over, or any other usual indication of furniture upheaval that one so often finds in cases of this kind. All that was abnormal, or extraordinary, was the fact of these playing-cards being on the floor. Now, Andrew—supposing that the table with the playing-cards on top *had* been knocked over? And the murderer, after the murder, replaced the table but forgot to pick up the playing-cards."

"Why should he?"

"We don't know. The time factor, possibly, was operating. He hadn't time to pick them up. Was in too great a hurry."

"If he troubled to put the table in place it seems to me that it's a thousand to one that he would have picked up the playing-cards at the same time."

This time Mr. Bathurst shook his head. "It's by no means a certainty."

MacMorran refused to surrender his position. "Now you look here, Mr. Bathurst; you've got the idea firmly in your head—and I'm not blaming you for a moment—that these cards were upset by an accident. That they were lying on the floor accidentally. That's not my idea at all. On the contrary, I believe that they figured in the affair for a purpose! And—what's more, Mr. Bathurst, I'm prepared to prove the truth of my contention."

"Good man," replied Anthony. "Let's have it, then."

The Inspector's eyes twinkled as he accepted the invitation. "Here's a dose of your own medicine for you. A hair of the dog that bit you. Supposing a pack of playing-cards were lying on a table. They hadn't been used for a game, which is pretty much what you are suggesting. Would you expect to find those cards stacked loose or contained within the usual cardboard case?"

Anthony replied promptly: "In the covering case, without a doubt. Why?"

MacMorran's face showed the pleasure that Mr. Bathurst's reply had given him. "Right! So that if the table had been turned over in any struggle which took place, and the cards had fallen on the floor in consequence thereof, you would expect the two parts of the outside case on the floor with them? Yes, Mr. Bathurst?"

"Undoubtedly."

"Well, then, that's how I prove my contention. The two outer cases *weren't* on the floor. They were still in the drawer of the table! I'm dismissing the idea that the murderer put the cases back and left the cards themselves lying where they were."

"Andrew," said Anthony Bathurst slowly, "I congratulate you on what I consider a sound piece of deduction. I take back what I said. I agree with you. To this extent. That the cards had been used. But I can't think for what purpose."

MacMorran, secretly delighted at Mr. Bathurst's eulogy, nodded sagely. "For what purpose, you say? Well, that's where I can come along with my little theory concerning the nine of diamonds near Mrs. Traquair's hand. I've been flattering myself that it's highly ingenious on my part."

"Which hand was it, Andrew? The right or the left?"

"The right, Mr. Bathurst. So Inspector Rudge tells me."

"I suppose that might reasonably be considered as a strengthening of your theory, Andrew. It certainly doesn't detract from it. I must try to remember what I know of the Curse of Scotland. Let me see, now! I think that it's been held that the word 'curse' is in this connection a corruption of the word 'cross'."

"Couldn't say. You've taken me out of my depth."

"I think the term was first recorded somewhere about the early eighteenth century. Now what have I stirring in my mind about that?" Mr. Bathurst closed his eyes and passed his hand across his brow. "It's coming to me. It's in Houston's *Memoirs*. Somewhere round 1740, I fancy. The reference was to the Lord Justice-Clerk Ormistone. The gentleman was so universally detested in Scotland that when the ladies played cards at that time, instead of calling the nine of diamonds 'the Curse of Scotland' they called it 'the Justice-Clerk'. Yes, I'm sure I'm right. I remember it distinctly."

Sir Austin Kemble coughed. "I've never heard that. I always thought that the reference was to one of the Scottish noblemen. I can't recall his name, but I—"

"I can supply the name that you're thinking of, sir," inter-posed Anthony. "You're referring to Dalrymple, Earl of Stair. The direct relationship was to his coat of arms. I can remember reading it. It was *or* on a saltire *azure* with nine lozenges of the first. Note the number, Andrew—nine. That, I believe, is generally regarded as the most plausible suggestion of the term's origin. After the massacre of Glencoe, the Earl of Stair was naturally in bad odour, and he was also detested in Scotland for his share in bringing about the Union with England. That would be about the beginning of the eighteenth century."

MacMorran nodded in admiration and his eyes were sparkling. "I reckon I'm well behind when it comes to the book-learning. And it makes me a wee bit ashamed in consequence. But I'm a Scots-man and I've heard tell from my mother that Mary Queen of Scots introduced a card game, of which she was wonderfully fond, called 'comette'. Now, in comette the nine of diamonds is the great winning card, and the game came to be known as 'the Curse of Scotland' because it was the ruination of many Scottish families."

"Cards—eh? What about this, then?" Sir Austin Kemble laboured under an excitement. "I used to play Pope Joan when I was a youth. In that the nine of diamonds is called the Pope, that is to say a sort of Anti-Christ of the Scottish reformers. I can remember that fact very well."

Anthony smiled. "Now, I can go one better. Yet another reminiscence has come to me. I've been delving in my mind for it for some minutes, but I've got it at last. It's yet another suggested explanation of the name. That the nine of diamonds was the card used by the Butcher-Duke, Cumberland, on which to write his cruel order, after the Battle of Culloden. Too much credence, though, isn't given to this. Culloden was fought in 1746, and that fact would seem to make it too late, according to friend Houston. But—stay a minute—let's turn up the reference. We may as well know all there is to know about it before we leave it." Mr. Bathurst rose and walked over to Sir Austin Kemble's bookcase.

"Here we are." Anthony took down the book that he wanted and flicked the pages. He ran his finger down a page. The Commissioner and MacMorran watched him as he read the particulars. He nodded from time to time. "This pretty well agrees with all that we said, sir. But there happens to be one additional item of information. Grose, who wrote the *Tour Thro' Scotland* in 1789, says this of the card the nine of diamonds: 'Diamonds signify royalty, and every ninth King of Scotland has been observed for many ages to be a tyrant and a curse to the country.' But, unhappily, sir, from our point of view, the estimable Grose omits to give the names of these ninth kings." Anthony closed the book and returned it to the Commissioner's bookcase. "Well, sir—and where are we now that we know all this?"

"What do you think of things yourself, Bathurst?"

"I should like Inspector MacMorran here to take me to Doctor Traquair's surgery at Brooke. If that can be arranged. And as soon as possible."

"That shall be done, Bathurst. I'll arrange that for to-morrow morning. Suit you?"

"Couldn't be better. Good-bye, sir—and thank you for the opportunity. Bye-bye, Andrew. See you to-morrow. And good hunting." Anthony shook hands with the two men and took his departure.

MacMorran rubbed his cheek with pleasurable anticipation.

CHAPTER II

In The House of Dr. Traquair

(Told by the Author)

INSPECTOR MacMorran pointed to the carpet. Rudge, the Brooke inspector, stood at his side. Anthony Bathurst faced them. "That's where the body of Mrs. Traquair lay." MacMorran made various indications. Rudge nodded from time to time. "Head there. Feet here. The right hand, stretched out, came about as far as here."

Anthony assessed distances. "So that our friend the nine of diamonds lay just about here. Yes?"

"Quite right, Mr. Bathurst," responded Rudge. "Just about this spot here."

"I see. Now where was that table, in the drawer of which was the outer case of the playing-cards?"

"Exactly where it's standing now, sir."

Anthony looked at the table and looked at the drawer. "The cards, generally, I suppose, were scattered in profusion?"

"Undoubtedly, sir."

"By the way, sir," put in MacMorran, "there's one point of the case that I don't think has been put to you yet. I meant to tell you yesterday, but it slipped me. Inspector Rudge here has discovered that there were two bullets fired that found their mark on the side wall over there. If you come over here, Mr. Bathurst, I'll show you where they were. You can see the marks for yourself."

Anthony bent down and examined the marks on the wall. "Unusually low, aren't they? Don't you fellows think so?"

"They are that," Rudge spoke.

"Different calibre bullets, I suppose, from the bullet that killed Mrs. Traquair?"

"Yes, Mr. Bathurst. From a smaller-bored revolver."

"So there was a little firing squad, eh? Dear, dear! Things grow even more interesting. Tell me, Andrew. Can you remember the details of the autopsy? Who was the doctor that first saw Mrs. Traquair's body?"

"Dr. Cutler, Mr. Bathurst. From the Brooke station. Why, what's the point?"

"Did he make any remark, do you know, as to how and when she died? I mean—was death considered by him to have been instantaneous?"

Inspector Rudge took it upon himself to answer Mr. Bathurst's question. He nodded affirmatively. "Yes, I can answer that. I can remember that Dr. Cutler told me that death had been instantaneous. He had no doubt about it. Mrs. Traquair was shot clean through the heart."

"I see. So that it's feasible that *she* fired the two bullets that found their way into the wall over there. I take it that those two had been fired from the same revolver?"

"Yes. From the same revolver. I follow your point, sir."

"Thank you, Inspector Rudge." Anthony walked slowly round the room. Twice he measured the distances between the door and the place on the floor where the body had been found. "I've seen all I want to see in here, Inspector," he said to MacMorran. "What else have you for me?"

"Bring Mr. Bathurst into the bathroom," said Inspector Rudge. "There are one or two things I'd like him to hear about concerning in there."

"Philo Vance's 'yon lavatorium', eh? Right you are, Rudge," said Mr. Bathurst. "I'm game. Lead on."

Inside the bathroom, Rudge halted in front of the big washing-basin. "There was a spot of blood on the side of this basin, Mr. Bathurst. I noticed it the first time that I came in here. The murderer washed his hands before he decamped."

"Yes, I think you're probably right. And washed his hands, I expect, because one of the bullets that found its way into the lounge wall had, in its passing, wounded him somewhere. Cheek, perhaps. Or even on one of his hands, possibly. The room isn't a large one—the lounge, I mean—and the revolver must have been fired at close quarters."

Rudge turned and looked at him queerly. "Fired by whom?"

Anthony smiled at the sharpness of the question. "I couldn't say, Inspector. But I would suggest, I think, by the murdered lady, Mrs. Traquair."

"More that than by a third party?"

"Oh yes, most definitely. If you examine the marks on the wall, and then consider where Mrs. Traquair must have been standing when she was hit, you'll find that they correspond splendidly with the idea that Mrs. Traquair fired at somebody. Her assailant, in all probability."

"And yet I've a strong idea that there were more than two people in that room when the murder took place," said Rudge.

"Very possibly. But we can't tell at the moment. Anything else in here, Rudge?"

"Yes, sir. This was picked up from the floor. It had rolled, or fallen perhaps would be the better word, almost underneath the bath." Rudge handed Anthony a small pearl button, light brown in colour. "May be nothing in it, of course, Mr. Bathurst. A button may easily come off in a bathroom at any old time."

Anthony looked at the button with some curiosity. "I don't know," he said. "There may be an association here which may prove valuable to us. At any rate, Inspector Rudge, we won't allow ourselves to forget that we have it. The time may come when we can prove its worth."

Mr. Bathurst stood there thinking. Suddenly he looked up and spoke to MacMorran. "Take me into the doctor's bedroom, will you, Inspector? I'd like to have a look round in there. My brain has just been delivered of an idea."

Rudge nodded. "Very good, Mr. Bathurst. Come this way, will you, please?" Anthony and MacMorran followed Inspector Rudge into the Traquairs' bedroom.

"Did you pick up anything in here, Inspector?" inquired Mr. Bathurst.

Rudge shook his head. "No, sir. Although I had a pretty good look round. The bed hadn't been slept in. I should say that the room hadn't been used for anything at all since the previous night."

"I see. Were there any letters lying about? Or papers of any description?"

"No, Mr. Bathurst. Nothing at all of that kind. But, if I may say so—would you expect to find them in a person's bedroom?"

"Very often I find that a woman—and even occasionally a man—will keep private papers in his or her bedroom. The idea being, I suppose, that fewer people visit the bedroom. Anyhow, you say that you found nothing. That settles the matter." Anthony Bathurst wandered round the room, eyes on everything. At length he came to a halt in front of Dr. Traquair's wardrobe. He opened the doors. "Clothes may not make the man," he said, "but according to Freddie Lonsdale 'many a bride has been disappointed when he has taken them off'. Let us see what manner of clothes Dr. Traquair affected." The wardrobe was beautifully tidy and of very modern design. Suits, hats, shoes, ties, shirts, pull-overs were all here, and obviously in an arranged order. Mr. Bathurst took down a blue soft hat. "Head about my own size," he remarked—"6⅞, I should say, from the look of it." He took down several others from their pegs—a grey, a brown and a black. MacMorran and Rudge watched him with a certain amount of amusement. "All the same size," he remarked again, "and all of exceptionally good quality." He put the four hats back on the four pegs and his eyes roamed again over the contents of the clothes-cabinet. Suddenly MacMorran, who, naturally, knew his Bathurst better than did Inspector Rudge of Brooke, knew that something in the cabinet had arrested his attention. "A hat-box," declared Mr. Bathurst. "At the bottom of the wardrobe, too. What kind of hat does Dr. Traquair keep in here? Even money that it formed part of his wedding garments. Taking me on, MacMorran?"

"No, Mr. Bathurst, I'm not taking you. I've argued with you before concerning the ethics of betting." Mr. Bathurst bent down to look closer, when a more curious look came over his face. "I say, you fellows," he declared, "have a look here, will you?"

They stooped down, all three, as he pointed to the level of the hat-box. "See that?" They looked again at where he was pointing. The lid of the hat-box was covered with a thin layer of dust, but on one side of it there were distinct impressions of finger-marks. "These are recent marks," said Anthony interestedly, "and I find myself wondering why. I suppose you didn't look at this, Inspector, did you?"

Rudge shook his head, but chagrin showed on his face. "No, Mr. Bathurst, I didn't. I looked in the wardrobe, but nothing seemed to have been disturbed, and everything looked to be in such . . . well . . . apple-pie order that I passed on to other matters."

Anthony nodded. "Quite understandable. Still, let's have a look inside this hat-box. One never knows what one's going to find on a quest of this kind. I'll be extra careful, though, not to interfere with these hand-prints on the dust of Time." Anthony put the palms of his hands against each side of the lid and lifted it off. MacMorran gestured towards the silk hat that showed in the box.

"And ye'd ha' won your money, Mr. Bathurst, if I'd been misguided enough to bet. There's the hat that Dr. Traquair carried with him to the altar. A real touch of St. George's, Hanover Square."

Anthony grinned at him as he lifted out the hat. "I want to have a look at this topper, Andrew. Those finger-marks have interested me. I don't know anything *about* the 'Why', but I've a hunch that there's a 'Why' knocking about somewhere and that we aren't too far away from it."

The two inspectors looked at the silk hat held in Mr. Bathurst's hands. MacMorran saw the old familiar gleam come into Anthony's grey eyes.

"7⅛th," said Mr. Bathurst, "or I'm a Dutchman. Sizes bigger than all these other hats of Dr. Traquair's that we've just looked at. Again—why, oh why, oh why?"

"That's a verra peculiar thing," grunted MacMorran. "I see your drift, Mr. Bathurst."

Rudge looked as though the problem at stake were entirely beyond him. Anthony turned the hat over and looked inside it. He was rewarded immediately. There, stamped into the discoloured satin-like lining were two letters: "'F.C.'," quoted Mr. Bathurst with quiet emphasis, "and 'F.C.' certainly doesn't stand for the initials of Dr. Stuart Traquair. What about the nine of diamonds now, MacMorran?"

MacMorran, thus appealed to, contented himself with nodding his head slowly. "Ay! As I said to the Commissioner, there's a lot more in this case than meets the eye. A rare lot more."

Anthony began to follow up on a line of definite reasoning. "Now, gentlemen," he said, "what can be deduced from this? No fantastic theories—but hard common sense. Do you get anything?"

"Do you mean that a man with initials 'F.C.' must be looked for in the affair—a man who obviously has the freedom of Dr. Traquair's wardrobe? Another example of the eternal triangle?" This from Inspector Rudge.

Mr. Bathurst shook his head. "No. I don't mean that. I hadn't been thinking of that. No—my deductions had run on these lines. This hat is in this box for the simple reason that when Dr. Traquair disappeared on the night of the murder he walked out of the house *wearing his own top hat.*"

MacMorran frowned. "Why? How do you get that?"

Anthony held up the hat. "Consider these facts, gentlemen. The fact that we have found a silk-hat-box here is evidence that the doctor *had* a silk hat. The finger-marks which showed in the dust on the lid of the box imply that he opened the box quite recently. Why? Surely to obtain the hat! Why—again? Because, I suggest, the hat which he *intended* to wear was unfortunately much too large for his head. Therefore—he changed the hats. Put this one that we have here into the box and took out his own. Well, gentlemen? I await all your comments."

"What I don't see," remarked Inspector Rudge thoughtfully, "is why Dr. Traquair, having a silk hat, should want to wear a hat which belonged to another person. Especially a hat which, as you say, was too large."

Anthony smiled and nodded. "What do you say to that, Inspector MacMorran? I should find your opinion both valuable and interesting."

"I know your methods, Mr. Bathurst, better than Inspector Rudge here, and I take it that your point is that Traquair was desirous of wearing the strange hat because the clothes that he was wearing wanted a silk hat to go with them. No—stop a minute, I've got it. He wanted the other fellow's hat . . . because he was wearing the other fellow's clothes. How's that for you, Mr. Bathurst?"

"You've seen it exactly as I saw it, Andrew. Congratulations."

Rudge nodded. "I get you. Good! And all that explains something which has been baffling us."

"You mean that the description of Traquair in respect of the clothes which he's supposed to be wearing is all wrong? Is that it?"

"That's it, Inspector MacMorran. I can't imagine that Dr. Traquair is walking about wearing a brown tweed suit, brown shoes, etc., etc., plus a silk topper."

Anthony scratched his cheek. "I'll go a step further, Rudge. A helpful step, too. And that's this. If Dr. Traquair wanted the hat before he left here, he must have already changed his clothes. Therefore, the brown tweed suit must have been discarded *here*, and, equally therefore, should be somewhere here still. Are you following me, gentlemen?"

The two inspectors signified their assent. "Question is," continued Mr. Bathurst, "where? Assuming that Dr. Traquair, when he made his get-away, had no time to waste, the clothes which he took off shouldn't be too far away. I think that may be regarded as a logical conclusion." He replaced the hat inside the hat-box and put the box on the floor at the side of the cabinet. Then he opened wide the two doors of the cabinet. His eyes took in the contents of every shelf. At the bottom of the wardrobe was the line of shoes—black, brown and dress. Mr. Bathurst sat on his haunches to look more closely. Tucked away in one of the corners, and lying on top of a pair of black shoes, was a neatly tied brown-paper parcel. Mr. Bathurst pulled it out. "Open that, Inspector Rudge, will you, please? Parcels of this kind in a wardrobe such as this is strike me as unusual, to say the least of it."

Rudge took the brown-paper parcel and began to untie the string. MacMorran and Anthony waited for the revelation. Rudge's fingers fumbled with the knots. To the two other men it seemed an age before he had the parcel undone. At last the task was accomplished. There, in a heap, lay a collection of clothes. "As I anticipated, gentlemen," came the quiet tones of Mr. Bathurst, "there you have the clothes which the missing Dr. Traquair is supposed to be still wearing. Or, in other words, you know now that he pulled a fast one. First blood to Dr. Traquair."

"Ay," added Inspector MacMorran, "or even second. Thinkin' in terms of his puir young wife."

Rudge examined the heap of clothes and checked off the different articles one by one. "Brown suit, jacket, vest and trousers. Brown shirt and collar. Tie. Brown socks. Hand-kerchief to match as well. Yes, Mr. Bathurst, the whole outfit, as far as I can see, seems to be here. And in the ordinary way, a brown-paper parcel like this, neatly put away too, wouldn't attract undue attention. You get my meaning, sir? There's nothing 'sinister' about it."

"I only partly agree," returned Anthony. "Nothing sinister perhaps, but I certainly think unusual. Anyhow, we've found it, and if we don't know what Traquair is wearing—we know now what he's *not* wearing. Which is a move in the right direction."

"Question is who is 'F.C.'? Or perhaps better still—who was 'F.C.'?" This contribution came from Inspector MacMorran.

"You've got it, Andrew," supplemented Mr. Bathurst.

"You've put your finger on the pulse of matters. Problem—find 'F.C.' I feel that this is where the maid Phoebe Hubbard is going to help us."

"It's a chance," said Rudge, "we'll try it. Since the murder she's been staying at a shop in the High Road. Has a room there—we'll fix up to have a word with her."

"Good. So the girl's close handy? I thought that perhaps she might have gone 'home'—and home might have been anywhere, meaning possible delay for us. It's good news to me that she's still on the spot."

"She's an orphan, Mr. Bathurst. She told me that when I was questioning her. It's a bad break for her, this collapse of the Traquair household. Puts her out of a job—and from some people's point of view, not exactly in the best odour. You know how damned particular some people are. Would think twice about employing a girl who'd been mixed up in a murder case."

"I suppose you're right. Especially in a place like this! Well—get into touch with Miss Phoebe as soon as you can, Rudge, will you? And let me know—through Inspector MacMorran. I'm stopping at the 'Golden Thistle'."

"Very good, Mr. Bathurst. In the meantime I'll modify the description that has been circulated of Dr. Traquair. I can do that quite easily. There's no doubt that what we have discovered to-day explains a lot."

"It does, Rudge," replied Mr. Bathurst, "but I'm afraid that there's still much more to be explained. However, we still have to-morrow—*and*, I hope, Phoebe Hubbard."

CHAPTER III
SOMEBODY SHUTS A FRONT DOOR

(Told by the Author)

ANTHONY Bathurst was coming down the main staircase of the Golden Thistle Hotel at Brooke after lunch on the following day when a message was given into his hand by one of the porters who was standing near the vestibule. When Anthony opened the envelope he saw that it contained a note from Inspector Rudge. MacMorran had been called back to the "Yard" for a day or so, but was expected to be in Brooke again as soon as possible—in any case, before the end of the week. Mr. Bathurst read the letter from Rudge:

Dear Mr. Bathurst,

I have arranged for Miss Hubbard to meet us at 8.30 this evening. She couldn't manage the appointment earlier at such short notice as she had already arranged a journey to town to do with her obtaining another situation. This, you will readily admit, is a reasonable position. Thought that it would suit you better in every way if we saw Miss H. at the Traquair house, so have fixed matters up in that way. Trust that you agree.

Your obedient servant,

George Rudge.

Anthony pushed the letter into his jacket pocket and made his way to the lounge of the "Golden Thistle". There, awaiting him, were the various daily copies of *The Morning Message* since the day of the murder of Mrs. Traquair, which he had taken the trouble to obtain before he should interview Phoebe Hubbard. Mr. Bathurst read each daily account with care and patience.

There wasn't a hint in any one of the accounts concerning the scattered pack of playing-cards; still less, therefore, of any association with the crime, of the sinister "Curse of Scotland". After a time, Anthony, having exhausted all the papers, folded them neatly and placed them in an ordered heap. He then gave himself up to an exercise in concentration. If Traquair had killed his wife, as the purely circumstantial evidence suggested that he had, what was the probable motive behind the crime? Jealousy? Revenge? Gain? The first-named motive would be probably the most likely. Who was the owner of the silk hat that was too large? Extraordinary thing, that! And, if his theory were correct, how did Dr. Traquair get hold of the other man's clothes? Coincidence? Or definite plan and design? Anthony was uncertain. However, at the moment he was short of data, and he made the immediate resolve that after he had seen Phoebe Hubbard with Rudge that evening he would take another look round Dr. Traquair's surgery and premises.

In these musings and similar contemplations Mr. Bathurst passed the afternoon. Shortly after tea he had a 'phone call from Sir Austin Kemble. The latter, as usual, took a great deal of trouble and time to say nothing rather badly. Anthony smiled at his end of the receiver and spoke reassuring words to the Commissioner. MacMorran had evidently reported early concerning their first visit to the Traquair house. Eventually Sir Austin rang off and Anthony prepared to await the coming of eight o'clock. Punctually on the stroke of the hour Inspector Rudge met him in the lounge of the "Golden Thistle". At twenty-two minutes past eight Rudge opened Dr. Traquair's front door and he and Anthony made their way towards the surgery. Rudge looked at his watch. "She should be here in a few minutes," he remarked. "We'll wait for her."

"What sort of a girl is she?" asked Anthony Bathurst.

"Oh, all right. Bit dopy. But I suppose she'd be about average as girls go, on jobs like hers. I've seen her two or three times since this business started, and on the whole I must say, if I'm quite fair, that she's not done too badly. However, you'll see her for yourself in a few minutes and you'll be able to judge."

Anthony nodded. "After this interview, Rudge, I want to have another look round the place. Remind me, will you?"

"Before we go this evening, Mr. Bathurst?"

"Yes, I think so. Provided that we don't get away from here too late."

"Very good, sir." Rudge looked at his watch again. "Not long to wait now," he remarked. "Jolly quiet in here, isn't it? All Dr. Traquair's panel patients have been transferred to Dr. Broome down the road. The local Insurance Committee had to make special arrangements about them."

Mr. Bathurst nodded. But it seemed to the Inspector that Mr. Bathurst was not paying full attention to him. Indeed, his thoughts appeared to be a long way away. Rudge, watching, saw a strange expression cross his companion's face. "Do you know, Inspector," said Anthony with due solemnity, "that I believe I heard a noise that came from upstairs?"

Rudge shook his head disclaimingly. "Very likely, sir. But nothing to worry about. The wind in all probability. Caused a door to slam, I expect. There can't be anybody here—if that's the sort of thing you were thinking of. The place has been locked up since we left it yesterday."

"All right, Inspector. I'll take your word for it. But I certainly thought that I heard something."

Rudge looked up. "I can hear somebody at the front door. More than one of them at that. I'll see who it is."

When Rudge opened Dr. Traquair's front door he was surprised to find that Phoebe Hubbard was accompanied by no less a person than Inspector Andrew MacMorran.

"Good evening, Inspector Rudge," said the latter—"I'm not the only one who wants you, seemingly. I've brought Miss Hubbard with me. I managed to get back more quickly than I had anticipated. Is Mr. Bathurst here yet? I've had a word this afternoon with the Commissioner, so that I know pretty well what's doing. Step right in, Miss Hubbard, and don't be afraid of anything."

Rudge answered him. "Come in, Miss Hubbard, and you too, Inspector. Mr. Bathurst and I have been here for some little time. He's inside—waiting."

Rudge noticed that Phoebe Hubbard looked very pale. Doubtless the girl had gone through much since she had returned from her walk on the evening of the murder and found, firstly, Dr. Traquair's note and, secondly, the morning after, the dead body of her mistress. Rudge and MacMorran piloted her to the surgery, where Anthony Bathurst sat awaiting her. The former introduced her. "This is Miss Hubbard, Mr. Bathurst. Phoebe Hubbard, to give you her name in full."

Anthony saw a tall, thin, almost gawky girl in front of him whose age he put at about twenty-five. She had a sharp, rather well-shaped nose, short dark hair and quick-moving brown eyes. Nature had intended her for a boy, Anthony considered with quick assessment, as he addressed her.

"Good evening, Miss Hubbard," he said. "I am glad that you have come along to see us. Because I want to ask you one or two questions."

"Yes," she answered him pleasantly, in a clear, rather strong voice. "Good evening, sir. May I sit down?—then I'll try to answer your questions—that is if I can."

Anthony waved her to a seat. As she took it, he noticed her hands. They were well kept, if a trifle large, and he judged that her duties with the Traquairs had not been too arduous, from the point of view of manual labour. The hands were neither rough nor coarsened.

"How long have you worked for Mrs. Traquair?"

"About ten months, sir."

"Where were you before that?"

"Nowhere, sir. I started work here. This was my first situation."

Anthony looked at her closely. "Your first, you say?"

"Yes, sir. You see, it's like this. My brother and I are orphans. We lived together—I kept house for him—until he got married. When that happened I had to get a place. So I came here."

"I see. Were you comfortable here?"

Anthony thought that she hesitated just a shade before she replied to his last question. But when she did answer her words came quickly enough. "Yes, sir. Quite comfortable. If my next place is as good as this one was I shall consider myself a fortunate girl."

Anthony noticed that she spoke well and that her accent was good. He returned to the attack. "Were Dr. Traquair and his wife on good terms? As a married couple? Would you say so?"

"Ordinary, sir. Nothing unusual about them that I ever saw. There were no public quarrels between them, for instance."

"So that you had no warning, as it were, that there was anything like a disaster on the way?"

"No, sir. None at all, sir."

"Their behaviour on the last evening before the tragedy was entirely normal?"

"Yes, sir."

"You noticed nothing that gave you the slightest inkling of the terrible events which were to follow?"

"Nothing, sir."

"Everything to do with the household, then, was absolutely as it would be day in and day out?"

Phoebe Hubbard shook her sleek head.

"No, sir. I wouldn't go quite so far as to say that."

Anthony showed signs of surprise, and MacMorran and Rudge pressed forward a little.

"Why?" questioned the last-named a trifle sharply. "You've not mentioned anything of this kind before. Why didn't you?"

"You never asked me, Inspector. Not as this gentleman has. I answered the questions that you asked me. I'm sorry if I've done any wrong."

Anthony intervened. "Better late than never, Inspector Rudge. Let's hear what Miss Hubbard has to tell us now she's here. Fire away, young lady. What was your point?"

Phoebe's brown eyes flashed Mr. Bathurst a look of gratitude. "Just this, sir. That day, on the afternoon of the day of the murder, Mrs. Traquair had a visitor. And as we didn't have visitors every day, I couldn't agree with you quite when you used the expression 'day in and day out'. Have I made my meaning clear, sir?"

"Quite, Miss Hubbard. And I accept your explanation. But tell me—who was this visitor? A friend or a stranger?"

"A friend, sir. At least, I suppose he was. You'd call him that, I think. He had been to see Mrs. Traquair and the doctor several times before."

"And the doctor? Was he a friend of Dr. Traquair as well?"

"Well, sir—they appeared to be quite friendly together."

"Who was this man? Do you know his name?"

"No, sir. I have never heard his name that I can remember."

Rudge interposed brusquely. "That's strange—taking you at your own words. You said that he had been to the house several times before. Doesn't that mean that you have let him in?"

Phoebe Hubbard was unperturbed by the almost direct attack.

"No, sir," she replied again. "The mistress, Mrs. Traquair, always brought him in with her. As though she had met him somewhere and brought him home. I can't recall that I have ever heard his name."

Rudge's eyes spoke volumes, but MacMorran's face was grave and set. Anthony sought detail. "Is this man a young man, Miss Hubbard?"

"About the same age as Dr. Traquair, I should say, sir. Perhaps a little older."

"Thirty-five to forty—eh?"

"About that, sir. At least I think so."

"On this particular afternoon you didn't hear any of the conversation, I suppose?"

"No, sir. I took in the tea on the tea-wagon. Then Mrs. Traquair told me that I could go. I didn't see the gentleman again."

"Can you describe the man?" demanded Inspector Rudge.

Phoebe Hubbard nodded her head briskly.

"Tall and dark. Black eyes and hair. White teeth. Rather foreign-looking."

"Did he speak with a foreign accent?" asked Rudge.

The girl hesitated before replying. "Perhaps—a little. But not *very* much."

MacMorran leant forward in his chair. "Miss Hubbard," he said purposefully, "tell Mr. Bathurst the story of your disturbed night. From the moment when you found the doctor's message to you."

"Just a minute," said Anthony; "where exactly did you find Dr. Traquair's message to you?"

"On the—mantelpiece, sir . . . in the—"

Rudge was in like a flash: "You said before that you picked it up off the kitchen table."

Phoebe nodded quickly. "Yes. So I did. I'm wrong. Thank you for correcting me, Inspector. I did find it on the kitchen table in the first place. I must have put it on the mantelpiece myself afterwards and that's what made me say that just now."

"You are sure that this note was written by Dr. Traquair? Quite positive?"

"Oh, quite certain, sir. I know the doctor's handwriting far too well to make a mistake over it."

"I see. You are certain of it. Good! And in view of what Dr. Traquair wrote to you, you went to bed?"

"Yes, sir. I went to bed directly I was able to."

"After a time you were awakened, I understand?"

"Yes, sir. I was asleep very quickly. I was very tired that night. I didn't hear Dr. Traquair come in either. I suppose that I must have dozed off almost at once. Then, about a quarter to two I should think it must have been, I heard a lot of noise that seemed to be coming from all over the house. I was very frightened. There was so much noise. As though many men were in the house. I was afraid to move. So I stayed in bed for what seemed to me hours. Then I heard noises on the stairs, so I jumped out of bed and bolted the bedroom door. Made a barricade too with chairs. Then I heard doors opening and shutting. And I prayed that nobody would come into my bedroom. My prayer was answered. At last the house was quiet again."

"What time would that be?" Anthony put the question quickly.

But the girl's reply was equally as quick: "Just before five o'clock, sir. When I knew that the men had gone, I slipped on a few clothes and thought that I would try to find out, if I could, what had been happening in the house. Of course, you know now what I did find. In the lounge was the body of Mrs. Traquair. She was quite dead and I could see that she had been dead for some time. So I went to the telephone at once and told the Police all I could." Phoebe Hubbard finished her statement quite simply and unaffectedly.

"Thank you, Miss Hubbard," said Anthony Bathurst, "your story has helped me considerably. There's nothing like information that comes to one first-hand. Now that the Inspector and I have—" Mr. Bathurst stopped suddenly.

For a reason! The eyes of everybody in the room were as alight as his were. Rudge sprang to his feet. He put into words the thought that was in everybody's mind. "That was the front door. Being closed—somebody has been in the house and has just gone out."

Rudge dashed out of the room. Anthony spoke to MacMorran: "We shan't get him now, Andrew. Too many people about in the street there. A few steps and he'd be lost in the crowd."

Rudge was back with them almost as quickly as he had gone. "What does this mean?" he asked with some emotion. "Who is it that comes to this house now?"

Anthony looked across at Phoebe Hubbard and scratched his cheek. "You know, Inspector," he remarked quietly, "I'm beginning to think that I was right some little time ago. You will remember that I suggested we had some unexpected company upstairs before Miss Hubbard arrived, but you overruled me. I'm not blaming you—but I think that you would have done better to have listened to me."

Rudge conceded the point. "I'm afraid that you're right and that you *were* right, Mr. Bathurst. Though I can't think who'd come 'gate-crashing' to this establishment."

"I think we had better search the house," contributed MacMorran.

"You've taken the words from my mouth, Andrew," returned Anthony Bathurst. "In my opinion, the sooner we look over the place the better. There's one thing—we have Miss Hubbard here with us—she should know the lie of the land as well as anybody. We'll take her with us on our voyage of exploration."

"Let's hope it will turn out to be a voyage of discovery," said MacMorran nonchalantly; "that will serve us a great deal better."

"Depends on what we discover," supplemented Anthony. "Lead the way, Miss Hubbard, will you? Don't be afraid."

The girl showed what, in the circumstances, were natural signs of hesitation.

"We shall be with you all the time. There's nothing to fear. I suggest that we try upstairs first."

"Where?" asked Phoebe Hubbard.

"Say to Dr. Traquair's room, shall we?"

"We know the way," said Rudge rather curtly. "Come on."

They ascended the staircase, the girl and Inspector Rudge in the van. As they went up, everything in the house seemed quiet. To MacMorran's sensitive ear it seemed an ominous quietness. They went to the staircase landing. Anthony noticed that the stair-carpet was thick. In quality he judged it much better than the average. The rugs, too, on the landing were all of equally excellent quality. "How was the doctor situated financially?" he asked Inspector Rudge.

"Oh, very well. I should say that he must have a private income of some kind. He's far better housed than the ordinary G.P."

Anthony was watching Phoebe Hubbard. "Would you agree with that, Miss Hubbard?" he asked her.

"With what, sir?"

"With the opinion that Inspector Rudge has just expressed?"

"I should say that Dr. Traquair was very comfortable," she answered slowly. "Though, of course, I know nothing about such things as his private income. He always seemed to have plenty of patients."

Rudge stopped at a bedroom door. "Here's the doctor's bedroom," he announced, "which I suppose is the room that Mr. Bathurst wants to have a look at first."

"Not very long since we were in here," said Mr. Bathurst. The four of them entered. Phoebe Hubbard came last. It was as well. For, the moment they entered, Anthony pointed to the floor and to a hand that protruded from beneath the bed.

CHAPTER IV
THE DEAD MAN UNDER THE BED

(Told by the Author)

"Unless I'm very much mistaken," said Anthony Lotherington Bathurst, "the dead hand speaketh."

Phoebe Hubbard paled at the shock which the first sight of the hand must have given her, but she made no startled sound, as many girls in her position must have done. MacMorran and Rudge went on their knees by the bedside. Anthony saw them pull out the body of which the sign had been the gruesome hand. The body of a man. He knew at once, directly he saw it, that the man was dead. Although he had obviously not been dead for very long. Anthony heard Rudge swear under his breath. MacMorran grunted and Phoebe Hubbard stood with her back to the bedroom door with a horrified look showing on her face. Anthony stood away from the body so that she should be able to see it better. Not that he had any desire to lacerate her feelings. What he thought was this. That if any identification were to be forthcoming there was much more probability that it would come from Phoebe Hubbard than from Inspector Rudge himself.

The man was young. Black hair, black eyes and a swarthy colouring gave him an undoubted foreign appearance. Anthony thought of Phoebe's description of the man who had visited the Traquairs on the afternoon of the murder. He began to wonder and to toy with the allurement of theories. "Shot," he heard Rudge say to MacMorran as the two of them huddled over the body. "Shot through the heart. Tiny wound, judging by the hole in the clothes here. Fired, too, at fairly close quarters. Well—this is a facer and no mistake. Body still warm. The murder may actually have been committed during the time we've been here. That's a nice thing for us to have to tell people. My lucky day—I don't think."

MacMorran said something to his colleague which Anthony wasn't able to distinguish properly. Rudge replied to him: "Yes. I'll 'phone and get the Divisional Surgeon along as quickly as I can. Stay here for a moment, will you? I'll do the job at once."

Rudge motioned to Phoebe Hubbard to stand away from the bedroom door so that he might have passage. This action on the part of the Inspector brought the girl nearer to the body. Anthony beckoned to her to come and stand by him. "Miss Hubbard," he said to her, "an idea has just come to me. To be strictly truthful, it came to me a few moments ago. It was suggested to me by your description of the man who was here with the Traquairs on the day that Mrs. Traquair was killed. The details, as I remember them, were—age thirty-five to forty, tall, dark, black eyes, white teeth, and generally rather foreign-looking. Well, Miss Hubbard, those particulars wouldn't be out of the way as applied to this man here. What do you think yourself?"

Mr. Bathurst watched her carefully as he put the question to her. Phoebe Hubbard stared at the corpse with a sort of horrified fascination in her eyes. She shook her head from side to side with a strange regularity. But she made no direct reply. Anthony pressed her. "Well, what do you say, Miss Hubbard?"

"Yes," she almost whispered her answer, "the description that I gave would almost fit this man. But—" She paused.

"But what?" demanded Mr. Bathurst. "Is it the man or isn't it? We want you to tell us one way or the other."

"I am not—sure," said the puzzled Phoebe. "It is like him. It looks like he looked . . . and yet . . . I am not sure." She repeated the last words almost challengingly. Anthony was mystified. There was something here that he wasn't able to understand.

"What is it exactly that you're uncertain about, Miss Hubbard?"

"It looks like him as I look this side . . . but when I turn my head and look this way it doesn't. I know that it must sound silly, but I can't put it to you any differently."

MacMorran, who had been listening to the dialogue, took a hand. "Maybe he's dressed differently from the time you saw him before, miss? Clothes, and costume generally, can make a great difference. Isn't that what's troubling you?"

Her eyes brightened perceptibly at the MacMorran assistance. "It may be that, Inspector, that's making me so uncertain of things. Very likely. But I'm not sure and it's not a bit of good my saying I am. I mustn't mislead you, must I?"

Before either Anthony or MacMorran could reply, Rudge was back in the bedroom. "I've 'phoned through. Dr. Meldrum is already on his way up here. I was lucky enough to catch him there. Until he comes we'll leave the body as it is. Have you had a look round, Mr. Bathurst?"

"No. Not yet, Inspector. While you've been away I've been asking Miss Hubbard a question on this dead man's identity. Whether this man was the friend of Mrs. Traquair whom she has already told us about. But she's not sure, Inspector. She'll go as far as to say that it's like him, but she won't go a step farther than that."

Rudge nodded. "I expect it's the man all right. At any rate, that was the idea I had, directly we spotted him here. The eternal triangle all over again. That's what it will turn out to be. I'll run over him. See what's on him. Then we'll get him identified in two shakes of a cow's tail. Hark! There's a car stopping outside. That'll be Dr. Meldrum from the station." Rudge turned and rattled down the stairs. They heard his voice at the door. Another voice mingled with it. The front door closed. Steps ascending the stairs could be heard again.

"Need I stay through all this?" asked Phoebe Hubbard in a tone of quiet resignation.

"Don't go for a moment or so," returned Anthony to her. "I'll speak to Inspector Rudge about it. Better still—go and wait in one of the other rooms. You know the house. Come with me." Anthony took her out. "I know what," he said, on the threshold, "go and sit in your own bedroom until Dr. Meldrum's finished. There he comes with Inspector Rudge. Go on."

The girl nodded gratefully at Mr. Bathurst's suggestion. Rudge and the Divisional Surgeon came past her. Dr. Meldrum was a thin, long-faced man with drooping eyes and loose lips. His blue eyes betrayed but little excitement as they took in the body on the floor by the bed. He proceeded to his work methodically and completely unemotionally. Anthony heard him repeat the words that Rudge had previously used to Inspector MacMorran. "H'm! Shot. Through the heart. At close quarters. Small-sized bullet. From one of those small automatics, I should say, that are so commonly in use these days. Been dead less than an hour and must have died almost instantaneously. When I get the bullet out, gentlemen, I'll let you have the dimensions." Dr. Meldrum rose to his feet. "Foreigner, I should imagine. Thirty-eight or thereabouts. Judging by the usual external evidences. Well dressed. And a man, too, who is in good condition, moreover." He turned to Inspector Rudge. "Well—there you are, Inspector! You've heard what I said. Make arrangements for the mortuary, will you?" Then he spoke more generally. It seemed that certain ideas had come to him. His remarks appeared to embrace both MacMorran and Anthony Bathurst. "What's this chap doing in here, gentlemen? Any idea?"

Rudge went back to the body again. "Now that you've had your look at him, Doctor, I'll run him over. I may get a clue of sorts to his identity." Rudge knelt on the floor and systematically went through the dead man's pockets. A small amount in cash, three keys (all small), a stub of lead pencil, and a card with a row of numbers marked on it were the sum total of Rudge's discoveries. The card, in size, shape and texture was very similar to those cards attached to which part-skeins of wool are sold. Rudge stood up and held his findings out for general inspection. "No papers, visiting-cards or documents, gentlemen. This is the lot. So that we're no nearer to knowing who the man is than we were when we first found him." Anthony took the card from him and inspected it curiously. The numbers were arranged in the following order: 8. 22. 58. 66. 85. 99. Through the first four numbers a line had been struck as though they had been cancelled. "Eight, twenty-two, fifty-eight and sixty-six struck out," commented Anthony Bathurst. "H'm! The first number still standing is eighty-five. Code of some kind, I suppose." Dr. Meldrum spoke dispassionately. "More in this Traquair case than appears on the surface. I've thought that right from the beginning. Well, I'm off. See to the mortuary arrangements, Rudge. Good evening." Dr. Meldrum waved to them and took his departure. Anthony faced Rudge and Inspector MacMorran. He put a direct question to them. "Well, what do you make of this latest business, gentlemen?"

"What do you?" countered MacMorran.

Before Anthony could reply Rudge cut in. "What about that girl? There's no point in keeping her here any longer, is there? Where did she go?"

"She went into her bedroom and waited. Call her and tell her you're through with her for now—if you really feel that you are." Rudge nodded. "I can't see that we need detain her any longer. Can you, Inspector MacMorran?"

MacMorran expressed his agreement. Rudge went to the door and called her. Her answering voice was heard immediately and then her approaching footsteps. "Come in, Miss Hubbard," said Rudge. The girl followed him into the room. "We're sorry that your visit this evening has coincided with a second tragedy in this house, but, unhappily, things like that are beyond any human control. I take it that if we should want you again the same address will find you?"

"Oh yes, Inspector. At any time. Until I get another place, that is. But if I do I'll let you know at once where it is and when I'm going to it. Is that all for this evening, Inspector?"

"Yes, thank you, Miss Hubbard. I'll see you out. And another thing—for the next hour or so at least keep your mouth shut with regard to what's happened in here to-night. No sensational stories—mind!"

Phoebe nodded her head briskly, said good night all round and followed in the wake of Rudge downstairs.

"What was your point just now, Mr. Bathurst?" This from MacMorran as Rudge left them. "I feel sure that there *was* something when Rudge butted in about that girl."

Anthony took a cigarette from his case and lit it with the utmost deliberation. "I'll tell you what occurred to me, Andrew. I'll admit, though, that I'm taking a good deal for granted. But Rudge is undoubtedly barking up the tree labelled 'the eternal triangle', isn't he? He's harped on it more than once."

"Yes, I'll give you that. And I'm not saying he's wrong either."

"For the moment then—we'll go with him, Andrew. Right! Then how's this? I'll guarantee that I give you a surprise. The question that's agitating you and all your people and that has *been* agitating you and them for some time now is 'Where is Dr. Traquair?' Yes?"

MacMorran nodded. "Ay. Go on."

"Well, how's this? I mean as an answer to that question. Dr. Traquair, less than an hour ago, was in this house."

MacMorran started to his feet, his eyes blazing with incredulity. Mr. Bathurst's statement regarding surprise found its mark. "You mean that seriously? Or is it just a mere theory that you're toying with?"

Anthony shrugged broad shoulders and smiled. "I'm afraid I mean it seriously, Andrew. Honest Injun! But here's Rudge back from seeing Miss Hubbard off. Try *him* with it. See what his reactions are."

Rudge bustled in.

"What's this about my reactions?"

"Just this, Rudge. Mr. Bathurst thinks that the man on the floor there was bumped off by our friend the missing Dr. Traquair. Or in other words, that Traquair, for whom we're all searching, was actually here this evening in person. How do you react to that?"

Rudge replied to him with ready coolness. "Well, to tell the absolute truth, I was considering the very same point as I came upstairs just now. As I see it, it's the eternal triangle." Rudge rolled the phrase round his lips. "Traquair first of all killed his wife and then came back and killed her lover. For I'm pretty certain in my own mind that this stiff here is the same one who had bread and butter and cake on the afternoon of the day when the missus was killed. Tea for two—until number three came on the scene. You see if I'm not right." He turned to Anthony. "Is that your line of country, Mr. Bathurst?"

"H'm! Partly perhaps. There are weaknesses about it, you know. Here's one to go on with. If Traquair came back this evening to get his dead wife's lover, how did he manage to arrive so entirely opportunely? Had you thought of that, Rudge?"

"Yes," returned Rudge promptly. "In some way, either Traquair or this man that's been shot had contrived to make an appointment with the other. That's my explanation. It's perfectly feasible, isn't it?"

Anthony made the semblance of a grimace. "Would the other man, as we will continue to call him, have fallen for such an appointment, knowing Traquair's state of mind at the time? That's the point which it seems to me requires the most explanation, Rudge."

"Perhaps it does, Mr. Bathurst. By the way—another little matter I want to have out with you before I forget it. Where did you say just now that Miss Hubbard had gone to wait?"

Anthony looked at him with strong interest.

"I suggested that she went and waited in her own bedroom. It struck me at the time as being the natural place to which one would send her. Why do you ask?"

"Well, it's rather funny, but you remember a minute or so ago when I called to her and asked her to come in here, don't you?"

Anthony and MacMorran both nodded. Rudge continued his illustration. "I went to this door, if you recall the incident, and I called to her from here. That was so, wasn't it?"

The other two gave him agreement. "Well, she didn't come out of her own bedroom. She came out of Dr. Traquair's spare room. I'm certain on the point because I saw her. Struck me as peculiar—that's all."

There was a silence after Rudge had spoken. Anthony flicked the ash from the end of his cigarette. "D'you know, Inspector, I find that fragment of information decidedly interesting. So she came from Dr. Traquair's other room, did she, and not from her own? That young lady certainly has an appeal. Let us go into the room ourselves . . . the gentleman on the floor there won't be any more lonely on account of our departure. I have an idea."

The room, however, yielded nothing. There were no signs of disturbance.

Anthony led the way back into the bedroom of Dr. Traquair. He walked over to the clothes-cabinet which had aroused their interest on the day before. He pointed to the doors of the cabinet. "Have a look in that hat-box again, Rudge, will you, please?"

Showing signs of surprise, Rudge obeyed the instruction. He bent down, took out the hat-box and opened it. "I think," said Mr. Bathurst, "that you will find that the hat initialled 'F.C.' is no longer there."

Rudge shook his head—it is feared with some satisfaction. "On the contrary, Mr. Bathurst," he remarked, "the hat initialled 'F.C.' is still in here. As far as I can see, just as it was when we last looked at it."

Anthony quietly placed his cigarette-stub in a convenient ash-tray. "H'm," he said, "so I've drawn a blank there—have I? Not so good." He sat down. "Let me think for a minute, gentlemen. My mind has become untidy. I must retrace many of my steps."

Anthony Bathurst stretched the length of his legs. Rudge and MacMorran stood and watched him—one at each end of the mantel-piece. Rudge's right elbow rested on the mantelpiece. Against his left side he held the hat-box. MacMorran rubbed his chin. There was silence in the house of Dr. Traquair. Silence and death!

CHAPTER V
FRESH CAST. BY ANTHONY

(Told by the Author)

MINUTES passed—and the silence was unbroken. The only sound that disturbed the silence came from the occasional movement of Rudge's feet. MacMorran heard it and judged that Rudge was impatient. Anthony Bathurst took another cigarette from his case and handed the case to his two companions. Two matches were struck. Again the silence. Then Rudge relaxed and placed the hat-box on the floor. Anthony smoked hard and quickly. He had almost finished this last cigarette before he spoke. "Andrew," he said to MacMorran—"this Miss Hubbard of our to-night's companionship—the more I think things over, the more I find myself intrigued by our Phoebe. Our most certainly superior Phoebe."

"What about her?" inquired the practical MacMorran.

"Why, this, Andrew. When you arrived here this evening you said that you had brought Miss Hubbard with you. You told Inspector Rudge when he opened the door to you. I was listening and I distinctly remember you said that."

"Quite right, Mr. Bathurst. I did say that."

"Tell me then, Andrew—how far exactly was that statement of yours correct?"

"All the way, Mr. Bathurst—and then some, as they say across the water. If you want to check up on her movements—and I take it that's your idea—I'll tell you this. Miss Hubbard got into my train at Eastminster, on my way down from town. I recognized her. I had seen her once or twice before on this inquiry, you know. I spoke to her, she confirmed my impression of her, she came and sat next to me, we talked all the time on the journey down—and she accompanied me from the station here. I can give her a completely satisfactory alibi for some two hours and more. Now—how do you like the sound of that?"

"Not much, Andrew. I'll willingly admit it. But there's something wrong somewhere—I know that. Where—I don't know."

Rudge looked up at the sound of a vehicle stopping outside.

"There's the ambulance," he said simply . . . Rudge went back to the bedroom to superintend the necessary arrangements. There were inevitable noise and disturbance. Anthony and MacMorran waited and listened. Anthony put questions to MacMorran. The latter knew what this activity signified. Mr. Bathurst was on the track of something again. Fresh spoor strewed on the ground in front of him—the ground at which he looked.

"What do *you* think of Phoebe Hubbard, Andrew? I'd like to know. Your views on the matter should be important. Because your journey down from town this evening gave you opportunities of judging her, which have certainly been denied—if not to Rudge— to me. You conversed with her when she was more or less normal. Not so much 'on duty' and therefore much more inclined to be off her guard. Conversation must mean a certain amount of mental exposure—that's almost a *sine qua non*. Thoughts are dragged from their hiding-places, as it were, and, because of this, see the light of day even before they are intended to."

MacMorran's face was as impassive as a mask. "Before I answer that, Mr. Bathurst, let me put a question to you. What do I think of her, you say? In what way do you mean, particularly? I've a verra good reason for asking you that."

Anthony demurred. "But I didn't want to give you any sort of a lead, Andrew. To do so will defeat my object. I don't want to put words or even ideas into your mouth or your mind. Look at it like this. How would you describe her to Mrs. MacMorran when you're giving her an account of this evening's doings at supper one night?" Anthony pressed because he knew that the Inspector never failed to respond to a hook baited as this had been.

MacMorran nodded.

"I see what you mean. Better now than I did. I'll not be deny- ing that—well, how can I put it? She's intelligent enough. Not bad-lookin'. Too modern, perhaps, for my likin'. You know what I'm gettin' at. The girls aren't so feminine as they used to be in my time. Ape the boys. Speaks nicely. Well-mannered. Still—I suppose you'd expect that—bein' attached to a doctor's household. Well dressed—as far as I've been in a position to see. On the whole, Mr. Bathurst, and summing up, as it were, I'd describe her as a 'superior' girl. The same word that you yourself used just now. A long way in front of most maids whom you'd meet doing a similar sort of job to the one she's been doin'."

Anthony smiled in cheerful agreement. "Then you're with me, Andrew—all the way. You've described Miss Hubbard in very similar terms to those that I should have employed."

MacMorran eyed him with puzzled interest. "Well—now that you've got that out of me, where are you? Better off—I suppose you'd say."

"Yes—in a way. Two heads are better than one—even when one of the two's yours, you old villain." Anthony grinned at him.

"What are you leading up to, Mr. Bathurst?"

Anthony began to pace the room. "Candidly, Andrew, I don't know. I'll be perfectly frank with you. Although Dr. Traquair fills the bill in many ways as the man who was in here this evening—yet in many others he doesn't. And it's no good my shutting my eyes to this latter fact. It will be as well, though, if Rudge redoubles Police vigilance in this quarter, especially in view of what's just happened."

"He'll see to that all right. I've been thinking again of those numbers on that card which the dead man had. You mentioned the word 'code'—didn't you?"

"That was my suggestion. Purely a chance shot, though. Little to back it up. Why do you ask?"

"Well, I've been thinkin' about those numbers, Mr. Bathurst. Quite a lot, as we've been sittin' here. And I'll tell you something that's occurred to me about them. It strikes me that they may signify certain things which have got to be obtained. Possibly from this Dr. Traquair. Now, do you know what he had in his possession? Papers, letters, documents?"

Anthony seemed surprised to hear MacMorran's line of argument.

"Incriminating letters do you mean?"

"I don't know. Maybe. There may even be a touch of the 'black' in it. Somebody may have been 'puttin' on the black', for all we know. There are more unlikely things."

Anthony looked at him. "Are you hinting at such things as love-letters?"

"If you like. They'll do as well as any other. Let me develop the idea. We'll assume, for the sake of the argument, that Dr. Traquair had certain letters in his possession. Written either by his wife to a third party or by the third party to his wife. There were six of these letters all told. They were numbered as we saw on that piece of card we took off this last dead man. The first four of these had been picked up. There were still two remaining. Numbers eighty-five and ninety-nine. They were the two that he had come for this evening—and instead of getting them he took a lump of lead instead. There you are, Mr. Bathurst. Pick the bones out of that."

Anthony shook his head. "Too easy, Andrew. Bones all over the place. Don't need any picking out. For instance, why give ordinary letters such unusual numbers as those the card bore? Ranging from eight to ninety-nine with no definite progression intervening. Why not number them just one to six or even letter them from, say, 'A to F'?"

"We don't know all, Mr. Bathurst. Those numbers that have been used may, for all we know now, have especial significance." As he spoke, MacMorran shrugged his shoulders.

"You may be right, Andrew, but I very much doubt it. Another thing—how about the cards? The playing-cards? How about your Curse of Scotland? Have you forgotten all about that?"

MacMorran stared at him but said nothing.

"No playing-cards in the bedroom to-night, Andrew, where the dead man lay. As I see it, the two murders don't tally. There's a vital piece missing from the pattern somewhere." Rudge returned as Anthony finished speaking. "That job's all right. They've cleared. Not sorry. Rotten business at the best of times."

He took his handkerchief and wiped his forehead. "Don't know where we are. Didn't know when I came. Know still less now. That girl puzzled me. Such an air of confidence about her this evening. Always has been, right from the first occasion when I interviewed her, but I noticed it more than ever to-night. Funny! Can't put my finger on anything wrong—but there you are. Sort of leaves you all unsettled." Rudge replaced his handkerchief with a gesture that might have meant disappointment and might even have meant resentment.

Anthony nodded his corroboration. "I know how you feel, Inspector. As a matter of fact, I feel much the same myself. I fear that we shall have to mark time more or less until you've had this dead man identified. Before that happens, an investigation is too much like chasing a needle in a haystack."

"I agree, Mr. Bathurst. All the steps that we can take towards getting him identified I've already arranged. The machinery is actually in motion. Any moment from now may bring something in. Perhaps even a 'squeak' of a kind from somewhere. You never know." Anthony turned to MacMorran. "I'd like to go through Dr. Traquair's papers. I presume that you've made the usual list."

"Inspector Rudge passed a packet over to me. You can see 'em whenever you care to, Mr. Bathurst."

"Good," returned Anthony; "and as far as I'm concerned, the sooner the better. Let's find a drink somewhere, Andrew."

CHAPTER VI
BENEFIT PERFORMANCE

(Told by the Author)

ANTHONY Lotherington Bathurst took the air of Brooke. He walked from his place of temporary residence down the High Road. He passed by the surgery of Dr. Traquair and also by the establishment of Morley & Son, but, unhappily from his point of view as an investigator, the latter place held no interest for him beyond the ordinary. Anthony walked up one side of the High Road and returned down the other. He had a great deal to think over and he had come to the conclusion that it might be wise for him to look round Brooke generally.

He reasoned in this way. Dr. Traquair had lived in Brooke for some years. Few people have the opportunities to know the conditions and circumstances of the various inhabitants of a town such as Brooke was better than a popular and much-sought-after general practitioner. Anthony had determined, therefore, to keep his eyes and ears open as he made his way in and around Brooke, in the hope that a fragment of vital information might come to him down the avenue of one of these two senses. Mr. Bathurst reached a convenient turning-point at the corner of a side street and resolved to retrace his steps. As he did so he suddenly caught sight of a bill that was showing in the front of a shop window. The manner in which a certain name had been arranged by the printers of the bill attracted Mr. Bathurst's attention. Inspired by curiosity, he walked to the window so that he might the more easily read the contents of the bill. The terms of the announcement were as follows:

RENDLESHAM HALL, BROOKE.

Mr. Bathurst noted the venue and the date which followed. Neither of these was important to him. In the words of the immortal Hanaud, "the importances" of the advertisement showed below. Mr. Bathurst read on carefully. "A Grand Benefit Concert will be given on behalf of the widow and dependants of the late Frederick Curtis." The initial letters of the beneficiaries' names had been printed in such a way that they hit the eye and immediately arrested the onlookers' attention.

"F.C.," he murmured to himself. "Coincidence or something more? At any rate, I can do the cause no harm by reading on." Mr. Bathurst thereupon read on. "Frederick Curtis . . . who was the victim of a tragic accident on . . ." He checked the date. With grim satisfaction he noted that the date was the exact day of the first Traquair murder. "The following artists have positively consented to appear and in every case their services will be gratuitous. Your old favourites . . ."

Anthony read through the list . . . but the names of the performers as given were of little interest to him. He racked his brain for ideas. "Fred Curtis." There were the initials staring him in the face right enough. *Could* it be coincidence? There was another issue, too, which merited his special consideration. This man Frederick Curtis had been "the victim of a tragic accident". And it had occurred on a date which already loomed large in his own particular problem. A closer investigation of the Curtis accident was certainly demanded of him. Anthony walked away from the contemplation of the bill and made his way down the High Road again. At the foot of the hill he had read that tickets for the concert could be obtained from "Mr. Samuel Bullivant, at the 'Dagmar Arms', Trelawney Road". Mr. Bathurst looked at his wrist-watch. The time was both convenient and opportune for a visit to Mr. Bullivant. Now, Anthony had seen that particular road-direction sign at some time during his enforced stay in the Borough of Brooke and he thought he would be able to walk to it with but little difficulty. His power of memory stood him in good stead, and within a few moments he found himself standing at the corner of Trelawney Road. He could see the building of the "Dagmar Arms" but a short distance down the road on the left-hand side. Anthony walked to it and went straight in. "The Guv'nor?" echoed an industrious barman. "Yes, he's in. Shall I tell him you want him?"

"I'd be obliged," returned Mr. Bathurst cordially.

The barman slid off on his errand and within a few moments returned with Samuel Bullivant. The latter was heavily fat, bespectacled and had strands of lank dark hair which flopped untidily over his ivory-white forehead. Anthony smiled at him pleasantly, but Samuel didn't appear to be in the cream of tempers. He was, to use his own expression, "rattled". Worries and anxieties had crowded upon him all day.

"What is it?" he asked, scowling. His speech was thick and guttural. Anthony judged him of the chosen people.

"I'm sorry to trouble you," he declared, "but I've called for just a trifling item of information." Anthony produced his card.

Bullivant read it, but the ill-tempered expression did not leave his face. "You'd better come along into my office. I hope you won't keep me long."

Anthony followed him into a small room. One table and two chairs occupied almost all the available space. "Who is it this time?" inquired Sam Bullivant. "What's the trouble? I'm prepared for anything in this place."

"No trouble, Mr. Bullivant. Despite the fact that 'Scotland Yard' is on my card I'm not always a bird of ill omen."

Bullivant's face cleared a little. "That's better. You gave me a bit of a turn. You can't be too careful in this place—especially in our line, you know. Really reliable managers are hard to find. Still—that's neither here nor there. What can I do for you?"

Anthony seated himself in one of the chairs. Bullivant took the other.

"You're running a Benefit Concert for the widow and children of the late Frederick Curtis. Yes?"

Bullivant nodded vigorously. "Yes—but it's all O.K. There's nothing 'phoney' about it. I'm in charge of all the cash side of it. The Committee that's running it made that an absolute condition, otherwise many of them would never have consented to take office."

Anthony smiled. But Bullivant, undeterred, plodded courageously on. "The tickets are all in good hands and Mrs. Curtis, the widow, will get the whole of the proceeds. So you can see that it's all Sir Garnet." Bullivant, with difficulty, pushed a fat finger between his neck and his collar. Anthony smiled again. This time, however, Bullivant was able to see that the smile was a smile of reassurance.

"Thank you, Mr. Bullivant," said Mr. Bathurst. "Although I didn't exactly want all those particulars, they will doubtless prove useful. But what I've called to see you about is this. Who was Frederick Curtis? And how did Frederick Curtis die?"

Bullivant looked at him in astonishment. "Well—why didn't you tell me that when you first started? You gave me quite a turn, I can tell you. Got me all of a dither. So that's all you've come to find out? Who was Fred Curtis?"

Anthony nodded. "That's it. That's what I want to know. Who was Fred Curtis?"

"Fred Curtis, poor fellow, worked for old Morley, the undertaker, as often as the old boy wanted him. Morley's place is in the High Road. Curtis was a sort of assistant at funerals—and—you know—interments."

Bullivant stopped. Anthony felt a pleasing thrill. "An undertaker's assistant." The silk hat fitted the picture. Bullivant continued his story.

"Poor old Fred—he used to use this house and I never heard him say an unkind word about anybody all the years I've known him—was run over. By a bloody great Rolls-Royce. The swine was doin' a cool sixty, so I've heard, in a built-up area. Fred was going down to Morley's to report for duty—he was walking across the street. The car caught him unawares and smashed him up fair and square. Luckily—well, luckily in a way—it was near a doctor's and they got him in there. Sent for his missus, too, they did."

Anthony was in like a flash. "Ah—that's the point, or one of the points that I've come to see you about. Which doctor's did they take the poor chap into? Can you tell me that, Mr. Bullivant?"

The man knitted his brows. "Well, now, I've never given that so much as a thought. But I ought to be able to tell you. Let me see a minute. The accident took place near Tricketer's Cross, in the market square, and that's not far from East Street. Why—they would have taken him into Dr. Traquair's for a certainty. Well—I'm blessed!"

Bullivant paused abruptly as though a strange thought had suddenly come to him. Anthony's eyes met his almost with a challenge. "What's troubling you, Mr. Bullivant?"

"Why—funny thing—never struck me before—it must have been the very same day that the murder took place. The murder at Dr. Traquair's, I mean."

"You're probably right. Now tell me this, Mr. Bullivant. I take it that Curtis died as the result of the injuries he sustained. *Where* did he actually die? Do you know?"

Bullivant produced a big silk handkerchief from the recesses of his sleeve and wiped the moisture from his face. "I do. Curtis died in the Marlborough Ward of the Brooke Hospital. It is called the Commemoration Hospital."

"He was removed there, I presume, from the doctor's where he was first taken? Was that the programme?"

"Yes. That's what took place, undoubtedly. If it was Dr. Traquair who saw him, he probably did all that he could for him and then had him sent on to the hospital. But what's your point, sir? What's all this leading up to?"

"I'm trying to trace all Traquair's movements on the day of the murder. I wanted to make sure as to whether Curtis had been taken into Traquair's surgery or not. Your information will assist me greatly, Mr. Bullivant. Do you happen to know the address of the widow?"

"I can give it to you," replied Bullivant. He took a small book from a back pocket. Anthony watched him as he slowly turned the pages. At length Mr. Bathurst's patience received the reward that it merited. "Here we are!" Bullivant's stubby forefinger stopped on a page of his book and closely indicated an entry that he had himself insisted on making when Mrs. Curtis took the house over. "Number twenty-two Catherick Avenue. She's taken a downstairs flat there. Ought to be moderately comfortable—but, of course, we're giving her all the help that we can in various ways, and in addition we hope to hand over a tidy sum of cash. There are other functions being run for her, you know, Mr. Bathurst, besides the concert."

Anthony nodded. He was thinking of other things.

Bullivant continued to justify the "Frederick Curtis Benefit Fund". "There's a whist drive at the Baptist Hall (specially hired for the occasion), another concert that's still to be fixed, and a social and dance down at the Pirie Library. The Committee mean to do it all well and they've wasted no time in getting right down to the job."

Mr. Bathurst hardly heard him. He had decided to make a further call. At a certain house situated in Catherick Avenue. Twenty-two was the number, to be precise. So he thanked host Sam Bullivant once again and took his departure from the comfort and kindliness of the "Dagmar Arms". A judicious and well-directed inquiry soon put him on the right road to Catherick Avenue and then to the house numbered twenty-two therein. According to Bullivant, Mrs. Curtis occupied a downstairs flat there. The house was an ordinary unpretentious-looking house of the commonplace villa type. One of many thousands which the last few years have seen erected in the land fit for pierrots to live in. Anthony walked to the front door and put a finger on the bell. A woman came in answer to the summons. She was dressed in deep mourning and the heavy black served but to accentuate the ivory pallor of her face. Anthony had little doubt that he faced the widow of the late Frederick Curtis. The task he had chosen to perform was a delicate one, but he had decided upon the opening that he intended to use. She looked up at him inquiringly.

"You will pardon me," he said, "but I believe that you are Mrs. Curtis?"

"Yes, sir," said the woman in black.

"I've just come from Mr. Bullivant of the 'Dagmar Arms'. He gave me your address, Mrs. Curtis."

The woman nodded understandingly. "Is it about the concert? The benefit concert?"

"Well, yes, in a way."

"Perhaps you'd like to come inside, sir?"

"Thank you, Mrs. Curtis. That's kind of you." Anthony was shown into the front room. The woman, it was plain to see, was still in the throes of her bereavement. She was now a widow and her children were fatherless. "I'd be obliged if you would let me have certain information, Mrs. Curtis, about your husband's accident."

"Is it for the newspapers?"

"Oh no. Regard me as a friend who is trying to help."

"It was Fred's own fault, sir. Everybody who saw the car knock him down says so. It wasn't the driver's fault. He might have been goin' a bit fast, but Fred never looked where he was going. He stepped into the road without looking to the right or to the left. Thinkin' of other things. He was a rare one to do that."

"I wasn't intending to ask you anything about that, Mrs. Curtis. It was about something else. When your husband was hurt, you were sent for, weren't you?"

Mrs. Curtis nodded. "Oh yes, sir. They came for me at once. As a matter of fact, I was in the middle of doin' a little bit of washing. Fred was knocked down in the market square just by the Cross. They sent for me and the neighbours broke the news. Then I went to the place where the accident had been and after that to the doctor's."

"Now that's what I want to ask you about. Which doctor did you go to?"

"To Dr. Traquair's, in the High Road. Fred was carried into his surgery and laid on a couch there. Dr. Traquair was ever so kind, too! Gave him every attention. When he found that he could do no more he helped get him off to the hospital. Funny, wasn't it? It was all sickness and death for the doctor that day. Fred in the morning and his wife in the evening."

"Yes, Mrs. Curtis, I agree with you. You're telling me now exactly what I wanted to know. You say that Dr. Traquair gave your husband every attention?"

"Oh yes, sir. Dr. Traquair did all that he possibly could for him. Nobody could have done more for him, I'm sure. You see, it was like this. Fred used to be a sort of odd man for old Morley, the undertaker. Used to get occasional jobs there when he had a rush of funerals. Well, he'd go down to Morley's early to see if there was anything doing. That meant he had to go down there in his professional clothes. Real smart Fred looked, too, when he had them on."

"I see. So that when your husband was knocked down by the car that killed him he was wearing the traditional black clothes of his occupation?"

"Yes, sir. That was what I meant, sir. Fred had on his black frock coat and trousers, black tie, black kid gloves, and, of course, his black top hat."

"Were the clothes damaged very much by the accident, Mrs. Curtis?"

The woman shook her head. "No, sir. Hardly at all. The car caught my husband and just knocked him down flat. At least, that's what I've been told. He was never rolled along the road at all."

"The clothes weren't torn badly, for instance?"

"No, sir, all dusty, but not torn."

"And he was carried into Dr. Traquair's consulting-room wearing them?"

"Yes, sir. His hat, too. One of the men that helped to carry him picked up the hat in his hand."

"I see. Now tell me, Mrs. Curtis, when Dr. Traquair attended him, what happened exactly?"

"About his clothes do you mean, sir?"

"Yes."

"Dr. Traquair took them off. Ever so gently. His back and his inside were where he was hurt most. His arms and legs were all right. The doctor got the coat and waistcoat and the trousers off— indeed, everything—without hurting him hardly at all. A woman couldn't have been kinder with him."

Anthony put his next question carelessly. "Have you the clothes here now, Mrs. Curtis?"

The woman seemed a little disturbed by the question. She began to shake her head and to exhibit just a little distress. "No, sir, I haven't. I suppose that I've done wrong in not raising the point before—but I didn't quite know what I ought to do. You see, when we took poor Fred to the hospital—the ambulance came for him—he was all wrapped up by the doctor and the attendants and his own clothes were left behind in the room at Dr. Traquair's."

"And you have never asked for them to be sent to you?"

"No, sir. Should I have done? What good could they be to anybody? They weren't any use to me, were they? Fred had passed over and none of my boys is big enough yet to wear them. And then there was—the murder—at the doctor's, and what with all the trouble and the police being there—and poor Dr. Traquair being missing—well, I just let things slide, as you might say, and said nothing about Fred's clothes. I'm sorry, sir, if I've done wrong over it. Will there be any trouble, do you think?"

"I don't think so, Mrs. Curtis. At any rate, you need have no worry over it. There'll be no blame attached to you. Your action was quite understandable in the circumstances. I'll tell you, though, what you might do for me now."

Mrs. Curtis looked at him inquiringly. "Yes, sir? I shall be only too pleased."

"Give me a complete list of the clothes your husband left in Dr. Traquair's surgery, will you? Describe to me everything that he was wearing."

"Yes, sir, I will."

"Wait just a moment and I'll write the descriptions down." Mr. Bathurst took out his note-book and began to unscrew the top of his fountain-pen. "Now, Mrs. Curtis, I'm ready. Call the items out to me, will you please, one by one?"

Mrs. Curtis went through the list and Mr. Bathurst jotted down the sartorial inventory. He then checked the details over again with the widow of Curtis. The particulars agreed. Mr. Bathurst rose to go. "Thank you very much, Mrs. Curtis. I am obliged to you. You have been most helpful. The Police Authorities couldn't make out what had become of your husband's clothes and they asked me to inquire."

Mr. Bathurst left the house in Catherick Avenue and made his way slowly back to his hotel. He understood now how Dr. Traquair had made his get-away. News for Inspector Rudge!

CHAPTER VII
CURRENTS AND CROSS-CURRENTS

(Told by the Author)

RUDGE moved quickly across his room at Brooke Police Station. He opened the door with a similarly decisive movement. Inspector MacMorran entered with Anthony Bathurst, who came close behind him. "I've news for you," said Rudge curtly. "The dead man from Traquair's bedroom has been identified. By a woman. According to her story his name is Reicher. Frederick Reicher. Address given is Colorado Street. West. I've discovered that it's one of the small turnings in Soho. Between Roman Street and New Casson Street. I expect you know it, Inspector MacMorran?"

"Ay! Very well indeed. Too well, in fact. I had my wrist slashed with a knife there in October, 1920. Well I remember it. I was down there after a dago concerned in the Paignton Club Scandal. Ay! I know Colorado Street all right! *And* the 'Silver Scimitar' in the near vicinity. Pretty warm shop, let me tell you."

Anthony cut in: "Anything known about this man Reicher?"

Rudge was quick to answer. "Very little, Mr. Bathurst. According to reports up to the moment. But he seems to mix with some pretty shady characters from what we can hear."

"Married?"

Rudge shrugged his shoulders. "I shouldn't like to bank on the ceremonial. But the woman who came here to identify him called herself Mrs. Reicher."

"Was she distressed?"

"Ye-es. I think so. A question like that is difficult to answer—but honestly I think she was."

Anthony looked grave. "What's a foreigner from Soho, of questionable habits and equally questionable antecedents, doing in Dr. Traquair's bedroom? Dead under Dr. Traquair's bed? Undeniably extraordinary. Especially after the murder of the same Dr. Traquair's wife. Don't get it, Rudge. And that's a solid fact, MacMorran. 'Pon my soul, I shall be dragged round to your 'Curse of Scotland' theory before very long, Andrew."

Inspector MacMorran frowned at him. "Say what you like, Mr. Bathurst, and have a jerk at my leg when you will—you can't get away from the fact that there's more in this case than meets the eye. I've said so before and I'll say so again."

"Yes, I'll give you that, Inspector." Mr. Bathurst turned to Rudge. He handed him at the same time a strip of paper. "Cast your eye over that, Rudge, will you?"

Rudge looked at the writing on the paper.

"There you have a complete description," said Mr. Bathurst quietly, "of the clothes which Dr. Traquair was wearing when he left his establishment at some time on the night of the first murder. With one exception."

"With one exception?" Rudge raised his eyebrows.

"I refer to his hat," said Mr. Bathurst. "Those clothes which are listed there are the clothes of Frederick Curtis, an undertaker's assistant. Or perhaps a more modern appellation would be a 'funeral director's deputy'. Unhappily, from Dr. Traquair's point of view, Curtis's hat didn't fit him, so he was compelled to go to his own hat-box for his own hat. When he took his own hat out he put Curtis's in—and we found it." Rudge tapped the paper. "This new description must be circulated at once then. It has made all the difference, no doubt. If we make a special point of asking whether any man dressed in *these* clothes was observed anywhere near Brooke on the night of the murder, or on the morning after, we may pick up some fairly useful information. Yes, Mr. Bathurst, this is going to make a big difference."

"I agree. I shall be interested to hear if anything does come through."

"I will let you know, Mr. Bathurst. Immediately I hear of anything."

"Any more news of Miss Phoebe Hubbard?"

Rudge shook his head. "Nothing definite. But I understand MacMorran is keeping her well in line. That's so, isn't it, Inspector MacMorran?"

MacMorran nodded. "Yes, I'm keeping her warm and cosy. Two of my best men are sticking closer to her than a grey tick. She gets about a bit up West—so they tell me."

"In what way do you mean, Inspector?" The question came from Anthony Bathurst.

"Well, since my blokes have been trailing her, she's been to a night-club and also to a house in Kensington. Not bad going for a domestic maid, you know, Mr. Bathurst."

"Modern days—modern ways, Andrew—or in other words, 'Tempora mutantur' and all the rest of the chorus. Might be nothing, though, in any of it, as Phoebe may be a vivacious little soul, sorely in need of transplanting. By the way, Inspector Rudge"— Anthony turned to the Brooke Inspector—"do you happen to have any copies of a local paper handy? I should like a copy for the week when Curtis was killed. Not so much for the Traquair case itself. I'd like to have a general look at it."

"I can get you one, Mr. Bathurst, if you'll wait just a second. I'll get you a copy of the *Brooke and District Herald.* Hang on for a minute or so, will you?" Rudge dashed from the room with his usual impetuosity.

"More ideas?" inquired MacMorran laconically.

"Just a glimmer, Andrew. Still, sometimes these 'glimmers' that come to us are more than ordinarily useful in a fog."

Rudge was back within a couple of minutes. He fluttered a newspaper in his hands. "Here you are, Mr. Bathurst. There's half a column on the Curtis accident in here."

Anthony took the paper from the Inspector. His two companions watched him as he read through the various paragraphs that made up the half-column. They then saw that he turned to the front page of the paper. MacMorran, although knowing him so well of old, had no idea what he was seeking. He went and glanced over Mr. Bathurst's shoulder. To his surprise, Mr. Bathurst was carefully examining the Obituary column. "Births. Deaths. Marriages," he commented semi-jocularly.

"Aha, my merry Andrew. Why not?"

"You won't find either Traquair or Curtis there, Mr. Bathurst," interposed Inspector Rudge. "The Traquair case would obviously not be sent along by reason of its—well—special conditions . . . and Curtis, I venture to assert, belonged to the wrong class of society."

Anthony shook his head. "I don't know that I'm looking for either the Traquair death or the Curtis death announcement," he said slowly.

Rudge looked puzzled. "Then I don't know that I follow you—quite," he contributed.

"No?" said an unruffled Anthony.

"No," returned Rudge with an almost dogged emphasis. Anthony smiled. "Read that," he said. He handed the newspaper to Inspector Rudge.

"This column on Curtis?" queried the latter.

"About the accident. Read it carefully."

MacMorran went and stood by Rudge as he complied with Anthony's instruction. MacMorran also read over Rudge's shoulder. Neither made any comment. Anthony waited for revelation. "Well?" he said at length.

Rudge replied curtly: "Sorry—I don't get you, Mr. Bathurst. What's the point?"

"It's a long shot, perhaps, but I observe from that account of the Curtis accident that the man's employers were Morley and Son, the undertakers—I beg their pardon—the funeral directors, of High Road, Brooke."

"What about it?" rapped Rudge. "I knew that. We knew it. What's original about that idea?"

MacMorran put a restraining hand upon his arm, but Rudge was impatient and would have none of it.

"Just this, Inspector," responded Mr. Bathurst. "If you look down the Obituary list that's shown on the front page you will find that the deaths therein number forty-four. In certain of the announcements you will find additional details given. I mean by that—additional to the usual text. If you read some of them carefully you will readily see what I mean. For example, let me illustrate."

Rudge handed him the newspaper. Anthony thrust a finger at the column which he was discussing. "Now, look here. My point. This third one. 'Austin. Interment at St. Clement's Cemetery, Grantley Road, on Thursday'. That's one. Now here again. Lower down. 'Groves. Funeral on Wednesday, 1.15, at the Parish Church of. St. Margaret's'. Again. Still travelling down the Obituary column. Look at this. 'Mardon. Funeral at St. Clement's Cemetery, Grantley Road. Thursday, 1 p.m. No flowers by request. Foreign papers please copy'. You can find similar details all the way through the notices. Here you are. 'Burton. Interment on the 22nd inst. at St. Clement's Cemetery, etc., etc. . . . Hunger and thirst she feels no more'. I won't go any further, gentlemen—but will proceed from that point with the development of my theory. The undertaking trade of Brooke—Inspector Rudge—who is the biggest man in the business?"

"Old Morley—undoubtedly. I should say that five people out of every six go to him. Old established, you see, Mr. Bathurst. Business been in the family for three generations. Old Morley's father coined a joke in Brooke—that he'd 'box' any man in the district and get him down."

"A fellow of crude jest, eh?" remarked Anthony.

"Yes. But go on—you haven't told me what you're after, yet."

"Well—I've been wondering whether I've so far understood *all* the reasons that lay behind Dr. Traquair's decision to use Curtis's clothes—with the exception of his hat. Let's put *our* heads together, Rudge. And you, Andrew, all the three of us. Why did the doctor make this change of clothes?"

"Disguise," retorted Rudge with strong assurance. "Not the shadow of a doubt about it."

"Ay," said MacMorran, "but I think I see what Mr. Bathurst means. Disguise to what primary end?"

"To avoid arrest, of course," returned Rudge again confidently.

"That's, of course, a fact," said Anthony, "but I fancy Andrew here has fastened on to my idea. Go a bit further with it, Andrew . . . will you? Let me see if you're on the right lines?"

MacMorran spoke with care and deliberate emphasis. "Well . . . I'm looking at it like this. It has come to me through my putting myself in the doctor's place. Trying to imagine myself confronted with the same set of circumstances that confronted him. Besides avoiding arrest, he felt that he must *get away. Escape.*"

"Isn't it the same thing?" intervened Rudge impetuously.

MacMorran, the cautious, gave him his answer. "No—it isn't. Not quite. I'm an older man than you are, Inspector Rudge, and an older hand at our game. Perhaps that fact just helps me to see a wee bit further than you. A man might manage to avoid arrest (using your own actual words) and remain within a short distance of the place of his crime. Just lying in hiding. Not so Traquair! Mr. Bathurst means that he wanted to get away. He made that his special objective. His *aim*." MacMorran turned to Anthony. "I'm reckonin' that's about what you meant, Mr. Bathurst, is it not?"

"Yes, Andrew, you've put it over just as it has been appearing to me. My point is this. Traquair used Curtis's clothes for the main reason that he considered that they would assist him naturally in his escape. And by escape—I mean as you said. That 'escape' meant his putting a distance between himself and the scene of his crime—not the mere avoidance of arrest. Now consider that point in its entirety. What did Traquair do when he had dressed himself in Curtis's clothes?"

MacMorran and Rudge nodded in answer, but they said nothing. Whereupon Anthony proceeded. "I suggest that he did very much as you did just now, Andrew. I heard you say that you were putting yourself in Traquair's place. I think that Traquair put himself in Curtis's place. He regarded himself as an undertaker's assistant. Then—what did he do?"

"Cleared out," said Rudge, "as he was bound to, in the position in which he found himself."

"How?" pressed Anthony.

Rudge shrugged his shoulders. "Can't answer that. Yet awhile."

Anthony smiled. "Well . . . I think I'll startle you with a theory of my own. I've been considering it for some little time now. It's this! In my opinion, Dr. Traquair 'signed on' with Morley and Son and got away from Brooke in that fashion. The idea can be tested. Easily. I commend it to you, Inspector Rudge. If it's necessary—I'll eat humble pie for you as becomingly as I know how."

Anthony waved a complimentary hand.

"There you are, Rudge," said MacMorran, "you've heard Mr. Bathurst's opinion; now it's up to you. I shall be interested to hear how you get on."

"I dare say you will," replied Rudge, "but all the same—"

"Look here, Inspector," continued Anthony Bathurst, "take some of these cases that I've just pointed out to you in the local paper.

Interment at St. Clement's Cemetery—Grantley Road. Grantley! Think of the possibilities Grantley would hold for a man in Traquair's circumstances. You try the idea, Inspector . . . the more I look at it the more I like it—blessed if I don't."

Rudge reached for his hat. "Very good, then. We'll put the Bathurst theory to the test as soon as possible. Perhaps we might go along together. I know old man Morley pretty well. He's a bit of a card, but reliable on the whole. We'll go and shake him up. Come on, MacMorran. Ready, Mr. Bathurst?"

"Rudge," said Anthony, "I'm with you—we will clear the decks for action. Count on me."

CHAPTER VIII
THE FRAGMENTS THAT REMAINED

(*Told by the Author*)

ANTHONY Bathurst handed back the piece of paper which Inspector Rudge had placed in front of him.

"I should hate to say 'I told you so'," he murmured encouragingly, "but the situation almost demands something of the kind. Don't you agree?"

"I wouldn't contradict you, Mr. Bathurst," said the Inspector. "But tell me what you think of things as you see them down there."

He pointed to the paper which he now held.

". . . Let me see it again, Inspector, do you mind?"

The document again changed hands. Anthony Bathurst proceeded to make audible comment. "First of all, old man Morley's statement. A man calling himself Miller arrived with the story that Curtis had had a bad accident and was detained in hospital. Miller, Jack Miller, as old Morley mentions later on in his version, offered to take Curtis's place and do any job if there were a vacancy that offered itself. Morley engaged him to act at a funeral from a shop in High Road, Brooke. The name in the case was Burton. The interment was at St. Clement's Cemetery on the road to Grantley."

Anthony lowered the paper on which he had been commenting. "Blood to me, gentlemen! If I mistake not, 'Burton' was one of the names which I discovered in the Obituary column of the *Brooke and District Herald*. But I will continue with the statement of old man Morley. 'The man who called himself "Miller" carried out his instructions and took part in the funeral procession of Mrs. Burton, under the supervision of my son, Mr. Leslie Morley, who was directing on that particular occasion. Miller went from the shop (Plummer's) to St. Clement's Cemetery. While the last rites were in progress' ("Beautiful touch, that," murmured Mr. Bathurst) 'Miller contrived, in some way that we do not understand, to disappear, and neither my son nor I has seen him again. Strangely, from our point of view, he didn't trouble to show up to collect his day's pay. An occurrence which in my experience I cannot remember happening, either before or since.'

"When interrogated as to whether he knew the missing Dr. Traquair well, Morley says, 'I knew him pretty well, having, of course, seen him several times in Brooke, and I can honestly say that, to me, Miller was in no way like him, and I had no reason whatever to suspect the man's identity.'"

Anthony looked meaningly at Inspector Rudge.

"Thus Statement Number One. I will pass on to Number Two. The statement submitted voluntarily by Edmund Judson Lovelock, conductor, employed by the Grantley and District Motor Services Company. Licensed Number, 332. Lovelock stated this. These are his own words:

"'Early in the afternoon of the day mentioned on the Police announcement, I was on duty on a motor-'bus travelling between Brooke and Grantley. Just after we passed the road that leads to the west gate of St. Clement's Cemetery I was hailed by a fare, and I took the person on board. It was a man dressed exactly as described by the terms of the Police advertisement and, also, I noticed that he carried a suit-case. He booked a single-journey fare to Grantley when asked for his ticket. I formed the instant impression' ("did he really say that, Rudge?") 'that he was a person a cut above what he looked like. Because he spoke with a cultured accent. I dropped him at our Grantley terminus. That's in the market-place. I did not observe what he did or where he went after that.'"

Anthony put down the paper.

"Well, I think you've done well to collect so much vital and undoubtedly authentic information in so short a space of time. You've got this satisfaction, too. You do definitely *know* that, at last, you are on the right track. Good work, that."

Rudge nodded. MacMorran, who had been silent for a long time, saw that the Brooke Inspector was more than ordinarily pleased at Mr. Bathurst's complimentary remark. Before he could contribute anything, however, Anthony Bathurst was in again with an additional request.

"Dr. Traquair's private papers, Inspector? Those that you told me you had taken from his house here?"

"Yes, Mr. Bathurst, what about them?"

MacMorran wondered why there was a note of surprise in Rudge's voice as he replied to Anthony. Or was it surprise?

"I'd like to have a glance through them, if I may. That's all."

"Of course. Certainly."

"Are they handy at the moment? Delays, you know, are proverbially dangerous."

"I'll get them for you." Rudge went out through the door that connected with the inner room of his office.

"He's jumpy," said MacMorran. "The job's got him down a bit. Bigger, I expect, than he's usually called upon to handle. That's my opinion."

"Don't think that you're far out, Andrew—but here he is."

Anthony had heard the sound of steps coming from the inner apartment. Rudge bustled in, carrying various bundles of papers that he had, presumably, removed from a green docket which he now held under his arm. "Here you are," he said to Anthony. "They're more or less separated into convenient divisions. I sorted them out myself, the day after I took them from Dr. Traquair's house. The bundle marked 'A' contains bills and receipts of all kinds. That marked 'B' is a miscellaneous collection of medical forms which the doctor kept in his several drawers. 'C'—the third bundle—is a collection of what I've described as 'personal correspondence'.

You can see the three headings plainly if you look at the slip on top of each bundle. 'Bills, receipts, etc.', 'Medical forms, etc.', and 'Personal correspondence'."

Rudge handed the three bundles to Anthony. The latter put the two bundles marked respectively "A" and "B" on the side table. Carefully removing the strip of red tape from the third bundle, "C", he began to look through the letters, etc., one by one. Suddenly looking up from his task of inspection, he addressed a remark to Inspector Rudge:

"I take it, Inspector, from the account you recently asked me to look at, that you have been unable to trace Traquair beyond the town of Grantley. Or, rather, shall we say beyond the market square of Grantley? That's the position, isn't it?"

Rudge nodded. "Quite right, Mr. Bathurst."

"No threads at all picked up *in* Grantley?"

"No, Mr. Bathurst. Up to the moment we have drawn a blank everywhere. Two or three possibilities came through. One very likely story came from a house agent there, but all of them, when they were examined and tested, gave us nothing. But there's this one point still to be considered. I haven't had complete reports from all the various transport people in Grantley. Grantley, you see, from that particular point of view, stands in a very different category from a place like Brooke here. It is four times the size of Brooke, and transport to and from Grantley is a much more extensive and complicated matter."

"Thank you, Inspector." Anthony went on with his inspection of the bundle marked "C". The two others watched him curiously. Again he found a question for Inspector Rudge to answer: "I suppose Grantley serves most of the towns within a radius of fifty miles or so, doesn't it?"

"Oh yes. It's one of the best junction centres in this area. You can get to most places from Grantley fairly conveniently. Why, particularly? Have you any special place in mind?"

Anthony tossed over a letter. "Cast your eye over that, gentlemen. Don't worry about the date."

Rudge and MacMorran read the letter in turn. "It's oldish, Mr. Bathurst," said Inspector MacMorran, doubtfully.

"I told you to forget about the date. It's just on a year old. Forget it. Read the terms of the letter. And remember—it's from Lifford, which is easily and conveniently reached from our town of Grantley, which, we strongly suspect, harboured the missing Dr. Traquair for at least a time. Why, what's the matter, Rudge?" Anthony noticed that Rudge was standing there with a most peculiar expression on his face.

"This letter—this address," he said, his voice betraying considerable agitation.

Anthony's grey eyes gleamed. "Yes, Inspector? What about it? You interest me immensely."

"It's my brother-in-law's place. The 'Nell Gwynne' in Chandos Street, Lifford. This girl who signs herself here as Helen Eversley is my sister-in-law. She married the man who happens to be my own wife's brother. Donald Eversley. My wife was Alison Eversley. What an extraordinary coincidence!" Rudge's hands were shaking with excitement as he held the letter.

"Do you know what this is?" exclaimed MacMorran. "It's the finger of Fate. No more and no less. If Mr. Bathurst's hunch is right, we've got our man in the hollow of our hand. What a stroke of good fortune!"

Anthony said nothing. He was considering the situation as it had now developed. Rudge broke in:

"I can 'phone Donald Eversley from here. What better? He will tell me at once if anybody like Dr. Traquair has been seen down there since the murder. If so—well—we're home! It's all over bar the shouting."

MacMorran nodded. "Yes . . . that's a pretty sound idea, Mr. Rudge. I don't think that we can possibly hit on a better plan. Are you going to get through to him now? From here?"

Rudge replied at once. Now that he had an opportunity for immediate action he both felt and looked better. "I think so. Why not? That was my idea, at least."

"Good. Mr. Bathurst and I will wait here then and hear the result. What do you say, Mr. Bathurst? Are you on?"

"Yes. I'll wait with you, Andrew. I shall be most interested to hear what Inspector Rudge picks up."

"Right," said Rudge. "I'll get through to Lifford now. If things are O.K., I'll make all the necessary arrangements. You wait here."

Rudge went out and quietly closed the door behind him. Neither MacMorran nor Anthony Bathurst spoke for some little time. Then the professional looked across and shrugged his shoulders.

"What do you think?" he asked.

"I'm doubtful, Andrew, and I'm wondering about all manner of things. It's a rare thing for ripe fruit to drop from the tree-branches into one's eagerly outstretched hands. Rudge's brother-in-law has arrived, if I may say so, so beautifully opportunely, that, quite frankly, he seems too good to be true."

MacMorran frowned. "Or else too true to be good. I get your meaning."

"Rudge is a longish time," said Anthony. "I judge that fact to presage hope. A denial on the good brother-in-law's part would surely have been short and sweetly summary."

"Yes," responded MacMorran, "I entirely agree with you." He cocked his head up. "I think—I think that I can hear him coming."

MacMorran's hearing powers were good. Rudge came into the room and faced the two men. His face was whitish, but there was a pink spot showing in each of his cheeks. "Gentlemen," he said, "I hardly know what to say to you. But I've been on to the 'Nell Gwynne', at Lifford—my brother-in-law's house—and he's told me the most remarkable fact. He says that a man calling himself Fred Curtis is certainly in his employ at the 'Nell Gwynne', who, from the news that I have just passed on to him, he feels pretty certain is our missing Dr. Traquair."

"What?" Exclaimed MacMorran excitedly. "Traquair in the very house itself, and calling himself Fred Curtis? Why—it's on a plate with parsley butter round it! Talk about Snow-White and the Seven Dwarfs—this knocks that sideways. It's got them all stone-cold."

Anthony made no remark. Still silent, he listened to the two professionals. Rudge continued. "I've told my brother-in-law to carry on as though nothing had happened. And that we would do the rest with Mr. Curtis."

Anthony entered the arena. "Which, being interpreted, means—?"

"That I'm not leaving any of this to the local people. This is what I've arranged. We three will go down this evening and do the job. Eversley assures me that Traquair—Fred Curtis—er—will be there all right. Why shouldn't he be? He doesn't know a thing and he's far too snug and comfy in the 'Nell Gwynne' to skip without a good reason."

"What job is he doing down there?" asked MacMorran.

"Billiard-marker," replied Rudge.

"Billiard-marker, eh?" exclaimed MacMorran. "Very opportune . . . because he's snookered this time all right."

"Very likely," remarked Bathurst; "but two blacks, remember, have never yet made a white."

PART THREE
THE SECOND ESCAPE

CHAPTER I
TICKLISH MOMENTS

(Narrative by Dr. Stuart Traquair)

DAYS passed. My life, and duties as billiard-marker at the "Nell Gwynne", were quiet and uneventful. Eversley seemed sullen and resentful whenever I encountered him. He was not exactly openly hostile, but he made it very plain to me that he heartily disliked me and that my stay would end directly he had his way. But there was this to it. I disliked him just as heartily as he disliked me and would have been delighted to tell him so. Bert and Alf and Bernard were all decent fellows and treated me well in every respect. I saw Helen at odd times only, and as she gave me no special sign at any time, I discreetly kept my distance, realizing that this condition was the one that she desired. I judged that her relations with her husband were definitely strained and that I must wait until circumstances found improvement.

A week and a half went by. Then came a sudden startling shock. I had been off between two and four one afternoon, had wandered round Lifford as was my usual custom, and had returned to the "Nell Gwynne" a trifle earlier than had been my habit. I had snatched a glance at an early edition of the evening paper and had noted with satisfaction that the space being given to the Traquair murder was becoming beautifully less and less. I had just folded the paper, preparatory to putting it in my pocket, when my eye suddenly caught a blurred mass of print in the space reserved for news described "Stop Press". I caught sight of my own name, "Traquair", and also the name of the place "Brooke". I read the announcement hurriedly:

TRAQUAIR MURDER CASE
SENSATIONAL SEQUEL

A dead man, at present unidentified, was found to-day in the house of the missing Dr. Traquair, at Brooke, shot through the heart. It is expected that even more sensational developments may follow, as it is believed that the Police authorities are in possession of a highly important clue.

I stood there in that side street of Lifford in a semi-stupefied condition. My thoughts raced round in the maddest confusion and my brain went into a whirl. Then I calmed down. A sane, well-reasoned and ordered thought came to my mental rescue. I remembered Halmar. I remembered his activities and for what he stood. There must have been a quarrel in my house, and I knew the reason of that quarrel. This dead man, shot through the heart, was either Halmar himself or one of Halmar's men. I suddenly felt better. Then I realized that there was one thing which I must do! I must get into immediate touch with Armitage. I knew the rules and regulations by which he was surrounded and I knew that in many circumstances I could expect no help from him. But in the particular matter of my wife and Halmar I felt that I had a reasonable claim, which Armitage would recognize as such.

So I slipped into a telephone-kiosk and dialled his number. Luckily he was at his flat, but I soon learnt from what he told me over the telephone that I had been extremely fortunate. Had I left the call until a quarter of an hour later I should have missed him.

Within a few moments I had asked him a torrent of questions. But in such terms that only he understood them. He answered them rapidly one by one—and in the order in which they had been put to him. I learned that the name of the dead man who had been found in the Traquair bedroom was Reicher, and that he had been attached to Halmar. Then Armitage listened to more from me. Requests and an appeal. His last reply brought me up with a jerk. "You must meet me, Ganymede," he said emphatically. "Before this week is out at that. At Terroni's. In Vancouver Street . . . in the main dining-room. Yes—I know—I'm fully aware of it . . . right in the thick of it. When? Friday evening. Seven o'clock. Right. Suits me. Keep your eyes skinned and come with a revolver in your pocket. You will recognize me in this way—I shall wear a tiny pink rosebud in the lapel of my dinner-jacket. Right-o! Till Friday then—and keep your chin up."

I strolled back to the "Nell Gwynne" in a mood of meditation. The plot had thickened, and confusion was certainly worse confounded. I wanted Helen to be made aware at once of the new development in the murder chain. It was quite on the cards that she would miss the paragraph in the newspapers. I knew that she sometimes used the sitting-room behind the office to rest in of an afternoon. It might be, I thought, as I entered, that she was still there. But Eversley too might be in there with her and I wasn't going to risk the possibility of that. I entered by the side door of the hotel and went quickly up the narrow staircase that led to Helen Eversley's sitting-room. I tapped gently on the door and sniffed at the same time. Eversley usually smoked a pipe of strong-smelling tobacco, and more than once my nose had warned me of his sudden and unexpected approach. This time I could smell nothing . . . and I heard Helen's voice saying . . . "Yes—come in." So I chanced it and slipped into the room. Her surprise betrayed her. "Stuart," she cried . . . "What is it? Is there danger?" I put my finger-tips to my lips and the evening paper into her hand. "Read that," I whispered.

She gave me a startled glance and then hurriedly read the paragraph that I had indicated. She looked at me again after she had read it. This time in sheer incredulity.

"I don't understand," she said simply. "Whatever does it mean? What has this other man . . . who's been killed . . . to do with you?"

"You trusted me when I came," I replied to her. "You asked no questions. You did not press me for even the shadow of an explanation." I paused.

She nodded. "There was no need. There never would be any need."

"Thank you, Helen. I give you my word of honour that although I know who this man is . . . I don't know who killed him."

She started forward and put her fingers on my arm impulsively. "What is this trouble that you have mixed yourself up in? No . . . don't tell me . . . I shouldn't have asked. I think that I would rather not know. Because I have no doubts of you . . . no doubts . . . only fears."

"Thank you again, Helen. If I were to—"

"Just a minute, Dr. Traquair. Tell me this. I promise you that I won't ask you to tell me anything more than this. How have you found out who the other dead man is? According to the paper report here, he hasn't been identified."

"I have 'phoned . . . to a friend of mine . . . for the information. It was rather vital for me . . . that I should know . . . it's hard for me to explain . . . but I do know. I found out."

She nodded again, almost to herself . . . as though I wasn't in the room with her and that she was alone.

"There is another thing," I went on.

"What? Don't frighten me, please."

"I must go to London,"

She shook her head swiftly. "That scares me. How long for?"

"A few hours. I shall come back here."

"Must you go?"

"I'm afraid so."

"Is it safe for you? Are you sure that it will be safe for you?"

"No, I'm not. It is better that I should tell you the truth than lie to you. But—and this is important—it is safer for me to go . . . and take the chance . . . than to stay here . . . in ignorance of something. I will tell you now, while I have the opportunity, where I shall be. I won't write it down for you, for obvious reasons. Listen, Helen, I shall be at Terroni's in Vancouver Street. There's somebody I must see."

She repeated the words after me.

"You will remember that?"

"Yes, I won't forget."

Then she looked up at me again—quickly. "When do you intend to go? Soon? At once?"

I nodded. "This week. I have arranged for Friday. Now what about your husband? Eversley? What's the best excuse I can put up to him . . . in order to get the time granted? It will take me the whole day, you see."

"That's awkward. He's funny about you. I'm afraid he'll be difficult."

"Where's he now?"

"Out. He's nearly always out at this time of day. I should have warned you before this, if he had been anywhere indoors."

"Good. You think he may make things unpleasant for me if I ask him for Friday?"

"I'm positive that he will. He'll absolutely jump at the chance. I know him too well not to realize that. The slightest excuse—and he'll get rid of you. I dread that happening. Because, comparatively, you're so safe here. He would have sacked you before this, I'm certain, only he was afraid that by doing so he'd offend me. I don't exactly mean afraid—but he likes to keep in my good books. For obvious—" She stopped sharply and then blushed scarlet.

I thought that I knew what she meant and could understand how eminently desirable Eversley found her. I went back to the practical issue.

"I see. He'll be awkward, will he? Well . . . any suggestions? Or can't you get brain-waves to order?"

She put a hand under her chin and sat there thinking hard. After a while she looked up. "I've got it. And, what's more, I don't think he'll suspect that there's anything out of the ordinary afoot. We must have new snooker balls, and also some new cues. He's been intending to get a new supply for some time now. The previous marker we had here used to go up to Burrows and Wilson's fairly regularly for our new supplies. There's no doubt that they're by far the best people. That's where you'd better go. That's where you'll go on Friday. Now how can we force the issue?"

"That's the point. How about some sudden mortalities amongst the cues? Would that help to work the oracle? Is it worth trying?"

"It might be . . . but I'd like him to . . ." She stopped again and I saw a light come into her eyes.

"Well?" I asked her. "Thought of a number?"

"Not exactly . . . but I've an idea. Listen to me for a moment or two. I'll tell him that the billiard-room stock needs replenishing. Got that?"

I nodded.

"Then I'll tell him that I've half suggested to you that you go up to town on Friday, to Burrows and Wilson's. See?"

"Yes." I nodded again.

"Right. Then I'll say to him that you demurred from the idea of going. That you didn't exactly refuse, but that the look in your eyes suggested the next best thing. I'll say to him: 'I didn't *order* him to go, it was scarcely my province, but I think that you ought to. After all—he's a paid servant.' And I'll bet you a hundred to one, Stuart" (this time the name did slip out), "that he'll walk straight away from me to you and give you your Friday orders. Don't forget to play up, either. For your own sake and my sake."

"Helen Eversley," I said to her, "that's a damned bright idea! It combines natural cunning with just that soupçon of psychology that makes the perfect alliance. Well—I'll leave it at that . . . and you'll forgive my saying this . . . you're the top. One day, perhaps, I'll be able to make it up to you."

As I left her I saw her drop her head in her hands—and as I closed the door behind me I wondered when I should see her again and talk to her *à deux*. For I resolved that between now and Friday I must be as careful as I knew how.

CHAPTER II
FRIDAY

*(Dr. Traquair's Narrative—*continued)

I MADE no further move in any direction until the morning of Friday came. Also I had heard nothing from either Helen or Eversley himself. But I restrained myself from forcing the issue although the temptation to do so was a strong one. "Patience," I whispered to myself, "and shuffle the cards"; and then the sight of Madeleine lying dead on the floor with the scattered playing-cards around her came back to me and made me feel sick of life and the problems it brings to one. About ten o'clock on the morning of Friday I went up to the billiard-room to do one or two of the usual jobs in there, which occupied my morning time. I wished to be in a place where Eversley could find me at once if he wanted to. That was my plan. Because the more time that I had at my disposal, to do what I liked with, all the better for me. To my satisfaction the plan worked. Some little time before half past ten the door of the billiard-room opened and Donald Eversley came bustling in. He walked straight up to me. I knew that Helen's plan had been successful—in part, at least.

"Curtis," he said to me rather peremptorily, "I want you to do something today. You had better pop up to town this morning. To Burrows and Wilson's. You know their place, I've no doubt. It's in Cranham Square. It is time we had—" He broke off here into descriptions of billiards and snooker equipment. I remembered what Helen had told me. I therefore began to make excuses.

"It'll be rather inconvenient, sir, if I have to go—"

He cut into my words brusquely. "I'm the best judge of that. Here's a list that I've had made out for you. You had better catch the 10.52. It's fast to Everton Street."

I tried to look dissatisfied. I wanted to complete the picture that I had already begun to paint for the edification of his mind.

"Wouldn't it be better, sir, and much more convenient from the standpoint of the tables here, if I left it for the time being?"

"No, it wouldn't," he snapped at me. "And who's head Serang here? You—or I, Curtis? Damn it all, man, when I give orders, don't you dare question them. Fancy yourself, don't you?"

"I wasn't questioning your orders, sir. I wouldn't dream of doing such a thing. All I wished to point out was—"

"I don't desire to hear another word. Take that list of requisitions and clear out! You can be back here by half past six, if you look slippy."

"I can be," I thought, "but I shan't be." Aloud I said: "Very good, sir. That shall be attended to."

"Tell them I want the stuff before the end of next week. Tell them you must have it. Don't stand any nonsense from them."

I was through the door by this time and on the way to my own room. I soon changed into a ready-made suit which I had purchased in Lifford a few afternoons previously, secured the vital papers from my suit-case, crammed a hat on my head and at once made off for the station. I caught the train with some minutes to spare. There were few people in it and I managed to obtain a corner seat in a third-class smoking compartment. Two men were the only other occupants. On the way to Everton Street I passed the time, of the long journey in looking over the papers that I had brought up with me, and naturally my thoughts soon travelled to Rupert Halmar. Directly I got out of the train at the terminus a thought occurred to me which previously, strangely enough, I hadn't stopped to consider. I realized that I was a wanted man . . . which fact had never entered my mind when I walked round the streets of Lifford. Different conditions, I suppose, presented different personal reactions. By this time I had quite a presentable moustache, and when I wore my glasses my appearance had changed considerably.

I hailed a passing taxi a hundred yards or so out of Everton Street and directed the driver to Cranham Square. I'd get Eversley's commission at Burrows and Wilson's off my mind first of all. That would leave the rest of the day free for me to go about my own affairs. The job at Burrows and Wilson's took me the better part of an hour. Many of Eversley's requirements needed amplification and explanation. I had dismissed the taxi, and when I came out of Burrows and Wilson's I decided that I'd buy an evening paper and have a cup of tea somewhere that was quiet and unobtrusive before going on to Terroni's in Vancouver Street. I hit on a little place that called itself "The Gypsy Tea-room" (I've heard since that the Dean of Ilford always uses it) and bowled in there with my paper as large as life. As I went in I passed a policeman. He gave me a nonchalant glance and I chuckled to myself as I considered matters. If he only knew what I knew! Immediate promotion was jogging his elbow.

It was comparatively early for tea and the place that I had chosen was almost deserted. I had a couple of hours to waste before I was to meet Paul Armitage . . . the man with whom I had communicated so many times, and whom I had never yet actually seen. He would be wearing a pink rosebud in the button-hole of his dinner-jacket lapel. The affair was becoming theatrical. Still, I determined to put all matters of hazard out of my mind and go straight forward with the plan that I had decided upon, and do my duty as I considered I saw it plainly set out in front of me. A neat-handed waitress attended to me, white-aproned and smiling. I ordered tea and two rounds of buttered toast. Whilst I was waiting I opened the evening paper and scanned the headings of the various columns. There was little to interest me and I could find but a few lines of ordinary comment on the Traquair case. The waitress arrived with my tea and toast. As I was pouring out my tea I had one of the most shattering shocks of my life. For a girl had entered the tea-room with a male escort. The man was tall, slim and eager-faced. The girl I did not try to describe or analyse. There was just one thing about her that mattered to me. That was her identity. For she was none other than the girl who had been my maidservant at Brooke. The girl was Phoebe Hubbard!

The sight of her here, miles away from the environment with which I had always associated her, wholly amazed me. It gave me an entirely new angle on the whole affair right from the moment when I had discovered Madeleine's faithlessness, to my telephone conversation with Paul Armitage from the kiosk at Brooke. Phoebe Hubbard and her companion passed by my table without either of them giving as much as a glance in my direction. I was careful to notice that they selected a table just behind mine and slightly to my left. By turning just a little in my chair I could see them, whilst their major view of me was a back and a shoulder.

The conversation between them was eager and animated. Phoebe Hubbard seemed to be explaining something to her escort, for he punctuated her narrative with a series of quick noddings of the head. I attempted to catch something of what they were saying, but only a stray word or two reached my ears. I heard "Dr. Traquair" followed by "Inspector Rudge". Then there came a pretty lengthy interval during which Phoebe Hubbard dropped her voice considerably, and I was able to hear nothing at all. The man said something about "the bedroom" and I saw Phoebe Hubbard nod vigorously. He leant over towards her with a look of intense admiration which he made no attempt to conceal. After a time I realized that they were too far away from me for me to hear anything properly. Disconnected words, travelling towards me at odd times, were more or less without value. I began to think things over and ultimately decided that I did not desire Phoebe Hubbard to see and possibly to recognize me. Apart, that is, from any such consideration as her denouncing me for the man that I was and handing me over to the authorities. I did not want her to recognize me or to think that I was here in town, in case the consequences which would follow that event interfered with my arrangements for the evening as they affected Paul Armitage. So I did snappy work with my evening paper, keeping it well over to that side of my face which was the nearer to Phoebe Hubbard and her attractive young companion.

Eventually I finished my tea, called the waitress who had attended to me, paid my bill and took my departure. I had no reason to think that Phoebe Hubbard had been in any way conscious of my presence near her. I still had plenty of time to cut to waste before I need arrive at Terroni's, so I did a wander round, most of it absolutely aimless, until the hands of my wrist-watch advised me that it was time for me to make tracks for Vancouver Street. I had a "wash and brush-up" and was outside Terroni's restaurant in Vancouver Street at ten minutes to seven. I pushed open the revolving door and walked in. An attendant took my hat and coat and asked me which room I wanted. I told him the main dining-room and he directed me to the first floor. I made my way up a narrow staircase the whole of which was most thoroughly impregnated with the odour of exotic cooking. I had never dined here in my life, although Terroni's was well known to me by name and reputation. I marched into the main dining-room and took stock of my position.

Now, it must be understood that Paul Armitage and I had never met. I was, therefore, as unknown to him as he was to me. I stood in the doorway for some moments, endeavouring to find with my eyes the man whom I had come to meet. The man whose help I needed so desperately. The man in the lapel of whose dinner-jacket I should see a tiny pink rosebud.

I looked carefully round the room. It was a long, spacious room both well furnished and tastefully decorated. The tables were artistically arranged and cunningly placed. Those by the windows especially so. I suppose that the room held between thirty and forty people all told—mostly couples . . . but a few obvious "parties".

There was, however, no sign of Armitage . . . for there was no man there wearing the flower of identification. I thought, perhaps, that I was a trifle early and he a little late. I selected a table in one of the retired corners which were more or less out of the way and waited for him. I walked down the room towards the table which I had provisionally selected. Then for one day I had shattering shock number two! For there, at a table in an alcove, close to the table towards which I was making, sat Helen Eversley!

CHAPTER III
RED FOR DANGER

(Dr. Traquair's Narrative—continued)

As MY eyes met hers I almost gasped for breath. For I knew that her presence here could mean only one thing. And that was danger—or something as much like it as would make no odds! Her eyes beckoned to mine although she spoke no word. I pulled myself together. The people in the room, sitting at the various tables, should be made to think that we were here by definite assignation and that Helen was waiting for me. So I bowed to my lady and took the seat opposite to her. The table had been arranged *à deux* and Helen had chosen it wisely and well.

"Good evening," I said.

She accepted the greeting with a wistful look. A waiter was at my side in an instant, which effectively cut short any possible chance of an immediate explanation of the situation. "Shall I order?" I asked her. She nodded brightly, but there was the hint of a story in her eyes which naturally I was impatient to hear. I kept my head and gave the waiter my order as coolly, I hope and think, as I should have done under normal conditions. I was able to extract one comfort, however, from the situation as it was. It was certain that, with Helen sitting there patiently, the danger, whatever it might be, was not yet imminent or acutely critical. The waiter left us to execute my order. Helen at once seized the opportunity that had been afforded her. She leant across the table to me and in the rosy glow of the table-lamp spoke to me in a low, thrilling voice.

"Stuart." She paused just a little as she spoke my name, but recovered quickly and went on again. "You must listen to me carefully. Please don't interrupt what I'm going to say. Don't say anything at all until I have finished. Promise me!"

I nodded quickly to show her that I accepted her imposed condition. "Early this afternoon a 'phone-call came through to the 'Nell Gwynne'. I heard the ring. As usual, I was in my room. The room where you came to me the other afternoon. Oh—what a stroke of luck it was that I heard the ring when I did! Because another stroke of luck went with it. A stroke of luck the wrong way. He was in— my husband. As you know from what I've already told you, he's scarcely ever in at that time of the afternoon, but to-day he'd been disappointed over a golf game he'd arranged with Littlestone—he's the Town Clerk of Lifford. Only mixes with Donald because Donald has money. The old story," she declared bitterly. At that moment the waiter arrived with our oysters. We murmured commonplaces to each other. The waiter hovered for some little time and then effaced himself again. By this time, I may as well confess, all thoughts of Paul Armitage and the real reason why I was in the restaurant had vanished completely from my mind. Helen took up the thread of her story again.

"Well, he heard the 'phone go and, as you have already guessed, I expect, he answered it. You know where the 'phone is at the 'Nell

Gwynne'. Well—something told me to listen. It must have been my sixth sense functioning. I kept the door of my room ajar. I heard him pick up the receiver and I heard what he said quite distinctly. Don't eat your oysters too quickly or that industrious waiter will be back here again."

I smiled and nodded. I was too keyed up to do anything else.

"I knew at once, although I don't know how I knew, that the person at the other end was his police brother-in-law. His name's Rudge. I told you, if you remember. Directly I saw it in the paper—I knew that it was a bad omen for us. You can guess how I listened when the idea came to me. My heart almost stopped as I heard Don say—'There's a fellow here now. Employed here at the hotel. His name is Curtis. Fred Curtis.' Then, of course, he listened while Rudge was putting his reply through to him."

"Yes, yes," I said. "Go on, please. I feel that the worst is coming."

She nodded across at me. "You're right. That's just what did come. As I listened, the next thing I heard was your name mentioned. Dr. Traquair. That, of course, told me at once that the game was very nearly up. It all depended on what I could do for you. Mind! Here's that waiter coming again. He's dying to ask me whether I want 'thick' or 'clear'. Isn't it astonishing that I can wise-crack at a moment like this? But it helps to take my mind off things a little. Mind."

The waiter busied himself at the table and solicitously took our next orders. It says much for my self-control that I was able to sit there as I did. Impatience burnt me up. Every second that went by might be a second of vital delay and mean ultimate disaster for me.

"Go on, Helen . . . please," I said as calmly as I could manage.

"I heard Don say that he would do 'exactly as you wish'. They were the words he used. After that I heard this. 'He's out now on business. For me. Don't worry. I sent him out. As a matter of fact, he didn't want to go. He'll be back all right—I'll guarantee that for you—too snug and warm here, you bet, to want to move away. Right! You'll be down this evening then to make the . . . the . . . arrest.'" Her voice faltered on the final word.

I sat there—grim and hard-faced. I knew the worst now. At this very minute, possibly, the Police were entering the "Nell Gwynne" for me . . . with the handcuffs all ready. Then it came to me that there was still something which I didn't understand and which had still been left unexplained. I looked at Helen and the blue of her eyes.

"They may be there now," I said to her. "Asking for me. Two or three of them, I expect."

"Yes, I expect they are. But they won't find you. One of them will turn to the other and say 'the bird has flown'. They always say that—in similar circumstances." She smiled at me bravely. "At least . . . you have a temporary respite. You're still free—and while there's life there's hope."

"Yes. But what's worrying me is—"

"S'sh," she warned me. "The waiter again."

I took the hint from her as I had done before. The next course was brought to our table. When the coast was clear again I continued the sentence which I had so summarily broken off. "What's worrying me, Helen, is this. How on earth did you get here? I know *why* you came, my angel, but I'm still hoping for the explanation as to how you managed to pull it off. I must know that before we go a step further."

She smiled a quick appreciation of the gratitude which she knew I was feeling. "Well, I realized, directly my husband took that message from the Police, that only rapid action on my part could save you. Luckily I knew where you would be. You had told me the other day. My toughest job was to get to you in time. I had to stop your returning to the 'Nell Gwynne' at all costs. The problem, therefore, the immediate problem, resolved itself into this. How could I get up here without creating suspicion? I thought it all over and I had a brain-wave almost at once. Within a few minutes, indeed, of my husband's putting up the telephone receiver! Without troubling to put on either a coat or a hat, I slipped out to the nearest 'phone-box to the 'Nell Gwynne'. There's one less than a hundred yards away from our saloon-bar entrance."

"I know," I interrupted her, "I used it myself the other afternoon. But go on, please."

"I had my plan all ready when I went into the 'phone-box. I rang up an old school friend who would do anything in the world for me. As I think I would for her. Her name's Eileen Fleetwood. She has a flat in the Kensington district. I got her to send me a telegram. I dictated the message that I wanted sent. I had to think of my husband, you see. The message was: 'Come at once, Mother very ill.' 'Mother', of course, was meant to refer to my own mother, who lives at Rollins Hill. It all worked beautifully. The wire came. I took it to my husband directly it was received. . . . He accepted the inevitable . . . and here I am." She paused and then went on again. "Don't you think it was all terribly clever of me? Even though it was all in such a good cause?" Mischief tinged the anxiety that stood in her eyes.

"I do. Something more than clever. We'll talk about it later . . . I hope! Then we shall be able to get it in its true perspective. For the moment, Helen . . . I can't say more than thank you. But that 'thank you' covers a multitude." I saw that she was crumbling her bread on the table-cloth. I went on hurriedly: "Question now is . . . what do we do next—or, rather . . . what do I do?"

"Yes . . . it's some problem, isn't it? It will need a spot of intensive thinking."

We were silent—the pair of us. Suddenly Helen looked up at me. "Before we decide on anything . . . have you seen the . . . person you came to see?"

"Good Lord!" I cried. "I'd clean forgotten all about him. What a fool I am, to be sure! As a matter of fact, I was looking for him when I saw you . . . but he didn't seem to have turned up. He was due to meet me here at seven o'clock."

"He," she said, and I noticed that her voice was trembling—"it was a man, then?"

"Of course. Whom did you expect?"

"I was afraid—that it was a woman. But I *hoped* that it was a man."

I shook my head. "I don't meet women. Except you, of course. But help me, Helen. You can see parts of the room that I can't. Is there a man dining here wearing a pink rosebud in the lapel of his dinner-jacket? If there is, he's my man . . . and I must see him . . . despite the danger that I'm in. At any moment, you see, the Police may trace me to Burrows and Wilson's . . . because I naturally went there, you see."

"Yes. I've been fearing that for some time. They will 'phone there from Lifford. But wait a minute and I'll look round for you." Her eyes travelled round the room. I waited for their verdict. I hadn't long to wait. "Your man is here, Stuart," she said quietly. "He's sitting at the first corner table on the left as you enter. He's alone."

"Then I must speak to him. He's here on my account. And I must waste no time, either."

"What shall I do? Because we have come to no decision yet . . . as to what we are going to do . . . afterwards."

I thought hard. "Look here," I said. "I must take a chance. The Crabble Street tube station is only about two minutes' walk from here. You go there. Wait for me there. I'll be with you in . . ." I looked at my watch . . . "I'll be with you within twenty minutes."

She looked at me steadily. "You will come?"

"I shall come."

"You promise that faithfully?"

"I promise that faithfully. Unless I'm arrested in here or on the way to you."

"That's where I must take my chance. All right, Stuart. Within twenty minutes, then. I'll be there." She rose to go.

I watched her. Then I walked across to the table to meet Paul Armitage. As I came close to him he raised his eyes to me . . . and I began to wonder. For I scented danger.

CHAPTER IV
I Take—Another Chance

(*Dr. Traquair's Narrative*—continued)

As I came close to him he deliberately fingered the rosebud in the lapel of his jacket. I sat down in the chair that directly faced him. "We have an appointment, I fancy," I remarked with all the nonchalance that I was able to summon. His appearance surprised me somewhat. For no logical reason, of course. But I had expected to meet a much younger man. This man who faced me suggested a Belgian burgomaster much more than an Englishman. He was bald, with twinkling eyes and a good deal of hair closely trimmed on his face. I put his age at round about fifty-five.

"It is very probable," he replied . . . "for I take it that you are . . . shall we say . . . Dr. Stuart . . . we, will omit the other name for reasons of—discretion!"

I smiled at this expression of tact. I returned the compliment. "I presume that I have the honour, then, of addressing Mr. Paul Armitage?"

He held up a deprecating hand. "S'sh! It's better now not to mention anything so definitely personal as a full name. I have no name. For this evening, at least. Address me, please, as Number Twenty-two."

I nodded. "I see. I am to understand, then, that Number Twenty-two masks the identity of the gentleman whose name in a moment of indiscretion I just mentioned. If it is not troubling you too much I should value that assurance."

His eyes twinkled almost boisterously and he raised a wine-glass to his lips before he replied. He sipped the wine appreciatively.

"I feel that you are destined for a measure of disappointment. The gentleman whose name you gave . . . inadvertently, we will say, is unable to be here this evening. Had he been *able* to keep the appointment, you would have negotiated with him as Number Eight. But circumstances have conspired to prevent his coming here. . . . In consequence of his inability to be present I have been deputed to take his place." He replaced his glass on the table—his eyes were still smiling at me. The words that I had been about to say were checked on my lips. My mind, worn and harassed by the events of the day and by all that had happened before the day, darted here and there, questing the truth. I had a swift intuition that all was not right. Why wasn't Paul Armitage here as he had arranged to be? If he had not been able to come, why hadn't he warned me? It would have been easy enough, surely! He could have devised a way of communication. I cut into my *vis-à-vis*, therefore, with a quick question. "Why isn't . . . Number Eight here? I have received no intimation in reference to his absence. Is it too much for me to ask for explanations?"

"Oh no," he replied. "You may certainly ask . . . even though it is not permitted for me to answer you. Number Eight cannot be here. You must content yourself with that bare statement of fact." His voice was harsh.

"You refuse to answer me?" I was nettled.

"Not exactly. I have tried to make myself reasonably clear, I think." He leant towards me across the table. "Now let *me* say something. Don't let us prejudice interests that we both have at heart. Interests which you will agree are much greater than anything personal. I entreat you, sir."

But I would have none of him on these terms. Every possible suspicion in me was by now thoroughly aroused and active. I shook my head emphatically. "I am sorry. But I cannot accept the conditions. I have no possible way of verifying your credentials. You may, for all I know, be anybody. You speak of important interests. I agree with you. They are far too important—much too vital—for me to handle them with anything like blazing indiscretion. Therefore, sir, I must beg you to excuse me." I rose. Number Twenty-two half rose. It occurred to me as I looked at him that he was on the point of denial or expostulation.

But instead of putting over either of these, he sat down again quietly and said: "I am sorry that you should think fit to speak as you have. I can do no more than repeat what I have already told you. I beg of you to be reasonable."

"I *am* reasonable. I am taking precautions such as any sane man in my position *would* take. I cannot jeopardize myself, and, similarly, I cannot jeopardize those other vital interests that were mentioned a few moments ago. I am as sorry as you are." I looked at my wrist-watch and thought of Helen. My time was growing appreciably shorter. That factor decided me. "I will wish you good night," I said to Number Twenty-two, and then, as I was about to turn on my heel, I was unable to resist the temptation of a parting shot. "Remember me to Number Eight, will you, when you meet him, and tell him that his advices to me on the score of caution have been well noted? Good night again."

I obtained my hat and coat and within a few moments stood on the pavement, outside Terroni's, in the cool night air. There I paused for a second or so to light a cigarette. I cupped my hands to shield the flame of the match. In the act of so doing, and with my head well down towards my hands, three men passed me quickly. They had come from a car which, travelling quickly, had stopped suddenly in Vancouver Street just opposite the main entrance to the restaurant. To my utter astonishment, one of the three men was Rupert Halmar. Both of the others I had also seen before on the night that Madeleine died. They were in such a hurry to enter Terroni's that not one of the three gave as much as a glance in my direction. As I saw the doors close on them I smiled grimly to myself. More than ever before I congratulated myself on the way in which I had dealt with Number Twenty-two. "He's waiting for them," I thought. "I avoided their clutches not a minute too soon. They chose the wrong man this evening."

I made my way quickly to the Crabble Street tube station. Helen, to my relief, was waiting for me there as we had arranged. I rushed straight up to her. "Where shall I take to?"

"I have the tickets. I knew that you would come because of your promise. I've done quite a lot of business since I came away from Terroni's."

"Business—or thinking?"

"Both. First of all, though, is it all right? The man at the table, I mean?"

"It is—but it mightn't have been," I answered bitterly.

"Good. Now I'll tell you what I've done and then I'll unfold the full plan that I've thought out."

I smiled at her eagerness.

"Come over here." She beckoned me into a corner of the station. "Directly I left you in Terroni's I went to a 'phone-box and got through to Eileen's. That's the little pal I told you of in the restaurant. She's as sporting as they make them. It isn't every girl would do what she's going to do for us to-night. She's letting you have her flat for as long as you like. I'm going to take you along there now. It's in Pelham Crescent. You'll have to fend for yourself, I'm afraid, but it's not the worst of ideas, is it?"

She eyed me with a touch of whimsicality as she detailed her plan. I began to remonstrate with her. I couldn't in any circumstances allow these two girls, one of them a complete stranger to me, to make these sacrifices and suffer these inconveniences on my behalf. "But look here," I said. "What about you? What are you going to do? I can't desert you like this."

She placed a restraining hand on my arm. "Now don't bother about that. I shall be quite all right. When I've dropped you at Eileen Fleetwood's I'm going on to Mother's at Rollins Hill. Twenty minutes from Eileen on the 'Met.' There'll be heaps of time. Eileen will come with me. I'll think of a story that Mother will believe—don't you fret."

I began to see a little more light. Eileen's flat certainly might mean another sanctuary for me for a time at least. Helen saw what was passing through my mind, for she intervened again quickly. "That suits all the departments of the problem. Can't you see that? I shall be at Mother's, which is where I'm supposed to be. In fact, I've really *got* to go there, in case Donald rings through to her. Eileen's been there before with me, so there'll be nothing unusual about her turning up with me this time. Now, I ask you, Stuart, what could be better?"

I was silent for a moment.

Helen pressed home her advantage. "You must see that I'm right. Now come with me at once and don't argue. Eileen will be wondering what's become of us." She turned quickly, and I followed her down the steps. After all, perhaps it was the best thing that I could do, considering all the circumstances.

"I've booked to Pelham Square. The trains run every few minutes, so we shan't have to wait very long."

We stood on the platform and a westward train came in. The train was so crowded that both Helen and I had to stand. "It doesn't matter," she said, "it's only for a few moments. Five stations, I think."

We ran into Pelham Square and pushed our way out past the line of standing passengers. "How far's the flat?" I asked her.

"Not more than two hundred yards," she answered brightly. "Eileen will be waiting for us. Let's hurry and get there as soon as we can."

I nodded and we each quickened our steps. "Here we are," declared Helen eventually . . . "This is Pelham Crescent. Eileen's block of flats is about half-way down on this side. Why so silent?"

"I've a lot on my mind, Helen. And you're a part of the lot, my dear. God knows what the end of it all is going to be! I wish I knew."

"Sometimes I'm glad I don't, Stuart." She halted on my name. "This is Eileen's. Come with me." There were several lights shining behind windows in the block of flats outside which she had stopped me. I knew roughly where we were. I recognized it as the block which backs on to the railway line. Helen ran quickly past an open door and I followed her. "This is it," she whispered to me, and I tapped lightly on a trim-looking door. It was quickly opened by a brown-haired girl with merry, laughing eyes and all the joy of living showing on her face.

"Oh . . . come in . . . my dears. I've been wondering if anything had happened to you."

I entered behind Helen. She turned very simply towards me and put her hand on my arm. "This is Dr. Traquair, Eileen. I am very proud to call him my friend. This is Eileen Fleetwood, Doctor. I should like you to be great friends."

Eileen held out her hand with a spontaneous gesture that added to her charm. The merriment still danced in her green eyes. "Good evening, Doctor. Helen has told me all about everything. You must really believe when I tell you that I'm frightfully thrilled to have this chance of helping Helen and you. Everything's arranged. I've had time to do it all while I've been waiting for you."

I took her hand and pressed it with gratitude. "Thank you, Miss Fleetwood. I must count myself the luckiest man on earth. Surely no hunted man has ever before had such charming champions. Even now I don't know that I'm justified in accepting your sacrifices."

She laughed delightedly. "Good Heavens! How you exaggerate a merely friendly action. I'm just obliging Helen, as I know she would me if I were in need of a friendly nudge. Please don't talk about such things as sacrifices and glorify something that's just nothing. I tell you I'm too thrilled for words." She swept round to Helen with swift eagerness. "Now shall I tell him everything, darling, or will you? Would you rather?"

"No. You tell him, Eileen. After all—it's your flat." Eileen, still laughing, turned her attention to me again.

"Sleep where you like, of course. That's understood. The other point is grub. Since Helen 'phoned I've taken stock of what's in the cupboard, and, Scout's honour, Dr. Traquair, if you can wield a snappy tin-opener there's enough to last you a fortnight with care. You mustn't hog yourself too much, that's all. As for such things as milk and bread—you know—the daily supply stuff—it's left outside that door there, every morning. All you need do is to put your claws round the door and hook it in whenever you want to. You needn't show your face, so that nobody need know that you're staying here in my place. Everything else I must leave to you. Oh, by the way, there's a pair of my brother's pyjamas on the bed and there's also a safety razor in the bathroom. He leaves one there for when he comes to stay."

"Thank you, Eileen. One day perhaps I can repay you. When that day—"

"Shucks and Gertcher," she replied. "Now, Helen, get a move on, because I'm ready to come with you. Tell me, Doctor—did anybody notice you come in?"

"I don't think so. Helen and I didn't pass a soul as we came down the road. I'd swear to that."

"Good. Now suppose the 'phone rings?" She pointed to the instrument on a small table by the side wall.

"I won't answer it. Every time a call comes through—you'll be out. How's that?"

"Not too bad. But—wait a minute. Supposing Helen has to communicate with you?"

"She mustn't."

"She might have to. At least, it seems to me she might."

Helen supported her. "That's true, Stuart. I might be compelled to send you a message."

"Don't," I said. "Wire it to me—address it to Eileen . . . and of course wrap up well what you have to say. That means if a telegram comes addressed to Miss Fleetwood I shall take a chance and open it. Is that O.K.?"

The two girls nodded. Eileen, by now, had on her outdoor stuff. Cool as you like, she sat down and powdered her nose.

"That reminds me," said Helen. "I feel an utter fright and am perfectly certain that I look like one." Whereupon she seated herself and followed Eileen's example.

"I believe you girls would powder your noses if Gabriel sounded the last trumpet," I remarked with a jocularity which I was far from feeling.

"Well, good-bye, Dr. Traquair," said Eileen, "and all the luck in the world. I am certain that things will go right with you. Here's the key of the front door. Don't worry too much."

We shook hands. Helen offered her hand to me. I took it and clasped it warmly. No words passed between us. I knew what she was thinking and I fancy she knew what my thoughts were. The two girls went to the door. Helen turned and gave me a farewell glance. "There's one thing," I called out to them, "I shan't be idle. I've got a job to do . . . or rather to finish."

The two girls closed the door behind them, and I heard their footsteps receding into the distance. For the first time for many days I was alone. I sat down on the edge of Eileen Fleetwood's settee and slowly filled my pipe. I felt that a quiet, introspective smoke would do me a world of good. I took out the papers that I had brought with me from Brooke. I sorted them through carefully. They were all there . . . including the two vital sheets that I had always made a point of carrying in my personal wallet. I would finish my job before Eversley's brother-in-law put his hand on my shoulder. I was determined on that. I took out my fountain-pen and started work. In this respect Eileen's flat was better sanctuary than Helen's hotel. Within it were quiet and privacy. I soon picked up the thread of things and settled down to my job in all seriousness. I scarcely noticed the regular chiming of the clock on Eileen's mantelpiece. At half past eleven an idea came to me. I rose, went to the door and turned the key in the lock.

CHAPTER V
DEATH ON MY DOORSTEP

*(Dr. Traquair's Narrative—*continued)

I WORKED on hard until the clock's chiming told me that it was midnight. I put my papers away again. Then I realized that beyond the clock I hadn't heard a sound the whole time I had been there. I wasn't hungry—dinner at Terroni's was too comparatively recent—so I walked into the other rooms at the back of the flat. I might as well get to know the lie of the land as soon as possible. Directly I opened the door of Eileen's bedroom I heard the noise of a train going by. This confirmed the opinion that I had formed when Helen had first brought me here, and I had realized exactly where I was. This block of flats in Pelham Crescent abutted on to the Metropolitan line. But the walls of the rooms must have been well constructed, for the rumble of the trains was scarcely heard in the sitting-room. I could tell from the position of the room that away to the right lay Pelham Square station. I wound up my watch and made up my mind to go to bed. I thereupon returned to the room that I had just left and switched off the light.

Then I returned to the bedroom and, as I had done previously in the instance of the living-room, locked the door. As I did so I heard a long, low whistle. To my ear it seemed to come from the foot of the flight of steps that led up from outside to the outer door of the flat. I stood behind the door in the dark, my heart pounding against my ribs. It might have nothing to do with me . . . of course . . . but, on the other hand . . . I stood there listening for some time, but no other noise came to break the silence of the night.

Feeling that I had been over-apprehensive, I switched the light on and began to undress. On the point of getting into Eileen's brother's pyjamas, which I had found lying neatly folded on the bed, I felt certain that I could hear a light footstep outside my door, and I found myself wishing that I had brought a weapon of some sort with me.

I wondered if the light from my room were showing under the crack of the door. I sat on the edge of Eileen's bed and thought over the position. If anybody were outside the door, who had designs upon my person or my liberty, it would be either (*a*) the Police authorities or (*b*) one of Halmar's men. Possibly even Rupert Halmar himself! If it were the Police who had tracked me here in some way, they certainly wouldn't stand on ceremony, but would effect an entrance and arrest me at their selected time. On the contrary, if it were Halmar or one of his emissaries, I might reasonably expect something in the nature of a personal attack, which probably would be delivered allied with the element of surprise. There was no point, therefore, in any attack emanating from me. My counselled principles lay in defence, so defence, not defiance, it would most certainly be! I would lie doggo, therefore, until they forced me from my precarious cover. So I switched off the light again and made myself comfortable in Eileen Fleetwood's bed. But I didn't intend towards immediate sleep. There was a locked door between me and those who prowled outside . . . but only a locked door, and I wasn't relying on it too much.

Fortunately my wrist-watch had an illuminated dial, so that I was able to gauge the passing of time without calling on the electric light supply. Thus I lay, all my senses keyed to their limits, until a quarter past two. About that time, however, Nature would no longer be denied, and I must have dropped off to sleep. I knew that this must have happened, because the next time that I can remember looking at my watch the time showed half past three. When I awakened at this time, true to my former habit, I propped myself on my elbow in Eileen's bed and listened to discover if all were still quiet. My first impression told me that this was so, but after listening for a few more minutes I became uncertain as to the accuracy of this impression. A steady, monotonous sound assailed my ears. For a long time I was unable to identify it, as it were. It was familiar to me and yet at the same time unfamiliar. Like something that I had heard many times before and yet unlike it . . . not quite the same. I lay there in bed, puzzled.

Then I tried to locate the sound. After a time I succeeded in this endeavour. The sound . . . steady and persistent . . . was coming from outside my bedroom door! There wasn't a doubt about it. And as soon as I was successful in locating the sound, it came to me in a flash what the sound was that had suggested itself to me as being like the sound to which I was listening now. The steady dripping of a tap not turned off properly into a basin below it! Drip . . . drip . . . drip . . . the noise continued regularly and relentlessly. I could stand inaction no longer. I was resolutely determined to investigate it. If I came to harm in the investigation, I should have to suffer it. I got out of bed and switched on the electric light. Then I stole noiselessly to the bedroom door. Arrived there, I again listened hard. The noise, of course, was louder now, but I could hear nothing else. I was certain that there was water dripping somewhere very near to my door. I turned the key in the lock and softly pulled open the door. As I did so I was frozen with horror! For the body of a man that must have been propped in some way against the door collapsed when the support of the door was removed from it, lurched in a ghastly heap on to my shoulders and then toppled, flabby and inert, on to the bedroom floor.

The man was dead. I saw that at once. He had been stabbed through the heart . . . and the noise that I had thought to be trickling water . . . was the dripping of his blood!

CHAPTER VI
Two's Not Company

(Dr. Traquair's Narrative—continued)

To say that I was horror-stricken is putting the case mildly. A more exact description of my feelings would be to say that I felt almost petrified. I realized, however, with sharp suddenness, that I was encompassed by danger. This man was dead. The poor devil, whatever his original intentions may have been towards me, was past harming me now. But—and this fact was vitally important—the mere presence of his dead body in my temporary bedroom was pregnant with peril for me. What was I to do? My primary and immediate idea was for secrecy. So I pulled the body right over the threshold into the room and locked the door again.

Time! What was the time now? Twenty minutes to four! It was still dark, thank goodness! Then I thought again. The blood! The blood outside the door! I must remove all traces of that before the milkman delivered the morning bottle. I looked hurriedly round and then remembered the proximity of Eileen's bathroom. I rapidly obtained a big sponge and a ewer of warm water. After that I pulled the body further into the room away from the door so that it was no longer in the way of entrance or exit. Thank God the blood had stopped dripping on to the floor and was oozing much more comfortably on to the dead man's clothes. I couldn't hear a sound outside, so I opened the door again and went on my knees. Then rapidly, with the aid of the sponge and the warm water, I eradicated all sign of the blood on the floor. But I wasn't satisfied immediately that I had finished the job, and I was rewarded for my care. For there on the large panel of the door was another stain of blood. Quick work, however, with the sponge and warm water again got rid of this, and within a short time I was back in the bedroom, feeling relief that outside, at least, all signs of the tragedy had been eliminated. I cleaned the sponge under running water in the bedroom and poured away the stained water from the ewer. Then I went back to the bedroom again and sat on the bed. There lay the dead body in front of me.

I smiled grimly to myself. There was one thing about it. I could perform an autopsy if I so chose. I bent down and had a closer look at him. The man was unknown to me. He was dark and sallow-faced, somewhere in the middle thirties. I put his height at six feet and his weight at about twelve and a half stone. I looked at the wound from which the blood had come. It was a punctured wound which had undoubtedly been inflicted by a pointed instrument. The wound, too, was deep, and the man had died from primary haemorrhage from the carotid artery. The blood was bright and red, and when the wound had been inflicted must have jet-spouted. I got back on the bed again—this time to make a serious and intelligent attempt to think out what best I could do. The presence of blood *inside* the flat was not of great concern to me . . . unless I had unwelcome visitors . . . and if they came, the game might well be regarded as "up".

The main problem was the disposal of this wretched body. I obviously couldn't inform the Police. They were the last people in the world with whom I desired to establish contact. At that moment a most disquieting thought took possession of me. I realized, with a kind of sickening feeling, that it was a thousand to one that this man had died because *I* was the man inside this flat. That is to say, my whereabouts, the whereabouts of Dr. Stuart Traquair, marked for murder, were *known* to *somebody*. And if to somebody, it would surely be merely a matter of time before they were known to many. I chewed this unpleasant reality over in my mind for a considerable period of time. If the information were in possession of Halmar I was safe from the Police but not from him, which thought brought me a little more light.

This dead man lying on Eileen Fleetwood's bedroom floor was one of Halmar's men. They were on my track in some way and this man was the advance guard . . . scenting the present situation as it affected me. I had an inspiration somewhere about this time. I went carefully through his pockets. With scant recompense, however, for my pains. In cash he carried between three and four pounds, which I calmly took and put on Eileen's dressing-table for (I hoped) my own future use. Outside one or two entirely personal articles he had nothing else on him. Not a letter—not a card . . . not a document of any kind . . . that might have revealed his identity to me. Then a curious question raised itself and demanded to be answered. Where was his hat? I knew that many men in these times made a regular habit of going hatless, but this chap looked to me as belonging to the kind that would have worn a hat. Still—this was all pure conjecture on my part and it was waste of time my theorizing on such a point. The man hadn't a hat . . . he hadn't been wearing a hat when he toppled into the room and there was no hat outside the door. I was certain of that. So I dismissed the question and turned my mental attention to matters of more importance.

Again the main feature of my problem presented itself to me. What was I to do with the body? I considered several ideas, but none of them commended itself to me for very long. Suddenly I looked at the window, and the dawn breaking in the sky reminded me that I should be unable to solve my problem for some hours. I should not be in a position to move in the matter until darkness came again. So I took my courage and the body of the dead man in my two hands and carried him through the connecting room into Eileen's bathroom and dumped it into Eileen's bath.

I got a certain amount of blood on my hands but managed to keep my pyjamas clean of any staining. To wash my hands again was a matter of minutes only. Then I slid back into bed and, by a miracle of miracles, seeing all that I had gone through since I left Lifford in the morning, was almost immediately fast asleep.

CHAPTER VII
DESPERATE MEASURES

(*Doctor Traquair's Narrative*—continued)

IT WAS well past ten o'clock when I woke up and the sunlight was pouring through my bedroom window. And as an anxiety always waits upon one's morning pillow, so mine did with me. There was that body still lying in the bath. But there was this about it. I was fast becoming a fatalist, and it seemed to me that the question of getting ready for the day that had already come was more import-ant than my worrying about the dead man whose company I was still enjoying. I would first of all have my bath . . . no . . . I'd make it a wash, shave and brush-up this morning . . . on second thoughts . . . and would keep my back to the wall for the better part of the time that I spent in the bathroom.

Oh yes . . . I was a doctor, I know, and had seen as much as the next man . . . but my senses were getting a bit on edge, which fact must be my explanation. At any rate, I proceeded with the programme which I had outlined for myself and began to think in terms of breakfast. I found bacon and eggs and cooked them, opened the front door of the flat, and took in, not a dead body this time, but a morning paper and a sealed bottle of milk. To my surprise, I found on the front page a paragraph in relation to myself. Actually a new description of myself and the clothes of poor Curtis. So the Police were *au fait* at last with most things . . . as I had suspected and feared directly Helen had told me the story of the telephone-call to Lifford in Terroni's restaurant. Well, I was no worse off . . . I was in hiding again . . . and the glorious sunshine that was blessing the room and me was bringing at the same time new life and hope.

I breakfasted well and lit one of my few remaining cigarettes. Then, for some passing fugitive reason that I can't properly explain, I went back to the bathroom to have another look at my dead visitor. I stood there and looked down at him as he lay there in the bath.

Suddenly a shaft of sunlight played on the man's face, and as it did so an extraordinary idea struck me. I walked across to Eileen's mirror, before which I had shaved myself but a short time since, and looked at myself in the glass. I rubbed the ridge of my jaw, pulled my cheek down, mucked about with my top lip (I had quite a respectable moustache by now) and then went back again to have a second look at the occupant of Eileen's bath. What I saw merely confirmed my first impression. The man lying dead there in the bath *was not unlike me*. We were, as far as I could judge from what I had seen of him, much of a muchness as regards height and weight. Also, he was about my own age. Dressed in my clothes, that is to say in the clothes which I had recently purchased in Lifford, easily traceable to me if the Police so desired, and armed with one or two credentials that might well be mine, I could well imagine his dead body, upon initial discovery, being hailed as the dead body of the wanted Dr. Traquair.

It was an idea, certainly, and an idea that became more attractive to me the more my mind toyed with it. But the question of clothes for me then assumed the proportions of a problem. I didn't fancy changing into this fellow's duds one little bit. Besides—the coat and waistcoat were bloodstained, and on that account alone were an almost impossible proposition. All this made me scratch my head. I was tempted, after some lengthy consideration, to dismiss the idea. The more I looked at it, however, the more plainly I saw that if I *could* pull this substitution off successfully I should be bound to gain a few days, at a moderate estimate, of most valuable time. So I donned my thinking-cap again. If Eileen Fleetwood had only been a man and not a girl! In that case she might have had clothes here for me.

This thought of Eileen brought me to another thought, so rapid is mental transition. A thought of her brother, his pyjamas and his razor, impedimenta of his kept in his sister's flat for his convenience (and mine) when he happened to be staying there with her. Was there just a bare chance that he kept any week-end clothes in the flat as well? If he did—well, Eileen was tallish—there was just the possibility that they mightn't be too bad a fit for me. I determined, therefore, upon an exploration of Eileen's wardrobes. I carried out this plan straightway. For a long time feminine creations were all that I could lay my unscrupulous fingers on, but once again, just as I was on the point of despairing, my luck held. Tucked away in a corner of Eileen's modern wardrobe I came upon an old grey pull-over side by side with a fairly respectable pair of old flannel bags. They had seen better days, it is true, but they would certainly serve me at a pinch. Especially for knocking about inside the flat, which, I feared, was my prospective lot for the next few days.

I took out the pull-over and the pair of bags. At a quick glance they didn't look too bad at all—from the point of view of size, that is. My chief concern herein was the length of the trousers. I had been fearing that they would be unendurably short. I don't mind a jacket that's on the tight side but I simply cannot stand short trousers. I decided that the best thing I could do would be to try them on at once. So I repaired back to Eileen's bedroom, took off the clothes that I was wearing, and tried on my new discoveries. To my relief, they were quite of a size to suit my purpose, so I kept them on and went back to the bathroom carrying the Lifford suit to see what I could do towards the furtherance of my new plan.

Things went well with me. I had little difficulty in getting the dead man's clothes off him and mine, subsequently, on him. So far so good. Beyond what I had accomplished I had but little further idea. I reflected, however, that Rome wasn't built in a day and that there was still a goodly portion of the day to come. There was plenty of time for me in which to hasten slowly.

The dead man's clothes, lying on the floor of the bathroom, gave me another idea. I thought of the plan that I had adopted in my own house at Brooke when I got away after the death of Madeleine. I scouted round for brown paper and string, found both, eventually, in Eileen's kitchenette and made a neat compact parcel of the dead man's clothes. This I ironically addressed to Rupert Halmar. I wished fervently to myself that I could have the satisfaction of being there with him when the parcel arrived and he opened it. For my brain-plan was now beginning to leave the skeleton stage and to find flesh for its bare bones. Although I knew that I should have to wait until the evening before I could proceed much further with it. Before the evening came on I would continue with my own particular job of work. I worked on, therefore, with scarcely a break until the late hours of the afternoon. At a few moments before the clock chimed five I sat back and surveyed my handiwork. I found much pleasure therein. Another sitting and I should be, to all intents and purposes, finished. Then I didn't care if it snowed!

I made myself some tea and toasted some slices of bread on Eileen's grill. Tea and generously buttered toast to a tired man take a deal of beating. After tea I rested in the lounge. All this time I had no interruption whatever from the outside world. For all the contacts that it made with me on that first full day in Eileen Fleetwood's flat I might well have been on a lonely island in the Pacific Ocean.

When it began to grow dark I determined on a bold throw. I locked the door of the bedroom and put the key in my pocket. Then I slipped out of the front door of the flat, carrying my parcel, and boarded the first 'bus that passed me. Its destination was Hammersleigh. I was there in a quarter of an hour. I dashed into a post-office and dispatched my parcel, then into the station and bought a ticket to Pelham Square. Five minutes later I had purchased a ready-made sports jacket in an outfitter's and was on my way back to Pelham Crescent on another 'bus. I was back again inside the flat within three-quarters of an hour of my leaving it. Which wasn't bad going by any means!

I went straight to the bathroom once I was inside—in case . . .! You see, I wasn't certain whether Halmar knew yet that his business of the night before—whatever it had been—had met with a sticky end. Somehow, I felt in my bones that he *didn't* know, and while he didn't know I was safe from further molestation or attack. Anyhow, my defunct companion was still recumbent in the bath just as I had left him, which was O.K. with me.

The plan that I intended to pursue was by now fully developed in my mind. I went into Eileen's bedroom in the dark and deliberately opened the window. I wanted to listen to the trains. I knew that Pelham Square station lay to my right. The next station in the reverse direction was, I also knew, the junction, Somerset Green. In my opinion, as I thought it out, the distance to Somerset Green would be approximately three times that of the distance to Pelham Square. But there was another point about which I was in doubt and which I desired to settle. I wanted to make sure which of the two lines (I'll call them the "up" and the "down") was on the side nearer to the rear of the flat. I leant out into the darkness and listened to see if I could hear a train approaching from either direction. I hadn't long to wait. Soon I heard the rumble of a train. It was coming from Pelham Square and travelling therefore in an eastward direction. I labelled that in my mind as a "down" train, and as it passed the flat I saw quite easily that the down line was the line nearer to the flat. I watched the train as it passed on its way to Somerset Green, and away in the distance I heard it swerve when it reached a set of points that were probably reasonably close to Somerset Green junction.

I calculated that the distance between the window-sill at which I was standing and the roof of the train passing underneath was about ten feet, and I made up my mind then and there that the first eastward-bound train which stopped outside the bedroom of Eileen Fleetwood's flat would take away on its roof the dead body of the man who had stood last night against my bedroom door. If I could get it there by hook or by crook! I went back to the bathroom and started to prepare the body and its clothes for its last journey.

In the pockets I placed a little money, my return half-ticket from Everton Street to Lifford, a visiting-card of my own from my wallet, a letter of a general nature, also from the wallet, and (I regarded this as a master stroke) the railway ticket between Hammersleigh and Pelham Square which I had bought earlier in the evening. From this last ticket I cut a piece from the edge with a pair of scissors which I found in Eileen's work-basket. You can see that I didn't regard my own game as being anything like up yet. These things accomplished, I carried the body into the bedroom. After that I commenced, I think, to pass through the most wearing period that I have ever experienced. Seated in the darkness of the room, with the body right against the windowsill, I was forced to wait for eastward-bound trains on their way to the junction station at Somerset Green. They came, I suppose, at intervals of about five minutes, but these minutes of my keyed-up waiting and watching seemed hours . . . and never ending hours at that.

Ten o'clock went by . . . three-quarters of an hour in passage of time—to me like a century—and not a single down train stopped outside my window-sill. I didn't move, however, but stuck firmly and relentlessly to my self-imposed task. I supported myself against the window-sill, first leaning on my right shoulder and then changing over to the left. The time was getting later than I liked. I didn't know what Rupert Halmar's next move was going to be. And I had no wish to be preoccupied with a task such as the one on hand at the time when Halmar's next attack was launched against me.

I was musing thus when the miracle happened. I say "miracle" because that is what it seemed like to me. I heard an eastward-bound train approaching from Pelham Square. As it rumbled along in the darkness my quick ears told me that the train was slowing down. My heart raced perilously. The train came gradually on towards me, its pace getting slower and slower, and then something like a shiver seemed to pass right through it. With a series of jerks, which took the forepart of the train past my window, it came to a stop, and there, right below me, was the roof of a carriage. I knew that I hadn't a second to lose if I wanted to put my plan into effect. I hoisted the body of my man over the window-sill head first, lowered it down with my hands tightly clutching its ankles, and then let it drop and slither on to the roof of the carriage just below me. To my indescribable relief, I had found the middle part of the roof, and the body stayed in safety on the top of the carriage. No other sound came to my ears as I craned out of my window, and as far as I could see there wasn't another soul in the world taking the slightest interest in the proceedings.

Suddenly, without warning, the train started to move again and I saw it draw away, slowly gathering speed and carrying a passenger who hadn't paid his fare. I pulled down the window and turned away. As I hit the hay a few moments later I wondered when the body of Dr. Stuart Traquair, the Brooke murderer, would be "found" . . . and where!

CHAPTER VIII
AT BAY

(Doctor Traquair's Narrative—continued)

I HADN'T been in bed more than a quarter of an hour when there came a ring at the bell. The sound of it set me on the defensive immediately. Frankly, I was taken off my balance. I think that the suspense period through which I had recently passed was, in the main, responsible for my feeling as I did. I got out of bed and went to the front door.

"Who's there?" I asked.

The blessed voice of a telegraph boy answered me. The tones were halcyon. "Telegram for Miss Fleetwood."

I partly opened the door, stuck my hand and part of my head round it, and took the welcome buff envelope from the boy. "Good night," I said, and the boy returned the salutation. I quickly and impatiently opened the envelope to see what Helen had to tell me.

Mother all right. No need to worry. Many inquiries. All answered satisfactorily. Stay as long as you like. Detroy.

This was good news for me, indeed, from all points of view. I saw through the identity of the signature, of course, and as I crawled back into bed I understood that Helen had sent me the message as a measure of comfort and relief. It meant that so far I had managed to elude my pursuers and throw them off the scent. "No need to worry." This phrase undoubtedly was intended to apply to me. "Many inquiries" took me longer to explain satisfactorily. Eventually I decided that it meant that questions had been put through by Eversley, acting possibly on the advice and in the interests of the Police, as to the *bona fides* of Helen's sudden and unexpected visit to her mother. Finding her there with her mother must tend to allay suspicion. At last I went to sleep, feeling more confident as to a successful issue out of all my afflictions than I had felt for a long time. In the morning, when I woke, my first concern, naturally, was the daily paper. I took it in directly it arrived and searched its columns for the news that I so badly wanted. There was no news of the Brooke case, and after a time I came to the conclusion that nothing whatever was as yet through to the Press with regard to my actions of the evening before. I was turning the pages rather lazily when my eyes landed on the little square at the extreme edge of the paper headed "Stop Press". There, in special red letterpress, was the announcement for which I had been seeking. I read it with eagerness.

BODY FOUND ON RAILWAY LINE

At a late hour last night the body of a man was discovered on the line between Pelham Square and Somerset Green stations. It is believed from information that has been placed in the possession of the Police to be the body of Dr. Stuart Traquair, wanted by the Police in connection with the recent murder of his wife at Brooke. Further details will be found in our later editions.

I smiled to myself. Again—so far so good! The game had gone just as I had intended it should. Then my satisfaction was checked. I thought of something that should have occurred to me before. What would be Helen's reaction to this news when she read it—as read it she would be bound to? I felt mad with myself for having neglected a consideration so patently obvious. It meant that I must communicate with her in some way before she returned to the "Nell Gwynne" at Lifford. I spent the better part of the day cursing myself for my thoughtlessness. This was poor repayment for all that she had done and suffered for me. Like so many others before me, I had borne the famine worthily but lost my head at the feast! How long could I count on her staying at Rollins Hill? That was my trouble. I didn't know! Then another cold fear assailed me. Supposing Helen and Eileen or either of them saw the news in the paper, came round here to the flat in a sort of desperation, and the Police followed! It was quite on the cards that they might unwittingly lead the Police to my place of concealment.

I paced the floor of Eileen's sitting-room seeking a solution to my problem. Then I threw everything to the four winds of heaven and went back to my real job. I took out my pen and papers and set to work with the fixed determination of going straight through to the finish. However I might try to persuade myself to the contrary, I knew in my heart that this consideration came before my own safety and even before that of Helen herself. At eight o'clock that evening I pushed my chair back. I had just solved my last equation . . . the equation that had been a source of trouble to me for so long. At that moment I became the victim of my emotions. Mingled with a sense of glorious achievement, brought about after trial and tribulation, there was an emotion of deep sorrow. My mind went back to the beginning of it all, and as a result I visualized everything that had happened since I knew the truth concerning Madeleine, my wife, and Rupert Halmar. I saw her standing in front of me when I accused her. I saw her take the card from the pack which I held out to her. I saw her draw the revolver and fire at me . . . and I saw her crumple and fall into a heap as the bullet from my revolver killed her.

My sorrow warred with my sense of triumphant achievement and I wondered at a man's true assessment of his own personal loyalties. I scarified my conscience and castigated my soul, but I knew at the bottom of my heart that what I had done I should have to do again if ever I found myself in a similar position. Collecting my papers carefully in logical sequence and order, I put them away in my wallet almost tenderly. There was blood on them from one point of view, but it had not been, and would not be, if I could help it, paid in full. I went into the bedroom and looked out of the window . . . at the trains. Eastward they went and westward they went . . . but there was no body now on the roof of any one of them!

I stood there, I suppose, for about a quarter of an hour before I decided to go back to Eileen's sitting-room. I went to the bedroom door, half turned to put my hand towards the handle . . . and saw fingers showing from underneath the bed! My heart rattled against my ribs . . . for I saw those fingers move. I made no sign, however, and went out of the bedroom. Once outside, I stood stock still. Acute crisis evidently was perilously close at hand. At this moment, I think, I felt really scared. Feet stone cold! For perhaps the first time since the affair started. At any rate, I know without the slightest fear of contradiction that this was by far my worst moment. Then I resolved that I must pull myself together.

I stepped quietly into the sitting-room . . . and again took a jolt on the point. I knew directly I stepped into the room that there

was a man behind the curtain. I could just see the toe of his shoe
. . . he had a big foot. . . . I screwed my courage to the sticking-point
and whistled a snatch of a song. It was a poor attempt, I fear . . .
but I did my best. For a moment or so I pretended to busy myself
at the writing-table . . . but I wasn't staying in that room too long
. . . thank you . . . any more than I was staying in the bedroom! Still
whistling, I left for the kitchenette. As I grasped the handle of this
door I heard the faint scrape of a foot . . . and I knew that here hid
an enemy as well. I was surrounded at all points, and when the
understanding of the odds against me came home to me I suddenly
felt sick. There was but one thing . . . one sane thing . . . that I could
do. I must get away from the flat at once at all costs. That action,
seeing what I carried, was absolutely imperative. How could I get
away unseen and unheard?

I stood between the kitchenette and the sitting-room racking my
brains for an idea. At last one came to me. Ostentatiously I entered
the bathroom and very audibly closed the door. Inside the bathroom,
I turned on the taps over the bath itself and within a second or so
the water was running steadily. With the water running, I started
to whistle again and to make as much reasonable noise, generally,
as I could. When the water had reached a fair height in the bath
I splashed it about a bit with a back-scrubber that I had spotted
standing against the wall beneath the wash-hand basin. In short, I
went through the whole gamut of noise that may be expected when
a man is preparing to have a hot bath.

Now, the first thing that I had to do was to open the door again
without the sound of it giving me away. So I leant at the side of the
bath splashing heartily with one hand and with the other extended
I opened the door again. Directly it opened I saw that the noise of
the water worked. Then I went to the head of the bath and turned
both taps—hot and cold—on to the full—at the same time removing the plug. I had no desire for the charming Eileen to return to
a flooded flat. With both the hot and cold water taps flowing away
merrily and at full blast, I tiptoed to the bathroom door, out of the
bathroom, gently closed the door again, and then made my way
noiselessly through the doorway that would take me to the street. I
hadn't the slightest idea where I was going. All that I *knew* was that

I must get away from Halmar's gang, because to stop against that weight of numbers could only mean disaster. Disaster that would affect others in addition to myself. I walked quietly along Pelham Crescent. I was without a hat or overcoat, remember—just wearing the cheap jacket I had bought in the shop at Hammersleigh and young Fleetwood's pull-over and flannel bags.

As I neared the end of Pelham Crescent, and could see Pelham Square station, I noticed a girl hurrying towards me. Something about her walk and general appearance struck a note of familiarity. It was like somebody I knew . . . or somebody I used to know. As I approached her, for the life of me I couldn't definitely place her. We came face to face eventually, and to my utter amazement I saw that it was Phoebe Hubbard. She had walked by me in a flash before I could collect my racing thoughts. The more I dwelt on it the more it seemed to me a most marvellous coincidence. What was Phoebe Hubbard doing at Pelham Square or in Pelham Crescent at this time of night? I stopped and turned to see where she was going. I didn't think that she had recognized me. For a moment I had an insane inclination to go after her, but it was short-lived.

My common sense prevailed and I walked slowly on in the direction that I had been taking, still without a real idea as to where I was going. Suddenly, I became aware of a car hugging the kerb just behind me. Something about the rate that it was travelling aroused my suspicions as to its intentions. I quickened my pace noticeably. So did the car behind me. I diminished my pace. The car did likewise. I stopped and turned fiercely and impetuously towards it. The car crawled up to the kerb right against me and also stopped. The man at the wheel leant over towards me and opened the door with his left hand. Although it had grown dark by now I was able to see his face distinctly. My worst suspicions were vindicated. It was the man I had left at the dining table in Terroni's. The man who had instructed me to address him as Number Twenty-two. As I looked at him I caught a half glimpse of another man seated at the back of the car. Number Twenty-two put out his hand towards me, as though to drag me inside. Panic took possession of me. I adroitly dodged the open door of the car and ran headlong, for all I was worth, in the direction of Pelham Square station. As I ran I heard his voice cry out sharply, but I took no notice of it. I ran harder!

PART FOUR
THE SECOND CHASE

CHAPTER I
THE BIRD HAD FLOWN

(Told by the Author)

CHIEF Inspector MacMorran, accompanied by Detective-Inspector Rudge of the Brooke Police and Anthony Lotherington Bathurst, entered Lifford at least twenty minutes before the time that Rudge had intended for arrival. Mr. Bathurst's car had been on its best behaviour, the roads had been excellent, traffic contacts well ordered, and no hitch of any kind had occurred to cause delay. Instructed by Rudge, Anthony took a number of short cuts and pulled up quietly outside the "Nell Gwynne".

"Can I leave her here?" he asked Rudge. The latter looked round and nodded.

"I think so. At any rate, we'll chance it for the time being."

"Did you tell Eversley what to expect?" asked MacMorran.

"Yes. That's all right. He'll be in the bar now. He'll take us into his private room. Don't worry. I've seen to everything." Rudge pushed open the door of the saloon and the three men entered, Anthony Bathurst walking last. Donald Eversley, who by his manner had been eagerly expecting them, came quickly towards them.

"Not a word," he said; "come in here with me." The three of them followed him into his little parlour behind the bar.

"Where's our man? Is he back yet?" demanded Rudge sternly as soon as they were inside and the introductions made. To Anthony's eye, Eversley seemed a trifle uneasy.

"Well, as a matter of fact, he's *not* back yet." Eversley took out his watch. "He should be along within the next half-hour. That allows time for the next train to come in."

MacMorran stuck out his jaw. "I don't think that I altogether understand. Where's he gone? From what you told Inspector Rudge earlier I expected to find him here by now."

"He should be here. Any other day you would have found him here. To-day, however, he happens to have run up to town, as I told my brother-in-law on the 'phone."

"What's that?" snapped Rudge. "Not back from town yet? Why not?"

"I don't think you have any cause to be alarmed. He didn't go on his own suggestion. I sent him to town on some business connected with his work here. Actually, he didn't want to go. I had to put my foot down. So there isn't the slightest reason to worry about his not coming back." Eversley rose. "In the meantime, while we're waiting, what will you gentlemen drink?"

Rudge remonstrated. Anthony could see that Eversley's latest news had rattled him. "It sounds all right from your point of view, no doubt, but our game teaches us to be suspicious and to take no chances. I'm beginning to wish that you hadn't let him out of your sight."

Eversley busied himself with regard to the drinks. A barmaid brought them into the parlour. "There's one thing about it," remarked Eversley, "it'll put this little pub of mine into the news. When it gets round that the Brooke murderer was arrested here, the people will flock here in their hundreds. It's an ill wind they say." He drained his glass.

"How's the wife?" inquired Rudge.

"Got a spot of trouble in her family. Otherwise as fresh as a daisy."

"Oh—nothing serious, I hope?"

"The old lady. Taken ill suddenly. Helen's gone up to see how she is. They wired for her. I hope it's nothing too serious. Still, you never know when they get on in years, do you?"

Rudge and Eversley degenerated into familiar conversation. Anthony and MacMorran talked things over quietly in their corner of the room. The time passed quickly. At length MacMorran referred pointedly to his watch. "What about that train, Mr. Eversley? It should be in by now, shouldn't it? Your man—our man—doesn't seem to have been on it. It wouldn't take him all this time to come from the station, if I'm any judge."

Eversley followed the Inspector's example and looked at his watch. Again Anthony noticed that he changed colour. "You're right," he said: "he's not come by the train I expected. He'll be on the next one. He may have had a bit of bother at the place I sent him to. May have had to call back there a second time and been delayed in consequence. Drink up, gentlemen, and I'll send for another round."

"When's the next train due in?" demanded MacMorran with a trifle more than his accustomed brusqueness.

Donald Eversley looked at his watch again and made a quick calculation. "In about twenty minutes' time," he answered.

"Is that the last to-night?" demanded MacMorran again.

"H'm . . . let me see . . . as a matter of fact, it is. But don't you worry, Inspector. He'll be on the next train all right. You see."

"I hope you're right. Personally, I very much doubt it. Quite candidly, I don't share your opinion and I don't mind admitting it." MacMorran's face was grim and hard.

Anthony Bathurst made his first direct contribution. "We must wait and see what the train brings, Inspector. Until we know, taking these conversation classes is so much waste of time."

Eversley expressed his approval of Anthony's remark. "Of course it is, Mr. Bathurst. What on earth's the use of meeting trouble before it comes?"

An annoyed MacMorran shrugged a pair of eloquent shoulders. Rudge grew more and more impatient. The waiting period, allied now to a general feeling of uncertainty, had frayed his nerves. He kept looking at his watch and then across at the door. Eversley made repeated attempts to revive a conversation that had undoubtedly languished. Most of these attempts failed dismally, Anthony being the only one of the three visitors to respond to the endeavours of the willing spirit. Gradually the minutes passed. Eversley, who had a bottle of whisky at his elbow now, was drinking more than was good for him. His nerves had gone the same way as Rudge's. Suddenly MacMorran shut the case of his silver watch with a definitely pronounced snap. The movement of his fingers betokened expressive antagonism and bitter triumph.

"Your last train's been in twelve minutes, Mr. Eversley . . . and I still await the arrival of Dr. Traquair."

Eversley's face was as white as a sheet. He licked his lips as though they had the dryness of fear. He made no reply to MacMorran's taunting remark.

Anthony mediated. "It looks as though the Inspector's fears are justified, Mr. Eversley. What do you think, yourself?" Anthony intended the remark to draw the man out.

"I don't know what to make of it. It's no good pretending that I do. I know this! I'm worried! Worried to hell. Worried every bit as much as you fellows are. I can't understand it—and that's a fact."

Anthony could see that the man's depression was genuine and that he meant every word he said. Rudge let his feelings get the better of him. "Chance it—it's made damned fools of us . . . whether you can understand it or not. I'm not doing this job as fun and games. It happens to be my living." Eversley took umbrage at this remark and showed more spirit.

"You can't blame me. I've done my best for you. Another thing—you can rave as much as you like, you're no worse off than you were before you came down. Worse off! As a matter of fact, you're a damned sight better off!"

Again Anthony Bathurst sought to pour oil on the troubled waters. "Mr. Eversley is quite right there, gentlemen. Without the information that he passed on to us we should be in a much worse position. There's no doubt about that."

"Still—" MacMorran began to argue. Anthony checked him, however.

"Recriminations, Andrew, are useless. Particularly so at the stage of the case that we have now reached. I suggest that the best thing we can do is to get down to our new problem and see what we can make of it."

Rudge revealed himself in a new light. "I guess Mr. Bathurst is right . . . it's no use crying over spilt milk." He turned towards his brother-in-law. "Tell me, Don—where was this fellow supposed to go on your behalf?"

Anthony gave benison to the effort. "That's the idea. That's the way we must get down to things."

The three men prepared to hear what Eversley had to say.

"I sent this man to Burrows and Wilson's on a business errand. You know the people I mean—they're the billiards experts. I wanted some stock renewed. Traquair—I'll call him Traquair—didn't want to go. That's a solid fact. As I told you when you came in, I had to choke him off a bit. As you may anticipate, knowing what you know now, he's been a bit superior for his position, ever since he came here and I took him on."

Rudge looked at his watch. "Is it too late to get Burrows and Wilson's now? Or will they be closed for the night?"

Eversley shook his head. "No, I should think you'd get them. They run pretty late sessions up there. Try them. I can give you their number. Hang on for a minute." Eversley took certain papers from his pocket. "Here you are—'Mar. 822'. Get through now."

Rudge took up the receiver and asked for the number Eversley had given him. "It's a Trunk's," he said. Eversley nodded.

Rudge waited patiently for the operator to get the number. The other men stood round him. Rudge spoke. "Yes, I want Burrows and Wilson's. Detective-Inspector Rudge speaking. Officially—on behalf of Scotland Yard. I'm inquiring with regard to a man who is believed to have visited your establishment some time to-day. What? No . . . to-day. He called on business, something to do with Mr. Donald Eversley, the proprietor of the 'Nell Gwynne', Lifford. Can you tell me for certain if he did make that call on you? Thank you . . . very good. . . . I'll hang on, then." Rudge put his hand over the mouthpiece and spoke to the others. "They've gone to find out. From the order-book or something. If you ask my opinion, he never went near the place. Not so likely!" He turned suddenly and spoke into the receiver. "Thanks . . . yes . . . yes . . . what's that?" The others saw him stop and listen. Eventually they heard him say: "Thank you very much, I'm extremely obliged to you." He quietly replaced the receiver. "I was wrong," he said. "He did turn up there, after all."

MacMorran chewed at his under-lip. Anthony Bathurst looked across at the others. "Rather surprising, that, don't you think, gentlemen?"

"I suppose it is," returned Rudge thoughtfully.

"What do you deduce from that, Andrew?" asked Anthony.

"Well . . . there's this to it. Going to the place where he had been sent might not have interfered with his future arrangements. Let me put it like this. He intended to get away later, and calling at this place in the earlier part of the day didn't matter to him two hoots . . . all that he wanted to do could be easily seen to afterwards."

Anthony shook his head slowly. "I don't know that I can agree with you, Andrew. You may be right, of course . . . but, somehow, I don't think so. It looks to me something much more like this. I will resolve it into a plain question. What was it that happened to Dr. Traquair at some time during his stay in town to make him bolt? I say 'bolt' because that is what I'm very much afraid he has done."

There was a silence after Anthony had propounded his question. It was broken by MacMorran. "I see your point, Mr. Bathurst. I'll be frank and say at once that I think you're right."

"What do you think?" asked Anthony of Rudge.

"Looks to me as though you're right. All the same, I'm wondering what can have happened to him. Did he meet somebody in town who recognized him, and sheer off? Is that the probable solution?"

Anthony turned to Eversley with a curious expression on his face.

"Mr. Eversley—you will pardon my question . . . did you tell anybody of your conversation with Detective-Inspector Rudge— your telephone conversation of this morning, I mean?"

"Certainly not," came Eversley's reply with emphasis. "As though I should! I'm man of the world enough to hold my tongue when it's necessary. I can give you my word that I never opened my mouth on the subject to a living soul."

"Where's the 'phone on which you held the conversation? Is this the one?" Anthony pointed to the instrument in front of them.

"No. Not this one. I spoke on the 'phone upstairs."

Anthony considered Eversley's reply. "Could your conversation have been overheard by anybody? Was that possible?"

Eversley denied the possibility. "I don't think so for a moment, Mr. Bathurst. The telephone I spoke on is situated in a part of the house that I use as private apartments."

This reply of Eversley's brought about a second period of silence.

"Has he left anything behind him?" asked MacMorran. "Have you had a look round?"

"By Jove," said Eversley, "that's an idea. It never occurred to me to look. Let's go and scout round in the beggar's bedroom."

The three men followed the host of the "Nell Gwynne" upstairs and into the bedroom that had been occupied by Dr. Traquair. Nothing of account met their eyes when they entered. Rudge opened the door of a cupboard. A black suit of clothes was hanging there on various hooks and on the floor of the cupboard stood a brown suit-case on end.

"That's his," said Eversley, pointing it out. "I've seen him with it several times."

"Let's see what's inside it," remarked Rudge, "then our doubts will be settled."

"Is it locked?" asked MacMorran.

"Don't think so. No, I can open it." Rudge suited the action to his words. MacMorran and Anthony Bathurst crowded close to him as he did so. Rudge took out two revolvers and a tin box.

"What's this?" he asked at once as he handled the last-named.

"I can tell you at once," said Anthony. "That's a make-up box. The kind used by amateur actors—hundreds of 'em—all over the country. Open it and you'll see what I mean."

Rudge lifted the lid of the box and he and MacMorran saw at once that Anthony had spoken the truth.

"This is our man all right," said Rudge, "if any further proof were wanted. False hair, sticks of greasepaint, all the artificial aids to disguising himself. And now he's slipped through our fingers again. Curse his slipperiness!" He replaced the articles in the suit-case from which he had taken them. "Well, gentlemen," he declared, "I don't think that we can do any good by staying down here. What do you say yourselves?"

Anthony nodded. "I agree with you," he remarked before MacMorran said anything. "I think that our place is on Traquair's tail. We do know this about him. He was at Burrows and Wilson's earlier in the day. We've got to pick him up from there. New starting-point, gentlemen—the establishment of Messrs. Burrows and Wilson.

Good evening, Mr. Eversley." He shook hands with the host of the "Nell Gwynne".

MacMorran nudged Rudge with his elbow. Rudge took the cue and within five minutes Anthony Bathurst's car was travelling hard towards the city that Von Bismarck always desired to sack—the city of London!

CHAPTER II
THE THINKING-CAP OF MR. BATHURST

(Told by the Author)

As HAS already been stated, Anthony drove hard. The car had shot away from the little town of Lifford as though it, too, had the knowledge that not a fugitive second must be laid to waste. Donald Eversley, listening from his saloon bar, heard the boom of the exhaust grow fainter and fainter as Anthony's car sped down Cryst Hill, which is right by the "Nell Gwynne", splashed through the little ford at the foot of Cryst, took the wide sweep of the road and then straight through to London town. MacMorran moved uneasily in his seat. His eyes stared ahead of him.

"Hold her a bit, Mr. Bathurst . . . I really should if I were you . . . my wife, you know . . ."

"What do you want to say about the estimable Mrs. Mac, Andrew? Anything you think I ought to know?"

"We get on very well together—that's all—considering that we're married, I mean. Sorry, sir."

Anthony paused, for out of the corner of his eye he could see that MacMorran's usual complexion tan held more than a hint of pallor. From an impulse, actuated by sheer sympathy, he slowed down the pace of the car to a modest and artless forty-eight miles an hour. The road now began to rise . . . up hill after hill . . . and they ran between high hedges. But still Mr. Bathurst forced the pace inexorably. MacMorran had no words now. His senses . . . every one of them . . . were concentrated on one matter and one matter only. The road was smooth, even and level, but MacMorran, true

162 | BRIAN FLYNN

to his nationality, more than once held his breath. The powerful car heeded little but the pressure of the power that urged it on. The moon was coming up in the sky to the left of them and MacMorran fell to wondering seriously whether he would see it again on the night of the morrow. No sound fell on his ears now save the throttled booming of the exhaust.

The road began to turn now, and twist, and there came several miles that brought to MacMorran an added uneasiness. At length they reached the straight hardness of the way which runs along the whole length of Crosscope Common. Anthony swung the car along this stretch with greater zest than ever and adroitly pushed the needle of the speedometer to a cool and calculated fifty-five. MacMorran gave way to an influence that had by now mastered him. He crammed his felt hat on to his head, pushed his back as far as he could into the corner of his seat and his chin into his chest. He closed his eyes. If the end were coming to him . . . please God it came quickly. Anthony drove on, silent, cool and icily efficient. Four cross-roads were in front of them. "Left," called Rudge from the back seat. Suddenly the road dropped and they ran through, in quick succession, a number of tiny villages and hamlets. Betweentimes MacMorran opened his eyes.

"Incidentally," said Anthony, steel-armed at the wheel, "how long have we been going?"

Rudge checked up on the time for him. "Fifty-eight minutes, Mr. Bathurst."

"Good," returned Anthony; "I shall have to slow down before very long. We're getting a trifle too near town now to take any risks."

MacMorran stared, round-eyed. "Good Lord!" he said with a wealth of expression. "You surprise me."

Anthony grinned again. In most of his moods MacMorran pleased him. Rows of houses were now on either side of them and gradually Anthony diminished the speed of the car. Suddenly he became talkative.

"Been thinking, Andrew?"

"No—praying, Mr. Bathurst. Praying, hard and strong."

"You been thinking, Rudge?"

"Not a lot, Mr. Bathurst. Just wondering."

"H'm! Seems to me I've been making a corner in thought. Still—listen a while, you chaps, will you?" Traffic was all round them now and the car had once again become a reasonable proposition. Anthony began to speak again, very deliberately. "Got a *dossier* on Dr. Traquair at the Yard, Andrew?"

"Ay. It's taken some little time to collect, but it's there all right now. Why? What's your point?"

"Like to know a little more of his early history—that's all."

"When you like—that's to say, whenever it suits you," returned MacMorran laconically.

"Good. That'll be quite soon, Andrew, believe me." Anthony turned the wheel and the car took a corner just as it should be taken. "Well," he said again, "if you've been praying, Andrew, and you, Rudge, have been wondering, I've been doing a devil of a lot of thinking. Thoughts all in one direction, too. Going to tell you about them now. Want your observations. Individual and joint. So listen, my hearties."

Rudge leant forward to get nearer to the speaker. Inspector MacMorran half turned in his seat. Mr. Bathurst began. "As I was thinking over the untimely disappearance of Dr. Stuart Traquair, I kept hammering away at one point. Why did the estimable doctor change his mind about returning to the little place where he had somewhat surprisingly found so admirable a sanctuary? Eventually, I reached one conclusion. Whichever way I looked at things, I invariably and inevitably found myself returning to the same solution. That solution was this." Anthony sounded a warning horn to a moronic pedestrian who, evidently, had become tired of life. "I think that Dr. Traquair stayed away . . . *changed his plans about returning* . . . because some time during the day he received a warning . . . but not from the gypsies, gentlemen. Not on this occasion."

MacMorran cut in at once. "A warning as regards what?"

"Regarding, my dear Andrew, the unexpected arrival in Lifford this evening of a certain three gentlemen. Bathurst, MacMorran and Rudge. And Traquair, if I'm any judge, said 'no more "Nell Gwynne" for me if *they're* in' . . . a squeak is as good as a nudge."

"I see," said MacMorran thoughtfully. "So you think there was a squeak—eh?"

"I'm absolutely certain of it, Andrew," replied Anthony with quiet but forcible emphasis.

Rudge, who had been intently following the conversation, intervened. "But from where, Mr. Bathurst? Who could put up a squeak? That's the point. Eversley swears that he didn't mention our intended visit to a soul. I believed him when he said it. I still believe him. I know very well that he's a peculiar sort of chap in many ways, but I'd trust him over what he's told us this evening."

"So you might and so you may, Rudge. Without proving me wrong either. Listen to this. Suppose Eversley wasn't aware that somebody else knew what he knew. That this third party had picked up the information without Eversley having an *idea* that such a thing had happened. How about it then, O wise and learned Rudge? Doesn't that meet the circumstances?"

Rudge nodded slowly. "Yes, I see! I admit that would make a difference."

"Well," said Anthony in a tone of finality. "That's what did happen."

MacMorran, ever practical, came across with the vital question. "Then who was the third party that you just mentioned. That put up the squeak. Seems to me that 'ud be worth knowing."

"Mrs. Eversley," returned Mr. Bathurst, "or the girl who went back to London to nurse her sick mother! Devotion *in excelsis*, Andrew. I commend it to your consideration."

Rudge stared at him in astonishment. MacMorran nodded sagely. "Ay—and I wouldn't be surprised if you're right. Women are rare sinful creatures. You can never tell where you are with them. Guid work on your part, Mr. Bathurst. Guid work indeed!"

"What's that you're saying, Mr. Bathurst?" demanded Rudge from the seat behind.

"Only that Mrs. Eversley heard your 'phone message to her husband and took it upon herself to warn the man we came to take. Just that, Rudge, and nothing more. A yellow primrose by the river's brim. And I'm wondering to myself all the time . . . *why*?"

Rudge was swearing to himself scientifically and with more than a mere touch of distinction.

"Tell me about her, Rudge, will you? As you know her. Who can tell—it may help."

"Bit of a stuck-up piece. At least my missus has always said so. It was a surprise to most of the family when she married Don Eversley. I haven't seen a lot of her. We don't mix much—distance for one thing. I don't run a car. Not paid well enough for that."

Anthony soon understood that he was not destined to receive too much help from Rudge of the particular kind that he wanted. Rudge was reacting to the question he had put to him from too much of a "family" angle. "Do you mean, Mr. Bathurst," went on Rudge, "that her mother's illness was a put-up job and that she's with this Traquair fellow?"

"The former certainly. I am not quite sure about the latter."

"Well—I'm jiggered! What a cow! No good ever comes from a man marrying above him—I don't care what you say."

"Or beneath him—come to that," supplemented Mr. Bathurst.

"Or in his own class," added MacMorran, "and that's a first-rate epitome of what they call holy matrimony."

"I've been thinking," declared Rudge. "I've got my sister-in-law's address here somewhere. Or rather her mother's. Where she herself used to live before she married Donald Eversley. We might be able to do a spot of checking up."

"Good!" returned Anthony. "Let's have it."

Rudge fumbled in a pocket and eventually produced a small pocket diary. MacMorran and Anthony waited for results.

"Here it is," said Rudge. "Sixty-six Casselton Avenue, Rollins Hill."

"H'm—Rollins Hill," said Anthony. "That's beyond Wimbledon, isn't it?"

"You're right," answered MacMorran—"about half an hour's run from where we are now. Take the car straight there, Mr. Bathurst. An inquiry this evening into Mrs. Eversley's little game may prove very valuable."

"I'll do it," said Anthony, "but our line of attack wants thinking out. It will never do to attempt a bull-and-gate stunt. Oh—I know. It's easy. Cut and dried for us—don't we travel in a perfectly sound line of brothers-in-law? Of course we do. What could be better?

Rudge will call on Mrs. Eversley with husband Donald's loving inquiries, and a message the purport of which is—that he cannot bear to be alone." Anthony chuckled gracelessly.

"It's an idea, certainly," conceded Rudge. "Drive on, Mr. Bathurst, and we'll try it out. There is one thing—we may get on Traquair's tail—which is our main object. In the meantime, I'll think one or two matters over."

Anthony made straight for the river and Putney Bridge.

"What's the time?" asked Rudge.

"Just on half past ten"—this from MacMorran.

Wherever and whenever he could, with reasonable safety, Anthony drove fast. "This is the road," remarked Rudge suddenly. "I remember that I came here once—some time ago. Number sixty-six we want. It's on the left-hand side going down." Anthony took the car round the corner. "Here we are. This is the house."

Anthony brought the car to a standstill before a neat and rather dainty-looking villa. "You'd better go to the door, Rudge. I'll support you. We'll leave Andrew in the car. It's quite likely that his solemn old countenance would frighten 'em out of their wits. Besides, as a sound lady's man, I want to have a good look at Mrs. Donald."

MacMorran acquiesced in the arrangement with a cynical smile. Rudge walked to the door of the villa, followed by Anthony Bathurst. He put a finger on the bell and pressed it. A white-aproned maid answered the summons. "Yes, sir," she said primly, in response to the request Rudge put to her. Anthony watched Rudge's face. He also heard voices within the house. Feminine voices. The maid returned to the front door. "Will you gentlemen please come in?"

Rudge and Anthony accepted the invitation and stepped over the threshold. The maid showed them into a small room, evidently used as a lounge. They waited in there for a few moments. Then a girl entered. At all events, Anthony regarded her as a girl. He quickly summed her up as fair, blue-eyed and altogether charming, but there was something in her eyes which, in homage to happiness, he would have preferred not to have seen there. All doubts as to her identity were dispelled when Rudge rose to greet her.

"Good-evening, Helen," he said cordially. "I don't know whether you remember me. You should do. I fancy that we have met before once or twice. I'm Detective-Inspector Rudge. I married your husband's sister Alison."

"Oh yes . . . why, of course," she answered brightly. She held out her hand to him.

Rudge turned to Anthony. "This is a friend of mine, Mr. Bathurst. Mrs. Eversley, my sister-in-law."

Anthony smiled. "Pleased and all that, Mrs. Eversley. It was Inspector Rudge's wish that I should come in . . . otherwise . . ."

She nodded. "Why not? But I don't know that I altogether understand." She laughed merrily and went on: "Tell me—why am I so honoured at such a late hour?"

Rudge endeavoured to reply disarmingly. "I thought you'd ask me that, naturally. As a matter of fact, I'm acting as a sort of good Samaritan."

Helen was round-eyed, and Anthony liked her. Her "come-back", he felt certain, would generally be worth hearing. "I thought you seemed a little out of your depth," she replied, without moving a muscle of her face.

Rudge hesitated, but carried on. "I'm not making things too clear, am I? It's like this. Alison asked me to call at the 'Nell Gwynne' early on this evening. She knew that I'd be in the district and she requested me to call in and give Donald a message. Well—I did—and while I was there he happened to mention that you'd had the bad luck to be called to town on account of your mother's sudden illness. He asked me to call to tell you that he was quite all right and that he hoped your mother was better. I promised him I would, and here we are. That's all there is to it." Rudge manufactured one of his best smiles to grace the occasion.

Helen Eversley returned him just what Anthony anticipated she would. "It's terribly kind of you . . . Mother is better, I'm pleased to say—thanks to my coming to her, perhaps . . . but surely you haven't come all the way to town to give me Donald's message . . . have you?"

Again her face was absolutely impassive.

"Oh no," replied Rudge; "I had to come to town on official business, and was able to fill this call in quite easily."

Anthony was listening intently.

"Oh, I see," remarked Helen with casual nonchalance, and once again Rudge was left high and dry. He made an effort to restart the attack, but the resources of his imagination were not rich enough. Helen Eversley almost clinched the matter with her next remark. "I thought that my husband would 'phone me. In fact, I've been waiting for the 'phone to ring practically ever since I've been here. Of course, now you've come with his message I can understand why I've had no 'phone-call . . . but you're about the last person on earth I should have expected to see . . . Mr. . . . er . . . Inspector Rudge."

"Er . . . yes, I suppose I am. Well, I'm glad the old lady's better."

"What old lady?"

Rudge looked surprised. "Your mother, of course."

"Oh, I see. How silly of me! But we never refer to Mother like that . . . and for the moment I didn't know whom you meant."

Rudge smiled a smile, but sickliness was its paramount feature.

"What was the trouble? Nothing serious, I hope?"

"We can't say yet—until we really know. It may be or it may not. You know how it is with a sudden illness, and, of course, Mother isn't as young as she was, is she? But there you are—we're all of us getting older every day and nothing that we can do will stop it. Good night . . . and thank you so much for calling." She extended her hand to her discomfited relation by marriage. Rudge allowed his hand to be held for a moment before she gave Anthony his turn.

"And good-bye to you, Mr. Bathurst. Fancy my brother-in-law travelling in such distinguished company! I had no idea he was so exalted in his profession."

"Good-bye," said Anthony, "and fancy you being short of an idea! Do you know, I can scarcely credit it."

The smile on his face tempered the shaft, and Helen Eversley took it good-naturedly. "That's very nice of you, Mr. Bathurst," she said. "I shall treasure that and bequeath the memory of it as a rich legacy unto my heirs." Her smile matched his. Anthony shook his head doubtingly. "I wonder," he said to himself as he took his leave of her. . . . "Lovely Helen . . . Perfect mate . . . Steel-true . . . Blade-straight."

He climbed into the driving-seat of the car. Rudge had no words. For a moment Anthony sat there—without starting the car.

"Well?" inquired MacMorran with something approaching eagerness. Anthony turned round to Rudge on the back seat. He repeated MacMorran's monosyllable. "Well?"

"You heard!"

"I heard, Rudge. We're up against an unusually intelligent and efficient woman."

"Tell me something I don't know," replied Rudge ungraciously.

Anthony started the car. MacMorran sought information. Anthony let Rudge do the transmitting.

"H'm," remarked MacMorran when the recital concluded; "there's one point that sticks out a mile."

"Oh," queried Anthony, "and what's that, Andrew?"

"We must put a man on to this woman Eversley. You think that she knows more than she admits."

"I didn't say so," said Anthony.

"What?" retorted Rudge, with an expression of surprise.

"I'm not at all sure of her, Rudge. That's my point. She certainly told you very neatly to mind your own business . . . but I don't know that she gave anything away beyond that."

Rudge looked at him incredulously. "You don't! Take it from me, Mr. Bathurst, that woman knows where Traquair is—beyond a doubt."

"If that's so," said MacMorran, "let her lead you to him—just as I suggested."

Anthony shook his head again. "You may be right. I think it very likely that you are . . . but you can't logically read guilt into anything that Helen Eversley said to us to-night. As I said, all that she did was to turn Rudge's nose firmly but justly in the right direction. That is to say—away from her affairs! Still—use your man, Andrew. Better play for safety than run a risk." Anthony accelerated. When the time came for him to say good night to Rudge and MacMorran, he felt that there was much that still demanded his keenest consideration. As he put away his car he was the prey of conflicting thoughts. Supposing that Traquair *and* Helen Eversley . . .

CHAPTER III
MR. BATHURST HARKS BACK

(*Told by the Author*)

Some twenty-four hours later Anthony Bathurst interrogated both Rudge and Inspector MacMorran. "Try as I will," he said, "I am unable to rid myself of certain deep interests. Let me get back to that dead man, Reicher, again. Anything more come through with regard to him?"

"Yes." Rudge sounded harsh. "One or two additional facts have been picked up. He was born in Stuttgart, and has been in trouble several times. Bad record all the way through. He's managed to keep out of the official eye for the last two or three years, and both the Paris and Berlin police have been wondering what new criminal activity was attracting him. A bad egg, Mr. Bathurst, without a doubt."

Anthony seemed satisfied with the information that MacMorran had passed on to him. "International work, eh? And dead under the bed in Traquair's bedroom? Now, Andrew—tell me some more. Miss Phoebe Hubbard? Still seein' the sights and the lights o' London?"

"Reports come through twice a week concerning her. Nothing against her . . . but she's not an ordinary maid—that's as plain as a pikestaff. Superior type altogether. Traquair, of course, may have advertised for somebody a cut above the average. Reasonable—in a G.P., I suppose."

"I see she's made no attempt to move, then, from the address that she gave to you?"

"None at all."

"Good. What is that address in Kensington she has been observed to visit more than once?"

"A smallish house in Heathcote Square. Wait a minute and I'll give you the number." MacMorran referred to his notebook. "Number eight," he added. "Occupied by a man named Onslow. I have had inquiries made about him. A much travelled man. Lived abroad several years and also in town."

Anthony smiled to himself at MacMorran's way of putting it. "And nothing against him, either, I suppose?"

"No. Not a whisper. Though he gets himself in some funny places, and socially he didn't ought to mix up with Phoebe Hubbard, did he, now?"

"Can I have the full Traquair *dossier*—oh, I take it that Mrs. Eversley hasn't found the doctor for you yet? In the absence of any statement from either of you to that effect . . . I . . ."

MacMorran handed him a file and shook his head at the same time. "So far, all Mrs. Eversley has done has been to go shopping with a young lady companion. Also . . . and I would stress this . . . we've had official help and co-operation, of course . . . she hasn't used the 'phone at the Rollins Hill house for an out-going call and all the incoming calls have been investigated. Not the slightest suspicion attaches to any one of them. And here's the Traquair *dossier* which you asked for."

Anthony took the file from the Inspector and carefully turned over the papers.

"What are you after?" asked MacMorran. "Anything in particular?"

"Traquair's early career. What were his special bents—any idea?"

"He's a clever chap—no doubt about that. Had a fairly distinguished career. Wrote a successful paper when he was at St. Cyprian's Hospital on the Black Formosa corruption. It seems to have attracted a good deal of attention. You'll find some reference to it in that file there."

Anthony nodded. "Yes, I've just had a look at it. I see that he was a Lecturer on several subjects at one of the bigger institutes before he took over the practice at Brooke. H'm . . . h'm . . . all very interesting."

"Sir Jasper Jolle's Institute, wasn't it? I know it. It's that big place near 'The Royal', Islington."

"Quite right, Andrew. A magnificent place and well organized. It has always been a success. I can remember it starting and the head-shaking that it aroused."

Rudge looked up rather impatiently. "Can't see why we are worrying about all this. We want to get him, not to sit here and discuss his career."

"Well said, Rudge!" cried Anthony heartily. "Don't let us travel too far from the beaten track." He handed the Traquair *dossier* back to Inspector MacMorran. "Thank you, Andrew. That has certainly been helpful." He rose and fingered his cheek. "This man who lives at eight Heathcote Square? Onslow! That's the name you said, isn't it? What's he like to look at? Got a photo of him by any chance?"

MacMorran was not perturbed. From another file at his hand he extracted a card and handed it to Anthony Bathurst. "There you are. Everything you ask for. We're as well organized up here as you say they are at the Sir Jasper Jolle's Institute."

Anthony grinned at the touch and inspected the photograph. "Know him?" queried Rudge. "Seen him before anywhere?"

"No," said Anthony; "I'm not looking at it for that reason. I'm looking at it so that I shall recognize him when I *do* see him. Which you will admit is a rather different proposition."

He handed the photograph back. From what he had seen, he felt confident that he could not only recognize the man should he run against him, but also give a perfectly good description to a third party, in the event of such description being required. For Anthony now had a definite plan.

"May I use your 'phone, Andrew?"

"Certainly, Mr. Bathurst. You know very well that you can."

"Thank you, Andrew." Anthony got the Exchange and dialled a number. Rudge and MacMorran failed to recognize it, and curiosity at once became uppermost in their minds.

They heard Anthony speaking and listened intently. "I want to speak to Murillo himself. Tell him, will you, please, that Anthony Bathurst wants a word with him—at once if possible?"

Anthony waited and the two others waited with him for that which was to come. MacMorran rose and stood by the telephone. There was a silence of some moments. Then they heard Anthony speak again. "Is that you, Murillo? Oh—how marvellous of you . . . I can well understand what you say. . . . A glorious sight, undoubtedly. Only your own touch, of course. They told you who it was wanted you? Good! I want to ask you a question, Murillo. I ask it of you because I regard you as the undoubted head of your profession. For years I've placed you as that. Now listen! You have heard of Reicher—the man who was murdered some short time ago? Yes ... his body was found under the bed in the room of a certain doctor ... that's right, Murillo. Very well. You won't mention names? I understand. Now, did that man Reicher, to your knowledge, ever use your establishment?"

MacMorran and Rudge saw that Anthony eagerly awaited Murillo's reply. They observed him nod his head several times. "Never? Well, I suppose you know. You should know. Very well. I'll wait for it." Anthony turned to his two companions with his hand placed over the receiver. "Murillo's gone for certain information. I think I'm getting hold of something. If Reicher was at all—" He broke off sharply and turned to speak again on the telephone. "Yes? Where? Spell it, will you please, Murillo? T-E-R-R ... oh yes. I know the place well. Terroni's ... in Vancouver Street: near the 'Silver Scimitar' ... thank you, Murillo. You've given me just what I wanted. I shall sing your praises more loudly than ever, you old wizard!"

Anthony Bathurst replaced the receiver. "The dead man Reicher was in the habit of visiting Terroni's restaurant ... that's in Vancouver Street ... which, in view of your information, Rudge, concerning him—that he lived in Colorado Street—seems quite feasible."

"I know Terroni's. It's not a bad place. Certainly not one of the worst," contributed MacMorran.

"What people use it—chiefly?" questioned Anthony.

"Well," replied MacMorran guardedly, "I should describe Terroni's as a cosmopolitan place. Certainly that first and foremost. In fact, a colleague of mine used to call it the League of Nations. Terroni's and the Leicestershire County Cricket eleven. It's a solemn fact, though, that people of all nationalities turn up regularly there ... but I wouldn't say that they were crooks or even suspicious characters. Far from it. Still ..." MacMorran stopped.

"Well?" interrogated Anthony ... "What was it you were going to say? Anything worth hearing?"

MacMorran seemed doubtful. "I'll admit that in this talk about Terroni's you've roused my natural fund of curiosity. I won't be denyin' that. For some time now I've had a shrewd idea at the back of my mind that Terroni's wasn't *all* that it seemed to be. You know what I mean, Mr. Bathurst. . . . I couldn't give a name to my suspicion . . . I hadn't anything whatever to go on . . . just my instinct sort of whispered it to me. And now you turn up with this." MacMorran wagged his head sapiently.

"Tell me, Andrew," said Mr. Bathurst, "has our little friend Phoebe Hubbard been known to visit Terroni's, this haunt of international interests?"

"Not so far as I know. There's nothing in any of the reports to that effect."

"Pity. I could have borne hearing that concerning our little Phoebe." Mr. Bathurst rose from his seat and paced the room. Rudge and MacMorran stayed silent and uncritical. Suddenly, Anthony addressed them.

"As I see this case now, gentlemen, it assumes much greater dimensions than I had anticipated. The light is beginning to break through, perhaps in one direction at least, but I fear now the entanglement of many complications. Traquair, believe me, is no ordinary criminal."

"I'm well aware of that," retorted Rudge with definite brusqueness. "That's no news at all. I've been certain of that since the beginning."

"I don't know that I mean what you mean, Rudge." Anthony regarded him gravely.

"You can only mean one thing, I take it, Mr. Bathurst," was Rudge's reply. "That Traquair, being an educated man and a member of the medical profession, obviously doesn't belong to the customary criminal class. And I said that I agreed with you."

"Perhaps I chose my words without proper care, Rudge. I'll put it in another way. That this murder of Mrs. Traquair isn't an ordinary murder. That's more what I intended to say in the first place. I am not sure where we shall be forced to go before we finish the problem satisfactorily. We are dealing with a case, gentlemen, I am convinced, which will lead us into channels of the most surprising nature. All of which goes to explain what I meant when I said that

Traquair was no ordinary criminal." He ceased his pacing and sat down again. MacMorran looked at his watch.

"Well, it's gettin' over-late. I promised the missus I wouldn't be late this evening. I've been late so far every night this week and she hasn't taken too kindly to it. I fancy that she's beginning to regret the day she married a policeman."

"A rose by any other name, Andrew . . . don't forget that! It may not be as bad as it sounds. Still, I sympathize with both of you. I'm sure that each of you suffers from one of the worst forms of tyranny. Have a 'spot' before we go. There's a little saloon near here which always attracts me. Afterwards I'm going to settle down to an exercise in intensive thought."

Mr. Bathurst picked up his hat.

CHAPTER IV
METROPOLITAN SENSATION

(*Told by the Author*)

A SUDDEN noise coming from nowhere, which obviously must be somewhere, made Anthony Bathurst sit up in bed and take notice. His reactions were as follows. A noise had awakened him. What was the noise? He must find out what the noise actually was. He rubbed his eyes, straightened his shoulders . . . and knew that the noise was coming in maddening persistency from the telephone in the next room. Mr. Bathurst promptly threw back the bedclothes directly this moment of understanding came to him and made for the next room under the impetus and impulse of investigation. The 'phone was still blazing away merrily. Mr. Bathurst lifted the receiver more in sorrow than in anger.

"Hullo . . . hullo . . . hullo." The words were lazily spoken, but Mr. Bathurst's laziness disappeared with them. "Good Lord!" he cried. . . . "Is that a fact? Well, that clears matters considerably . . . from one point of view . . . sad though it may all be. Where's the body? In the mortuary at Somerset Green police-station? Right. When? You'll be here in the car within half an hour? That suits me,

Andrew. It will give me time to slip some clothes on. I'll be waiting for you. Good. This may mean a clearance of the entire problem. Cheerio! 'Bye."

Anthony replaced the receiver and returned to his bedroom, deep in thought. So Traquair, hunted and desperate, had taken the matter into his own hands and committed suicide. Mr. Bathurst began to scratch his cheek. What had caused Traquair to kill himself in this clumsy manner?

Mr. Bathurst shook his head as he began to prepare himself for the early coming of Chief Inspector MacMorran. He was ready, with five minutes to spare, and was waiting on the pavement outside the flat when MacMorran drove up in a powerful police car. Rudge was with him, and Anthony was inside the car in a twinkling.

"It's Traquair," said MacMorran mournfully. "Not a doubt of it. Everything points to it. Clothes came from Lifford. Lifford railway ticket in one of the pockets. General description tallies as well. You come and have a look at him."

Anthony glanced at him shrewdly. "And after all that—what's really worrying you, Andrew?"

MacMorran smiled a semi-rueful smile. "A wound in the throat, Mr. Bathurst. That's no business to be there. The Divisional Surgeon will be at the mortuary when we get back. What he says may make a difference."

"What sort of a wound?"

"Sort of stab," replied Rudge laconically.

"H'm," remarked Anthony. "I begin to share your misgivings, Andrew. You told me on the 'phone that the body was found on the line. Well . . . railway trains don't stab people in the throat."

"Thought you'd say that, or something like it," growled MacMorran. "Anyhow—wait till you've had a look at things. You won't have to wait long." The great car devoured distance and stopped suddenly down a side turning. From its first appearance the street was unfamiliar to Anthony. "Here we are—and come in," panted MacMorran. "Come on and do your job of work."

Anthony followed Rudge and MacMorran into the building. Doors swung back before them and other doors were unlocked before their passage. They passed into a smallish chamber. Inside this apartment was something which looked as much like a refrigerator as anything else. MacMorran whistled from the side of his mouth and a uniformed constable came from a desk towards them. He produced bunches of more keys. At a sign from MacMorran he unlocked something and pulled at a handle. The door swung back and Anthony found himself looking at a dead body lying on a slab. Its head lay towards him. It was the body of a man.

"Shall I lift it out, sir?" queried the constable of MacMorran.

"Ay! Put it over here where you did before. Then we can get a better look at him." MacMorran indicated a long table. The constable lifted out part of the apparatus and laid the corpse on the table. Anthony and the two others walked towards it.

"Doctor been here?" MacMorran questioned the man in uniform.

"No, sir. Expected any moment, now, sir."

"Good. Then we may as well wait for him." He glanced at his watch. "Never did hurry himself. Thinks I can stand about all day waiting for him. Ah, well! He'll find out his mistake one day, I suppose."

The door opened on MacMorran's last word and a jovial, rosy-faced little man hustled in. "Hullo, Inspector, waiting for me? Now what's all the fuss about?"

"Good morning, Dr. Pryde. Just run your eye over this chap, will you? It's Dr. Traquair, the Brooke murderer."

"Good Lord!" said Dr. Pryde. "Fancy that, now! Dear, dear, a colleague of my own. And a very distinguished colleague at that! What an inglorious end to what might have been a great career." Dr. Pryde bustled over to the table that held the body. "H'm—punctured wound in the throat. Haemorrhage from the carotid. Let me look a minute . . . dear, dear . . . downward blow—pointed instrument . . . dagger of some kind . . . murder . . . undoubtedly murder." He turned again to MacMorran. "You heard what I said, Inspector? Murder! This fellow was murdered. Not a doubt. The wound could not have been self-inflicted."

Anthony motioned to MacMorran. The latter did the necessary. "This gentleman is Anthony Bathurst, Doctor. Dr. Pryde—the Divisional Surgeon." They peered at each other. Anthony thought that he liked the look of Pryde. "Doctor," he said, "what are the injuries on the body, in addition to that throat wound."

Pryde busied himself with the body. "Scarcely any. On the legs, shoulders, and arms there are slight bruises."

"Tell Dr. Pryde where the body was found, Inspector, will you, please?"

MacMorran made the necessary explanation.

"Really? On the track, eh, of the Metropolitan Railway? You surprise me!" He made a further examination. "No—only bruises. This body has not been run over—or even struck by a train. Must have been pushed out of the carriage door."

Anthony intervened with a question to MacMorran. "Anything on the body, Inspector? I must confess to a degree of interest." MacMorran transferred the question to Rudge. Anthony got his answer. "Three and sixpence-ha'penny in cash. His card showing his address at Brooke. A letter addressed to himself from a political club at Brooke. Conservative Club, to be precise. Also his railway tickets. The first a return half between Everton Street and Lifford dated the day that he presumably travelled up, and the second, a single ticket between Hammersleigh and Pelham Square. That's the bundle. Not a great deal, is it?"

Anthony considered Rudge's reply. "A ticket between Hammersleigh and Pelham Square. So that he had gone past his station? You say the body was found on the line just outside Somerset Green, don't you?"

"Quite correct," returned MacMorran.

"Looks as though he was murdered in the train," put in Dr. Pryde.

"I wonder," declared Anthony. Then he turned suddenly to Rudge. "What's the number of that railway ticket?"

"Which ticket? The one between Lifford and Everton Street?"

"No, not that one. The other one. The single ticket between Hammersleigh and Pelham Square."

Rudge showed it him. "Two-eight-six-six," he replied eventually. "Why? What's your point over that, Mr. Bathurst?"

Anthony indicated the telephone. "'Phone through to the booking-office at Hammersleigh, Metropolitan station, and find out when that ticket was issued. There'll be somebody on duty by now. I've a hunch, gentlemen."

Rudge at once went to the 'phone. The others heard him establish connection with the Hammersleigh station booking-office. Rudge gave necessary details. "Single ticket between your station and Pelham Square. Number 2866." Rudge waited for the answer. "At what? Between seven and eight o'clock in the evening. Thank you very much." He returned to the others. "Issued from Hammersleigh station between seven and eight o'clock in the evening, gentlemen."

"I see. What time was the body picked up, Inspector?"

"Just on midnight, Mr. Bathurst."

"Who saw it?"

"A guard of an eastbound train. He reported it to the staff at Somerset Green station."

"H'm! So between four and five hours elapsed between the issue of the ticket and the finding of the body. I don't know that I like the look of that, gentlemen! What's the matter, Dr. Pryde?"

All this time the Divisional Surgeon had been sitting there with a puzzled look on his face. "Why, Bathurst, your last remarks have set me thinking. Wait a moment. I've an idea that I may be able to help you on a bit."

Dr. Pryde went back to the body on the slab. He examined it again very thoroughly. Then he turned round to them rather dramatically. "Gentlemen, I've something to add to my previous statement. I was lax. I should certainly have spotted it before. This man has been dead over twenty-four hours. He most assuredly wasn't stabbed this evening. How does that fit in with your hunch, Bathurst?"

"What's that?" cried Anthony. "I say, Rudge, tell me again— where exactly was the body found?"

Rudge produced a plan from his breast pocket. "Here's the section of the Metropolitan railway line between the Pelham Square and Somerset Green stations, Mr. Bathurst. That cross you can see there marks the spot where the body was picked up."

Anthony examined the plan. "Let me look at that ticket again, please."

Rudge handed him the ticket. A gleam came into Anthony's eyes. He handed the ticket to Inspector MacMorran. "Would you say that this ticket has been clipped by the usual punch, Inspector?"

MacMorran inspected the clipped edge of the ticket. "Well," he said, after a careful examination, "I don't think it has."

Anthony nodded. "Why not, Inspector?"

"I'm judgin' by the edges. They look to my eye to have been cut rather than punch-clipped."

"I agree, Inspector. Or, in other words, this ticket never passed the collector at the station barrier."

MacMorran passed the ticket over to Rudge. "See what we mean, Rudge? Take a look at those cut edges."

Rudge nodded. "Well—where are we then, if that's the case?"

"I don't think," said Anthony, "that a body could be there close to the track, and so near a station, for very long before being spotted, do you?"

"No"—from both Rudge and MacMorran.

Anthony went on: "And we're all agreed, I take it, in the light of what Dr. Pryde here has told us, that Traquair was murdered?"

Rudge and MacMorran expressed their acquiescence.

"Well, then, gentlemen, here's my theory. The murder took place on the night before last and the body was placed on top of a District train at some time late last evening. It had, no doubt, been concealed somewhere during the day that intervened."

The Divisional Surgeon whistled his amazement.

"But how could that be?" demurred Rudge incredulously.

"That's what we have to find out. But it's so altogether logical from what we already know. You couldn't put a dead man inside a compartment . . . it's not done . . . but you could, in certain circumstances, dump his body on the top of the train. You must see that point, gentlemen."

"Damn it, Bathurst, but I think you're right!" exclaimed Dr. Pryde. "That would explain the man's death twenty-four hours previously."

"Get a map of the district between the two stations, will you, Inspector Rudge? Between Pelham Square and Somerset Green. Can you? Have they one here?"

"I expect so, Mr. Bathurst. I'll have a word with the Station Sergeant. Hang on here a moment, will you?" Rudge dashed out on his errand.

"This is what I should call a Victorian district," contributed the Divisional Surgeon. "You know the sort of houses I mean. They're flat-fronted and porticoed. With heavy pillars. There are many of their type still to be found in the West End of London."

"Yes, I know them," declared MacMorran. "There are any amount of them round this particular district. If we can establish the fact that—"

Rudge came in again before MacMorran could complete his sentence. "Here's a map of the district," he said, "on a fairly large scale."

He opened out the map in such a manner that they could all see it. Dr. Pryde's advice was most helpful. He quickly put his finger on a certain spot. "There, you see. I know the place well. Used to go to 'bridge' parties in one of these flats marked just here. Let's see. What's the name of these flats? On the tip of my tongue too. I know—Keppel Gardens. That's them. And, what's more, Bathurst, I'll tell you this—the back windows are close to the Metropolitan line."

Pryde was excited, and as he volunteered his information his excitement grew. "Also, I'll tell you this. Owing to the intersection of one of the other lines the Metropolitan trains are frequently pulled up just along that stretch of the track. Bathurst, my heartiest congratulations. I'm certain that you've hit the right nail on the head." Dr. Pryde paused breathlessly.

Anthony smiled. Pryde's praise pleased him. "Keppel Gardens, you say. It can't be more than five minutes or so from here."

Pryde nodded. "No—it's quite close, of course."

"I'm going to worry you again, Inspector Rudge. Can you get hold of a directory—of this district?"

"Easy," said Rudge. "Somerset Green is a well-conducted station, believe me. Shan't be two seconds. Hang on again."

"Rudge warms to his work," commented Anthony to MacMorran. "Promotion may come to him from the West."

"If it does, he'll be lucky. He's over-young for the rank that he's received already. Here he comes again, I fancy." Rudge entered flourishing a directory.

"Let Dr. Pryde find the place," suggested Anthony. "He seems to know the lay-out of the district better than any of us." Dr. Pryde turned the leaves of the directory. "Here you are," he remarked after a moment or so. "This is the place I mean."

Anthony read over the Divisional Surgeon's shoulder. "Keppel Gardens . . . yes . . . yes . . . here runs the Metropolitan railway line . . . that's the place, I've no doubt. We'll visit there, Andrew . . . and, what's more, we'll lose no time over the visit. Good job you've got the car here."

MacMorran made a sign to the Station Constable. The latter attended once again to the body of the dead man. The others underwent for a second time the ceremonial of the doors. "Coming with us, Doctor?" invited Mr. Bathurst.

"I think I will—there's nothing like being in at the death."

"I rather fancy," returned Anthony, "that you've already been there. Now, Andrew—step on it, man, as far as a certain block of flats known as Keppel Gardens."

MacMorran started the car.

CHAPTER V

A MATTER OF BACK WINDOWS

(*Told by the Author*)

"CAN you direct us, Dr. Pryde?" asked Mr. Bathurst from his seat next to Inspector MacMorran.

"Oh yes . . . straight along . . . then second left . . . first right. That, I think, should bring us into Keppel Gardens itself."

MacMorran acted upon Anthony's instructions and drove fast.

"Hark!" exclaimed the Divisional Surgeon with upraised finger. "Do you hear the noise of the trains . . . that shows us how close we are here to the line."

The car took a corner. Dr. Pryde was leaning towards the window. "This is the turning," he said somewhat jubilantly. "I was right."

MacMorran slowed down the pace of the car. "What's your next move, Mr. Bathurst?"

"I'm hoping to find one of these habitations empty. If there is one in that condition there'll also be a bill indicating from where we may obtain the key . . . but stop a minute . . . the house agents won't be open yet. It's too early. That's awkward."

Rudge broke in eagerly. "Look—our luck's in. There's a moving-job on. And it looks to me as though they're just about finishing their job. Perhaps we might get a break in there."

"Quite simple," said MacMorran. He stopped the car outside the flat before which stood the pantechnicon. Two men wearing green baize aprons, the badge of their trade, were negotiating the transport of a piano from flat to vehicle.

MacMorran and the others alighted. He went on a few paces ahead and spoke to the obviously elder of the two removal men. He produced papers to them before returning to his companions. "It's all right. We're lucky—as Rudge said just now. The occupants of the flat have already cleared out, so that we don't have to explain matters to them. I've told the men who we are and what we desire to do."

The two removal men stood aside to allow MacMorran and the others to enter. In its now unfurnished condition the flat appeared to be of considerable size and the rooms were both large and lofty. Anthony had noticed when he went in that the door was heavily solid. The passage was broad. The uncarpeted staircase was unfriendly—almost hostile. The roar of trains passing was conclusive evidence as to the nearness of the railway line. MacMorran led the others to the back rooms. Anthony wasted no time in getting to the window. No sooner had he done so than he gestured his disappointment. "We're barking up the wrong tree here. Look for yourselves." The others went and stood by his side. "It would be impossible to dump a body on to a train from here, now, wouldn't it? The trains are close, I admit, but nothing like close enough for anybody to bring that off."

Dr. Pryde uttered an exclamation of annoyance. "I certainly thought that the line was nearer than this. I'm sorry I've let you down."

"Not deliberately, Doctor, so there's no need to reproach yourself." MacMorran pushed up the window and leant out. "Let me see if these flats keep a straight line. I can't remember, though, that the road bends at all." He craned his neck as far as he was able. "No. No good. None of the places are any nearer than the one we're in."

The discussion was interrupted by the appearance of one of the removal staff in the doorway. "Excuse me for a moment, sir. I just wanted to make sure that all the stuff had been cleared from in here."

Anthony beckoned to him to come in. "I say, George, do you know this district pretty well?"

The man frowned as he drew a hand across his top lip. "Reckon I ought to, sir. I've been moving stuff from round about here for over thirty years. I started as a boy with Fisher, Neale and Company. But what's the trouble, sir?"

"Do you happen to know any flats or houses round here that back right on to the railway line? This is near, we know, but we're looking for a place that's even nearer than this is. The nearer the better as far as we are concerned."

The aproned man replied without the slightest hesitation: "That question's no sooner asked than answered, sir. The place you want is Pelham Crescent. That's over by Pelham Square station. There's a big block of flats there, sir, where the trains are unnaturally close to the back windows. I was on a job in one of 'em about six weeks ago. I said to my mate at the time—'Shouldn't care about Uncle Ned in here. Such a job to get a bit o' Bo-Peep with the rattlers at your blinkin' elbow.'"

Anthony smiled as he transferred the inevitable *pourboire*. "Thank you. Pelham Crescent—eh? You have a drink at my expense on the score of that information. Come on, gentlemen."

MacMorran started the car again.

"I know Pelham Crescent," announced the Divisional Surgeon, "but I've never been in any of the places there. Make for Pelham Square station, Inspector, and I'll tell you when to turn."

A matter of a couple of minutes brought them to Pelham Crescent. The car traversed the entire length of it. Every flat seemed to be occupied.

MacMorran addressed Anthony. "Mr. Bathurst, what's our best course, do you think? We must be careful not to take a false step, you know."

"I agree. I'll tell you what. Rudge and I will get out and survey the back of Pelham Crescent from the platform of Pelham Square station. We'll pick you up again along here and report. O.K.?"

"Right," returned MacMorran. "Suits me."

"Come on, Inspector," said Anthony to Rudge; "come and mingle with the crowd of morning workers and squint at the back windows of Pelham Crescent."

Rudge and Anthony left the car and were soon on the platform of Pelham Square station. They walked to the extreme end of the platform. Anthony pointed up the line in the direction of Somerset Green. "There you are, Rudge. Look at that. Our friend of the green baize apron spoke the truth. A train stopping up there would be right against those back windows. You can see that plainly from here. Agree, Rudge?"

"I think you're right, Mr. Bathurst. Our job is to find the house. How are we going to do that?"

"That's a problem, I admit. Needs thinking over. Anyhow, we'll report what we've seen to MacMorran. Come along. I'll tell him to drive us to the 'Yard'."

Consultation was deferred until Sir Austin Kemble was available. MacMorran essayed certain explanations. Anthony Bathurst listened in silence during the whole of the Inspector's recital. Then he surprised both the Commissioner and the Inspector. "I want something done, Inspector. I want Sir Austin's permission to do it."

"What is it, Bathurst?" demanded Sir Austin.

"It concerns Phoebe Hubbard, sir, one-time maid to Dr. and Mrs. Traquair at Brooke."

"What do you want with her?" queried the Commissioner.

"I should like another interview with her, sir, if you've no objection. An official interview."

"Statements have already been taken from her, Bathurst. Isn't that so, MacMorran?"

"Quite correct, sir. Also, Miss Hubbard has been kept under close observation ever since the first murder. Daily reports are submitted to me with regard to her. But so far nothing has come through upon which we could take any official action."

"Is she acting suspiciously at all?"

"Well, sir, that's a difficult question for me to answer. At the moment I'll content myself by saying that she's an unusual line in maids. That's all, sir."

Sir Austin looked at MacMorran with a certain measure of curiosity. "H'm. Very interesting. But you can pin nothing on to her? I see."

"I'll show you the daily reports, sir. Then you will be able to judge for yourself. I'll ring for the reports now, sir, with your approval."

"Good. Do so by all means."

MacMorran rang. To the man who entered he issued the appropriate order. "Bring in the daily reports on Phoebe Hubbard." The file was quickly handed to the Commissioner. MacMorran, at his side, went through the reports in daily order. From time to time Sir Austin Kemble nodded shrewdly at MacMorran's remarks. The sheets were turned over from day to day until the Commissioner came to the current day's report. Anthony, watching, saw MacMorran's face suddenly change colour. He looked up from the sheet of paper in question and caught the eye of Mr. Bathurst.

Anthony noticed that MacMorran was uneasy. Then he heard him speaking with an unusual but deliberate emphasis. "This is a most extraordinary thing, sir. This report for yesterday, I mean, sir. Look at the final paragraph. Chatterton's one of my best men at this game and can be absolutely relied upon. Listen to what he says here." MacMorran read out the words which had so attracted his attention. Mr. Bathurst was all ears. "'Between ten and eleven o'clock in the evening, she was observed to take a 'bus to Somerset Green station on the Metropolitan Railway. She alighted at the station and walked back towards Pelham Square. She was alone and met nobody on her journey. Just before she came to Pelham Square she turned down Pelham Crescent and stopped outside number eight. It appeared that she was either waiting for somebody to come out of the apartment or for somebody to join her. In all, P.H. spent over half an hour either directly outside number eight Pelham Crescent or close to it. At a quarter past eleven she walked back the way that she had come and travelled by 'bus back to her own address. Note! *P.H. spoke to nobody during the entire time that she was out.'"*

Anthony, rubbing his hands, made the first contribution. "Answer to prayer, sir! Neither more nor less. Blessed and heaven-sent. Here MacMorran and I have wanted a number in Pelham Crescent ever since this morning, and, lo and behold, the competent Chatterton hands it to us on a plate ringed round with redcurrant jelly. It's delicious. A thing of beauty and a joy for ever."

Sir Austin nodded. "I was right, you see, to send for these daily reports. Shows how you're always repaid if you use your intelligence."

MacMorran opened his lips to speak, but discretion became the better part of his judgment and he checked his impulse. As an alternative, he contented himself with staring at the Commissioner in undisguised astonishment.

Anthony deemed it an opportune moment to intervene. "Who's the occupant of number eight Pelham Crescent? That's our immediate problem."

"You shall have that information in a couple of seconds, Bathurst." Sir Austin spoke peremptory words into the telephone. His instructions were soon acted upon. "Here you are, Bathurst," declared the Commissioner. "A lady is the occupant of your flat. Name—Eileen Hassett Fleetwood—journalist. Doesn't seem anything particularly criminal about any of that. Do you know the name at all, Bathurst?"

"No, sir. But I'm open to bet that a dead body went through her bedroom window last night. Or; if not her bedroom, through the window, of one of the rooms at the back of her flat—journalist or no journalist."

Sir Austin appeared sceptical. "Doesn't seem to me to be absolutely—"

"Miss Fleetwood may have known nothing about it, sir. There is always that possibility. You need lose none of your faith in the sex."

Sir Austin turned to MacMorran. "Let Bathurst know when you're moving, Inspector. Fix your time for looking over the premises as soon as the preliminaries are completed."

"Very good, sir. Hear that, Mr. Bathurst?"

"I heard, Andrew. Give me a ring at my place as soon as you want me. But don't forget my wishes in the matter of Phoebe Hubbard, will you?"

"Is that still on, then, in the light of this?"

Mr. Bathurst smiled. "Certainly, Inspector. More than ever now." He reached for his hat. "You see—it's like this," he said, as he made for Sir Austin's door. "I want to get in touch with Phoebe in order that I may then get in touch with Dr. Traquair! Call it a sprat to catch a mackerel!" Mr. Bathurst closed the door. They heard his steps descending the stairs. Sir Austin Kemble and Inspector MacMorran looked inquiringly at each other.

For the reason that neither could find words with which to express himself!

CHAPTER VI
IN MISS FLEETWOOD'S FLAT

(Told by the Author)

IN ACCORDANCE with instructions received, Anthony Bathurst met Inspectors MacMorran and Rudge at the east corner of Pelham Square punctually at 10.30 that evening.

"Well, Andrew," said Anthony upon arrival, "what do you know?"

"A little that may be a lot before we've finished with it. Anyhow—we've established this, Mr. Bathurst. The Fleetwood girl's not been in the flat for a couple of days or more. The telephone people have reported that to us. According to them, 'phone-calls for Miss Eileen Fleetwood have not been answered. Seems to me that there may be even more foul play knocking about there than we imagine. I've seen Sir Austin again and we're going in to-night. I've a warrant for search."

Anthony nodded. "Good business, Andrew. I'll guarantee that I'll convince you of one or two things before we come away. If I don't, it will be one of the biggest surprises of my life."

MacMorran made a direct challenge. "Who's the dead man, Mr. Bathurst? I gathered early to-day that you don't think it's Dr. Traquair."

"Can't tell you who it is, Andrew, but I'm dead certain it's not Traquair."

"Why? What makes you so positive? I don't see your point of view at all. Everything tallies."

"Oh yes, everything tallies all right. Everything tallies too well. If you don't follow my reasoning, Andrew, answer me this. Why was Traquair (as you think it is) stabbed in the throat? Then, when you've answered that one, ask yourself another. Why, having been killed by a shot in the throat, was the man's dead body deliberately dumped on the top of a Metropolitan train? I'll tell you this, Andrew, that Traquair himself put that body on the top of the train, although I won't assert that he murdered the man first. Because I'm by no means sure of that part of it."

"Pelham Crescent," announced Rudge laconically.

"Number eight's just here," returned MacMorran a moment later. "Before we go in, see if there's anybody hanging about outside."

"If there isn't now there has been," said Anthony. MacMorran half turned as though to combat the assertion. Anthony was quick to amplify his statement. "I'm sure of my grounds, Andrew. Phoebe Hubbard to wit, for one." Rudge scouted round for a few yards either way. There appeared to be no one in sight. "The coast seems clear," he announced when he returned to the others.

They passed through an open door and up steps. MacMorran stepped forward quickly and rang the bell of eight Pelham Crescent. There was no answer to the ring. He rang again. There was still no reply. "I'm going in," said MacMorran. There was a coldness in his voice that made Anthony think of that interminable wait in the darkness which he and MacMorran had known when they crouched close to L'Estrange's ladder of death. MacMorran held out his hand to Rudge, who handed him a key. "This is a master-key," he whispered back to Anthony. "We had to wait to get it. Get ready, we shall be inside in half a second."

The door yielded to his effort and the three men stood inside eight Pelham Crescent. The passage was dark. Rudge ran his hand along the wall and found the electric light switch. Nothing to excite the slightest comment met their eyes.

"Go to the back room first, Andrew," urged Mr. Bathurst. "You'll probably find that it's Miss Fleetwood's bedroom. I am interested in Miss Fleetwood's bedroom."

MacMorran, thus enjoined, walked through to the room at the back with Anthony and Inspector Rudge close on his heels and again switched on the light.

"Up with that window, Andrew," cried Mr. Bathurst. As he spoke, a train sped out of the darkness and travelled past the window.

"Look at that," demonstrated Anthony; "is that near enough to you for fun and games? Just suppose that train had stopped directly outside. . . ."

Rudge put out the light and MacMorran produced an electric torch. He shone it upon the window and then motioned to Rudge. The latter pushed up the window as Anthony had asked. As he did so there came another harsh roar and a second train rumbled past in the darkness. MacMorran directed the light of his torch on to the windowsill. Anthony bent over and examined it. It was easy to see that there were marks upon the sill where the dust-places had been blurred. "See here, Andrew," said Mr. Bathurst, "this is where the body lay. They waited here for a train, which came along and stopped. I'd do the same for you now, to prove my point conclusively, but it's on the cards that we *might* have to wait as long as a couple of hours, and we can't spare the time. Just a minute, though, Andrew. Wait here half a second."

Another train was approaching with the same rumbling sound as before. On this occasion, however, it began to slacken its speed before pulling up immediately below the window by which Anthony and the others were standing. Anthony swung round on to MacMorran triumphantly.

"Behold, Andrew—somewhere about ten feet, I should say, between the window-sill and that train-roof down there! How convenient for disposal. Have your body ready on the window-sill, give your body a hefty heave over the top, and there's an even chance of its landing on the train-top. I am open to receive your congratulations," he concluded with a twinkle in his eye.

MacMorran grunted his approval, but Rudge put his appreciation into words. "I'll hand it to you, Mr. Bathurst. You're dead right."

"Yes," conceded MacMorran, "he has a habit of being right. You'll know that even more when you've worked with him on a job as many times as I have."

"Never mind the bouquets, Andrew," said Anthony. "Let's have a general look round Miss Fleetwood's flat. It's possible that we may pick up something more."

Although the light was still off, MacMorran's torch was sufficient to pick out necessities. As he turned from the window, it did its duty. Its light caught the space just below the bed. Anthony suddenly dropped on to his knees. He pointed to three discolourations on the carpet. "It looks to me as though the body lay here for some time. After the man was killed, I should say that the body was carried or pulled into this room. Question—where was he killed? Wherever it was, there's no doubt there was a good deal of blood shed before the body came in here. Let's have a look at the other rooms, gentlemen." They went into the living-room.

On the divan Rudge spotted a crumpled piece of paper. He picked it up and smoothed it out. It was a telegram. He read out the words that it contained. "*Mother all right. No need to worry. Many inquiries. All answered satisfactorily. Stay as long as you like. Detroy.* And addressed to Eileen Fleetwood," he added. "Significant—eh?"

Mr. Bathurst said nothing, but held out his hand for the telegram. Rudge passed it over. Anthony studied it carefully for some moments. Then he spoke directly to Rudge: "Mrs. Eversley, your sister-in-law—Inspector—may I call your attention to her Christian name?"

"Helen," replied the Brooke Inspector promptly.

"Exactly," replied Mr. Bathurst with quiet certainty.

"Why?" returned Rudge. "What's your point?"

"Merely this. She sent this telegram to Dr. Traquair. That's all."

MacMorran immediately shared Rudge's astonishment. "How do you arrive at that conclusion, Mr. Bathurst? A sheer hunch, or are you working on something definite?"

"I would not make a statement of that kind if it were foundationed on a mere hunch, my dear Andrew. Look at the name of the sender of this telegram. 'Detroy'. Obviously that means 'of Troy'. There is no need for me to fill in the name of the beautiful wife of Menelaus, King of Sparta, who eloped with Paris and was responsible for the siege and destruction of Troy. As Helen is Mrs. Eversley's Christian name, which I remembered, the deduction was moderately simple."

"But you went a step further than that. You stated that she sent it to Dr. Traquair. What has this flat to do with him?"

Anthony smiled at MacMorran's stubbornness. "I think just this! It's been the doctor's hiding-place since he cleared from Lifford the other day. Mrs. Eversley has been, I fancy, the *dea ex machina* for some time now. In fact, I regard it as quite probable that Traquair made for Lifford when he got away from Brooke in the first instance. He was aware that she was there and would help him could he but establish contact with her. There you are, Andrew. You have my complete conclusions in a nutshell. Now tear them to pieces."

"No, I won't do that," MacMorran dissented. "You've given me an entirely new angle on the case, Mr. Bathurst. One that I hadn't considered before. What do you say, Rudge?"

"I entirely agree, Inspector. And I'll say this as well. Mr. Bathurst's theory explains much away which needed it. How about looking through the other rooms? There's no knowing what we may find."

"Just a minute," MacMorran checked him with a gesture. "How about this Fleetwood girl? How does she come into it? And where is she now? Or is Fleetwood the town name of Mrs. Eversley? Is that the explanation?"

Anthony shook his head. "No, I don't think it's that, Andrew. I should say that the likelier contingency by far is that Eileen Fleetwood is a friend of Helen Eversley's. Perhaps a recent acquaintance. Perhaps an old school friend. Personally I incline to the latter probability. 'Two little maids from school are they'!"

"An old school friend who conveniently effaced herself at a critical moment, eh? Yes . . . I see your drift. Very likely." MacMorran nodded his head several times to punctuate his remarks. Then he thought of the point Rudge had just made. "These other rooms. Let's take a look at them."

Nothing caught their eyes until they went into the bathroom. Suddenly MacMorran and Rudge noticed Mr. Bathurst staring intently at the top of the bath. Rudge leant over the side and looked with him.

"What is it, Mr. Bathurst? Anything strike you about the bath?"

Anthony pointed to one end. "Mud, Rudge, unless I'm very much mistaken. Mud from a pair of shoes—or boots, of course!"

"Mud?" exclaimed MacMorran. He examined the end of the bath as Rudge had. "I see," he went on; "your idea is that the body was put into that bath before it went on the train. Yes, I follow. It all fits pretty well. Good. We're making progress at last." He turned to Anthony. "As I see things now we *must* get this Traquair fellow before very long, on your valuation that he's still alive. The net must be drawing more closely and more tightly round him every day. We are bound to corner him eventually, because he can't be far away. Then, when we've got him, we may also get at the actual truth. There are three deaths to be accounted for, don't forget. Not only that of Mrs. Traquair, but also of Reicher and this last unknown man. If you ask me, the odds are that Traquair murdered all three of 'em."

Anthony shook his head as he rallied his official colleague. "You may be right, Andrew, but I don't think he killed Reicher or even this last chap. Still—a shaft of light is breaking through on the case now—and when I've had that interview which I so badly want with Miss Phoebe Hubbard, the shaft may become a brilliant beacon. We'll see."

"You'll interview her to-morrow, Mr. Bathurst . . . in my office at the Yard. That's what I'm arranging for you. Well—come along, Rudge. We must tighten that net round Traquair."

"Good," said Anthony. "You, Andrew, to your Traquair and I to the cupboard with my young mistress Hubbard. We will wish each other the best of luck."

CHAPTER VII
The White Flag

(Told by the Author)

ANTHONY Lotherington Bathurst sat in the lounge of his flat. So far, no message had come from Inspector MacMorran to the effect that a certain Miss Phoebe Hubbard had arrived at the Yard for the purpose of the official interview which had presumably been arranged. The time went by, hour by hour, and Anthony was inclined to become restless. He wanted but one link now to complete the chain of the Traquair mystery, and he had banked upon MacMorran's assurance that this one remaining link should be quickly in his hands.

Anthony glanced at the clock on the mantelpiece. The time was already much later than he had expected for MacMorran's appointment at the Yard. Suddenly, as he marked and watched the hands of the clock going on towards the recording of yet another hour, he heard car-wheels stop outside and then a ring at the bell. He heard Emily go to the door. It was evidently a visitor for him. The sound of voices ascended to the room and he awaited the appearance of Emily with the inevitable announcement. Emily came upstairs and the announcement followed.

"A lady has called to see you, Mr. Bathurst. I understand from her that it's something very special. She says her name is Miss Beryl Armitage."

Anthony ransacked his brain in reminiscence, to decide that the name was not familiar to him.

"Bring her in, Emily," he said. "I'll see her, although I'm expecting a message which will probably cut short the interview. She must accept me on those lines. Tell her that, will you, Emily, before you bring her in? Don't bring her on false pretences."

"Very good, Mr. Bathurst."

A moment later Emily had done her duty. "Miss Beryl Armitage, sir."

Anthony rose to greet his visitor. She was well dressed—he saw at once. Everything she wore was in irreproachable taste. Also she was rather lovely. Her face was a clear oval, her eyes altogether charming and her legs were slim and long. Her little hat and her plain court shoes with her half veil gave her an appearance that was as trim and spruce as could be desired.

"Mr. Bathurst," she said, with a note of inquiry.

"Yes, Miss Armitage. I am Anthony Bathurst. Why am I honoured thus?"

"I want to speak to you," she said, "in the matter of the case of Dr. Traquair." Her voice was low-pitched and altogether delightful. The reply took Anthony rather by surprise. He gestured her to a chair. She accepted the invitation. He noticed that her face wavered for a second and then returned to normal.

"The case of Dr. Traquair? Well, I won't deny that I have a certain interest in it. What is it that you want to say to me?" Anthony, it must be admitted, was by now a trifle uneasy. He had an impression as he looked at her that her manner concealed smouldering fires and alien thoughts. It must be remembered that Anthony was not yet used to her, and he resolved therefore to stand guard over the phrases that would come from him lest some tiny word or mistaken emphasis should place him at a disadvantage.

"I want to say this to you, Mr. Bathurst—that there has never yet been a case quite on all fours with this case of Dr. Traquair." As she spoke she threw back her head and looked at him almost rebelliously.

Anthony made no sign. "Please proceed, Miss Armitage."

"Dr. Traquair was very gravely wronged," she continued, with her eyes full upon him, searching his face with the most obvious anxiety. Anthony made no answer. He had been well schooled to deal with situations of this kind. Suddenly Miss Armitage turned the tables. "But, of course, you are aware of that without my telling you."

"I wouldn't admit that for an instant, Miss Armitage. You forget perhaps that I knew nothing of Dr. Traquair until I was called upon to—er—chase him."

A half smile broke over her face. "I should have remembered that you would be unlikely to be indiscreet."

She saw Anthony smile as she uttered the word. "I am afraid," she went on, "that I am putting my case almost crudely. But it is my habit to speak directly and I have little skill in minimizing twists

196 | BRIAN FLYNN

of phrase or in diminishing the essences of meaning. I have to lay bare my thoughts just as they come to me. You, in a way, are my enemy. But please don't misunderstand the word. Let us say rather that you belong to an opposite camp. You intend, I know, to arrest Dr. Traquair—if you can. A few days ago, I should have dreaded that to happen. Now I dread it no longer."

Anthony was swift to interrupt. "Why is that, Miss Armitage?"

"Because the danger . . . the real danger . . . is past."

"You talk in enigmas, Miss Armitage. I take it that you know where Dr. Traquair is?"

"Yes," she answered simply.

"And yet I am unable to forget that there is a trail of three murders behind Dr. Traquair. Murder, I suggest to you, is something more than petty larceny. You have, I presume, thought of that and fully considered its implications?" She ignored the direct question.

"In a short time from now, Mr. Bathurst, Dr. Traquair will have left the country. It will be better in every way for that to happen. Complications will be avoided and awkward questions need not then be answered. I have come to tell you that because we feel that we have a much better chance of establishing an understanding with you than we should have with the official Police at Scotland Yard. I am sorry for the moment that I am unable to speak more plainly." She paused, as though seeking words which would express her meaning and yet enfold it with the dignity of seemliness.

Anthony seized on the plural pronoun that she had thrice employed. "'We', Miss Armitage? Whom am I to understand as 'we'?"

"Understand just my friends and me. For the present. Soon you will know the whole truth."

Both of them by now were superbly grave. Conscious of the direction each was intending to take. With Anthony's gravity there was allied a sense of bewilderment. He sought understanding.

"You will help me no more than that?"

She rose from her chair, and as she did so certain revelations came to Anthony. It came to him in a flash that he knew who she was! He accordingly hardened his heart as he awaited her reply. It came slowly.

"I am sorry. But at the moment I *cannot* help you any more than that."

An idea came to Anthony, swift-born in his brain. "You have helped Traquair all the way through the piece? You have been at his side, so that he might turn to you if he wanted help, or if you thought that he needed help. Why? I think that I *may* know . . . but as yet I am not sure."

She smiled a wistful little smile. "Although I have been, as you say, at his side—I am not in love with him . . . if that is what you mean."

Anthony rose and stood at her side. Her eyes met his fearlessly. He caught her by the wrist and looked at her hands. "I thought for a moment," he cried, "that I had seen you before . . . but now I know that I was wrong. But I know who you are and why you have come here this evening. I know, too, why Reicher died . . . that surprises you, doesn't it? And I'll tell you how I know these things. Your real name is—" There came a knock at the door and the speaking voice of Emily.

Miss Armitage drew back from Mr. Bathurst . . . who continued to hold her wrist.

CHAPTER VIII
THE PATH STRAIGHTENS

(Told by the Author)

SHE was, however, equal to the occasion. She withdrew her wrist from Mr. Bathurst's grip and gently inclined her shapely head towards the door. Anthony accepted the situation with similar grace.

"Yes, Emily?" he answered nonchalantly.

"Inspector MacMorran to see you, Mr. Bathurst. He says that it's vitally important. Otherwise, of course, sir, I shouldn't have dreamt of interrupting you."

Anthony's reply was grimly determined.

"Show the Inspector up, Emily. If the Inspector's business with me is as urgent as he states it is, Miss Armitage here will forgive my sanctioning the intrusion."

Miss Armitage raised the remains of her eyebrows but otherwise made no response. Emily, thus instructed, departed on her way to Inspector MacMorran.

"You seem to think, Mr. Bathurst, that Inspector MacMorran will make an appropriate addition to the company. Any idea on your part that he would be *de trop*, for example, appears to be conspicuous by its absence."

Anthony smiled and shrugged his shoulders. "A mere matter of opinion, Miss Armitage. Time will show which one of us is right. That noise which you can hear is Inspector MacMorran ascending my staircase."

"I notice that you still address me as Armitage."

"The Inspector is not yet here. Though you may have a passion for the truth, you really must curb a certain natural impatience. But if I mistake not, here is the Inspector."

MacMorran entered rather abruptly. When he saw Mr. Bathurst's companion he pulled himself up with something like a jerk.

"Your girl didn't tell me that you had a visitor."

"It's all right, Inspector," said Anthony. "Come right in. This is a young lady whom you should know. Rather, whom you should know better. For, to a degree, you already know her. Allow me to introduce you more formally. Inspector MacMorran—Miss—"

The girl's' voice broke across Mr. Bathurst's speech almost imperiously. "Be careful, Mr. Bathurst. My real name, if you please."

"Very well. I'll accept the challenge. Inspector MacMorran—Miss Beryl Armitage. But better known to you and me as Miss Phoebe Hubbard."

MacMorran surveyed this tastefully dressed, almost radiant vision of sophisticated femininity with a look of astonishment. When he had seen Phoebe Hubbard before, she had presented an appearance that had been vastly different from the girl whom he saw now. Before, however, he could translate his surprise into words, she broke in again.

"But my real name—it seems to be a matter of doubt—is Beryl Armitage. I mention that fact because it's an extremely important contribution."

"I was expecting you at the Yard," said Inspector MacMorran gruffly. "I didn't anticipate finding you here. And I don't understand why you *are* here—which is something else."

"I'm here," she returned archly, "because I wanted to see Mr. Bathurst much more than I wanted to see you."

"Don't upbraid the lady," remarked Anthony, "on account of her excellent taste. I'm surprised at you, Andrew."

"That's one way of looking at things," returned MacMorran, "but I don't know that it's going to be mine."

Despite Miss Armitage's *sang-froid* Anthony observed that she was far from pleased at the turn which affairs had taken. He decided, therefore, to force events to a clearer issue.

"I am sorry that Sir Austin Kemble isn't here," he said provocatively.

Beryl Armitage rose to the bait. "Who is Sir Austin Kemble?" she inquired with some show of uneasiness.

"The Commissioner of Police," replied Anthony curtly.

"Yes, I remember now. I should have known. But why do you regret his absence? I had hoped to settle a great deal before I left you."

"What is there to settle?" countered Anthony. "I use the word that you have used."

"First of all, there is the position of Dr. Traquair. I agree that the truth must be told—but it need never be made public."

"Isn't the doctor in safe hands? I understood that in a very short time from now he would have left the country. You see—again I use your own words."

"What's this about Traquair?" grumbled MacMorran. "Who says he'll leave the country? I'll have the bracelets on him before that happens, don't you worry."

Miss Armitage appeared to consider the situation. "May I speak to my chauffeur?" she asked at length.

"Why?" demanded Mr. Bathurst.

"Well . . . it looks as though I may be here some time . . . and I don't want him to hang about outside here unnecessarily."

MacMorran looked towards Anthony Bathurst. Then he shook his head.

"He'll be all right. Don't you fret yourself about him. Besides—how are you going to get home if you send your car away?"

Miss Armitage shrugged her shoulders. "Very well. It's of little importance. May I use your telephone? Is that such a tremendous concession?"

Anthony took upon himself to answer this question. "I shall be delighted to deliver a message for you. That is, if you could bring yourself to entrust it to me."

Beryl Armitage regarded him disdainfully. "You are really too kind. Very well then. I'll accept your generous offer. Will you please ring Pedlay 228? When you get through will you say just this: 'Beryl says "please come to Mr. Bathurst's flat at once"'? It's all right, the address will be known at the other end. We are quite thorough in our methods."

Anthony was unable to resist a smile at the aptness of the thrust. "I'll do that for you at once, Miss Armitage. In the meantime, you and Inspector MacMorran will be able to discuss whether murder should be treated by the courts as a matter of degree. I've no doubt that the Inspector will find your views highly interesting."

Mr. Bathurst went to the 'phone and established connection with Pedlay 228. A man's voice answered him. Anthony gave the message as he had been requested. The voice said "Thank you", but no more. Mr. Bathurst went back to the Armitage-MacMorran combine.

"I have delivered your message, Miss Armitage. I was thanked for my good offices. Beyond that, I have nothing to report."

"Thank you," she said simply. Then she turned to MacMorran. "My friend will be here in less than half an hour. I am telling you that to give you time to prepare your offensive. Although I think that both you and Mr. Bathurst are going to be surprised."

Anthony nodded as though in agreement with her. After a few minutes silence he slipped out of the room again and made his way downstairs. Shortly afterwards he might have been seen giving certain instructions to Miss Armitage's chauffeur. When he returned, Miss Armitage registered relief to see him. "I was afraid you had deserted us," she said, "and had left me to the tender mercies of Inspector MacMorran." Anthony shook his head. He smiled towards Miss Armitage.

"I shall see the case through to the end. Don't worry, Miss Armitage. Even though it may finish in failure for me."

"It depends what you mean by failure," she argued.

"Agreed. Some people might regard a failure as a success. For example, the bigger failure a politician may be, the greater success he usually becomes. Unhappily, that condition doesn't apply to the detection of crime, does it, Inspector?"

"I should say not. I shouldn't lie awake at nights—if that were the case."

"You see, Inspector," said Anthony, "it's like this. Dr. Traquair killed his wife. I think that I know why. Within certain limits, that is. I know, too, who murdered Reicher. I know why *he* was killed. And I think I know also why the man was killed whose body came from the railway line . . . although I am not yet aware of his identity. An identity which, I am convinced, matters to us but little. I am enumerating these various features of the case so that Miss Armitage may know exactly where we stand, Inspector, you and I. She invited you to prepare your offensive." Beryl Armitage went as pale as death. Her breath came in quick, short gasps. Anthony's statement had clearly shaken her confidence. For the first time since she had arrived her nerves began to master her. Suddenly Anthony saw her turn her head as though in the act of listening.

"Here comes the person for whom I have been waiting," she said.

Anthony looked towards Inspector MacMorran. "I think that Miss Armitage is right, Inspector. If you take my advice (and hers) you will prepare yourself for an entire surprise."

CHAPTER IX
Numbers Eight and Nine

(Told by the Author)

Miss Armitage, for good reasons, doubtless, allowed Mr. Bathurst's statement to pass unchallenged. Her fingers, however, were still restless and her hands inclined to tremble. Anthony, listening for familiar sounds, heard Emily go to the door. He made a sign to MacMorran which Miss Armitage failed to see . . . as had been Mr. Bathurst's intention. MacMorran moved his seat to one of more strategic value. Emily gave her usual tap on the door. Anthony responded to it. He heard what Emily had to say. "Show him in, Emily. Tell him that our party is incomplete without him."

Beryl Armitage sat tight in her chair. MacMorran knew from previous experience of Mr. Bathurst that he must lie low, watch points, and be ready for instant action. The door opened quietly. A man entered. A tall, thin, dark-haired man. Directly he saw him MacMorran uttered a sharp exclamation. Anthony turned to Beryl Armitage.

"I will leave you, Miss Armitage, to make the necessary introductions. Although, of course, we have all met before."

Stiff-lipped and unsmiling, Beryl Armitage obeyed Mr. Bathurst's request. "Allow me to introduce you, Paul! Anthony Bathurst, Inspector MacMorran of Scotland Yard—my brother, Paul Armitage."

The tall young man bowed. Anthony nodded.

"Good evening, Mr. Armitage. We were bound to meet, I'm afraid."

MacMorran jerked his head. At a moment of this kind he couldn't be bothered with the trivial conventions.

"Paul," said the lady, "from what Mr. Bathurst has already told me, no good purpose will be served by our continuing with the plan that we had decided on. Everything now will have to be made a matter of mutual arrangement. That's why I sent for you to come here."

"Meaning," declared Paul Armitage, "that they know too much."

Beryl nodded. "Exactly."

Paul Armitage hesitated. He looked rather helplessly at his sister. "It's difficult to know where to start. That's my trouble."

"Shall I help you?" said Anthony.

"Can you? The start must be the start, you know."

"I'll have a shot at it," said Anthony again. "You can correct me at every phase where I go wrong."

"Very good, Bathurst. I'll sit down, if I may."

"Of course. You sit here and I'll stand." Anthony and Paul Armitage changed places.

"I'll start," declared Mr. Bathurst, "on a sensational note. Inspector MacMorran!"

The Inspector looked up. There was challenge in Mr. Bathurst's voice. "Will you please arrest Miss Armitage on a charge of murder. You have the warrant, I believe, in your pocket."

Paul Armitage sprang to his feet. Beryl, his sister, put her hand nervously to her throat. MacMorran stepped forward from his position by the door. "Stop a minute, Inspector," cried Paul Armitage, "and listen to me! With what murder are you charging my sister?"

Anthony answered for MacMorran. "With the murder of Frederick Reicher in Dr. Traquair's house at Brooke."

"But how can that be," cried MacMorran, "seeing that she was with me in the train and afterwards with us in the house?"

Anthony shrugged his shoulders. "I would draw your attention, Inspector, to the fact that so far the lady has not denied the accusation. Which is, I suggest, at least significant."

Miss Armitage looked towards her brother. He made a helpless gesture and sank back into his seat. "I had better tell the whole of the story. I must ask these gentlemen, particularly the officer from Scotland Yard, for their discretion to be exercised until that full story has been told. For the reason that there are tremendous interests at stake—much greater than the personal."

"I must be the judge of that," contributed MacMorran.

"I must be content to leave it at that, then," returned Paul Armitage. He continued to speak and his eyes did not leave his sister's face. "My sister and I belong to Department X2 of the British Secret Service." He took a wallet from his breast pocket and handed a slip of paper to the Inspector. "There are our credentials. You will see from that that we work under a chief whose name should be well known to you. There is no need for me to repeat the name aloud. My sister is known as Number Nine. I am always referred to as Number Eight. Actual names are never mentioned in the departments in which we are proud to serve. The Chief is Number One. And there are times, many times indeed, when we are in conflict with the Secret Service of other European countries, when we can expect no help whatever from the Government of our own country. To help us, on those occasions, might well mean plunging the whole of Europe into war. The result is that our minor interests must suffer and we must fight our battles off our own bat. I mention that fact because it will help to explain much later on."

Paul Armitage took out his cigarette-case. "Do you mind if I smoke? Thank you." He lit a cigarette and then went on. "Our father was *the* Colonel Armitage, V.C., of whom you must have heard. Some months ago it was reported to me that a certain doctor living at Brooke was on the verge of a great discovery. The details were not quite complete. Certain agents of a foreign Government—the name is not vitally necessary—had come to be in possession of part of this discovery. And because they had been put in possession of this knowledge through the treachery of the doctor's own wife, we were requested to treat the entire matter as Secret Service duty and fight the menace with our own resources. Official assistance or recognition could not be afforded us because of the implication of this lady, and because of the strained relations that would almost certainly follow between the two governments—were any steps taken of a drastic nature. That doctor's name was Dr. Stuart Traquair. His wife was German born. Her maiden name had been Madeleine Halmar. Her brother was Rupert Halmar, one of the most competent and brilliantly efficient Secret Service agents that ever worked to the detriment and downfall of our own country, gentlemen. Dr. Traquair's suspicions of his wife were sent to me through a third party with whom the doctor had established contact. Another member of Department X2. In fact, until a few days ago I had never met Dr. Traquair, and shouldn't have known him had I met him in the street."

"Just a minute," interposed MacMorran, "you're travelling a wee bit too fast for me. What was the nature of this marr'vellous discovery of the doctor's?"

"It was called 'B. and N. 666'," replied Armitage. "I don't know that I can really describe it to you satisfactorily . . . you need the doctor himself to do that."

The door opened suddenly and a strange voice spoke: "Then I will do it, Armitage! After all, who should do the job better?"

A man stood in the doorway. A man in chauffeur's uniform. Beryl Armitage gave a little cry. Mr. Bathurst seized the opportunity.

"Let me introduce you, Inspector! I have no doubt that you will be delighted to meet Dr. Stuart Traquair."

MacMorran rose slowly to his feet. His eyes gleamed incredulity!

"Good evening, everybody," said Dr. Traquair.

CHAPTER X

MR. BATHURST HEARS OF B.
AND N. 666

(*Told by the Author*)

MR. BATHURST quietly controlled the situation. "This is all very irregular, Inspector, I know. But I suggest that before we act we hear the continuation of Mr. Armitage's story from the lips of Dr. Traquair."

MacMorran submitted, a trifle ungraciously.

"I'm in your hands, Mr. Bathurst."

Anthony found a seat for the man who wore the uniform of the chauffeur. He took a good look at him as he occupied the chair that was placed for him. Traquair's was a striking face, and Anthony recalled his own words, previously expressed to Inspector MacMorran, that Traquair was no ordinary murderer. He felt more convinced now than ever of the truth of this assertion. Traquair began to speak.

"I will accept this gentleman's invitation. I presume that I have the honour to address *the* Mr. Bathurst?" He paused—to proceed immediately. "Since I left hospital I have worked devilishly hard. Probably all doctors have to, but I've done more than my fair share. Harder, too, from the time I took up my practice in Brooke. I must tell you that before I went to Brooke I had put in a great deal of research work concerning that virulent disease which is more troublesome, perhaps, than any—a disease, too, which almost decimates armies in the field. Insanitary conditions, due to faulty drainage, wherein the bacilli may increase indefinitely, the contamination of drinking-water in places where wells or cisterns are exposed to sewage pollution, may convey infection to thousands of people, in the ordinary circumstances of civilization. But multiply these risks a thousandfold and you will have some idea of those run by an army under war-time conditions. I refer, of course, to the devastating scourge of enteric."

Anthony nodded in agreement. Traquair seemed to derive encouragement from the gesture. He proceeded, therefore, with more confidence.

"The bacillus was discovered first by Eberth in 1880. Now we recognize Bacillus Paratyphosus A, Bacillus Paratyphosus B and Bacillus Paratyphosus C. The last-named is responsible for the milder attacks of the fever. I will not worry you with technicalities beyond the necessary for the telling of my story, and will condense my remarks as much as I can. But in the course of the disease the bowels are affected, particularly the lower end of the small intestine where the solitary glands and 'Peyer's patches' on the inner surface of the bowel undergo certain changes. It was to these 'patches' that I began to pay special attention. I wanted a drug that killed the bacillus before these changes began to occur.

"I realized that if I could discover it, my country—our country—would hold one advantage in a long-drawn-out war, covering possibly many areas in Europe and the East, that might well prove the overwhelming and decisive factor in the campaign and an advantage which we must keep entirely to ourselves, when we consider the strength of the various Powers that it is feared may well be allied against us. I was successful. I killed the germ in experimental infections in mice, even in its most deadly strains. And during the last few days, thanks to opportunities afforded by Mr. Armitage here, I have treated a woman of 62, a man of 60 and a man of 34, all of whom were suffering from acute enteric. In the case of the man of 60, improvement has set in immediately. With regard to the woman aged 62 the drug was administered on the fifth day of her illness and within twelve hours her temperature had fallen to normal. The youngest man of my three cases is now out of danger. The peculiar course of the temperature in enteric fever, I may say, is one of the most important diagnostic evidences of the disease. The name of my drug is 'B. and N. 666'. Its full name 2—(p. Nubetasalcalofebrinamido) Phenaridine. It is, of course, antiseptic, anti-putrefactive and anti-pyretic.

"But I am probably boring you with these technical details and I will now leave the medical side of the affair, to relate the circumstances to do with the death of my wife." Traquair stopped for a moment. The others saw that he was considerably affected. "My wife was German born. She couldn't be blamed for that. But I did not know, when I married her, that her brother, Rupert Halmar, was one of the most brilliant and active members of my wife's country's Secret Service. For a time I viewed this fact as philosophically as I could. There it was. I couldn't alter it. I might as well school myself to put up with it. One day, however, my suspicions were aroused. I had a shock. I had reason to think that some of the papers in connection with my research work had been tampered with. I kept them in a locked drawer in my bedroom. My wife was the only possible person whom I could reasonably suspect." Traquair dropped his voice.

"I soon proved to my own satisfaction that my suspicions were justified. I was at a loss for a time as to the best course for me to adopt. Eventually, I got into touch with Department X2 of our own Secret Service. With Mr. Armitage here. I had his name from a third party, high up in the medical profession. This person, of course, did not know exactly what Armitage was. He merely suggested that he might be able to help me. Department X2 was interested and gave me certain instructions, but I was informed that as my wife's country was already involved I must rely almost entirely upon myself to safeguard my secret and that I could expect little official help or recognition should I be called upon to act 'indiscreetly'. I have since learned how they helped me clandestinely by placing

Miss Armitage as a member of my household." Traquair cleared his throat. "By removing certain papers, containing vital details of my discovery, from my drawer, I seriously interfered with the value of the knowledge that Halmar and his associates had already gained. However, as time went on, the dreadful truth came home to me—that they had learnt so much that I must take immediate action in the matter. My wife was nothing better than a spy! An enemy of mine in so far as she was a bitter enemy of my country. The loyalty to the land of her birth outweighed any personal loyalty that she might feel towards me. I knew that she and her brother meant to get rid of me when their time was ripe. The result was . . ." Traquair almost broke down here, but by a supreme effort he pulled himself together.

"The result was that I decided it was either my life or my wife's. My country or hers. That is how I narrowed down the issue. But I could not murder her. Scarcely can it be truly said that I even 'executed' her. I gave her an equal chance of life with myself. I will tell you exactly what I did."

Traquair described to them the story of the ordeal by card just as he has described it in his own account at the beginning of this history. When he had finished he spoke bravely and well. "I do not ask for mercy, I ask for Justice. Who dies if England live?" He buried his face in his hands and sat there saying nothing.

It seemed to the two Armitages that Anthony Bathurst held out help to them.

"Let me see if I can join some of the 'flats' for you, Dr. Traquair. I think it's possible that I can. The men who invaded your house just after Mrs. Traquair's death were Halmar's men, I take it?"

"Yes, he had several of his agents with him. I had to outwit them to get away. They thought I was still inside the house. It would have been my life or Halmar's had we met again . . . his sister was dead, you see, and he had found her in there."

Anthony turned to Miss Armitage. "You knew who the invaders were? When you were sleeping there as Phoebe Hubbard?"

"Oh yes. But I dared not say. It might have meant the most serious international complications. Especially with things as they are in Europe. Crisis is imminent."

Here MacMorran intervened for the first time. "Just a minute. If Halmar were seeking the doctor here, why didn't he try your bedroom? How was he to know that Traquair wasn't in there with you? A man defending his life doesn't find too many scruples, does he?"

Miss Armitage blushed deliciously at the Inspector's question and its implication. "Halmar did try my bedroom . . . and as Dr. Traquair wasn't there, but only Phoebe Hubbard . . . the maid . . . he left me alone. He didn't recognize me, you see, as Number Nine of Department X2." She smiled sweetly at the Inspector and Mr. Bathurst's heart warmed towards her. MacMorran coughed.

"Er . . . thank you, Miss Armitage."

Anthony took up the parable again. "You sought refuge at Lifford, Doctor, I presume, because an old friend of yours lived there? A friend whom you could implicitly trust?"

Traquair nodded. "Yes. Although when I got away I had no idea of going there. I saw the name of the place on a coach and it reminded me of Helen . . . Mrs. Eversley."

Mr. Bathurst went on again. "Mrs. Eversley overheard the telephone message with regard to the visit of the Police to the 'Nell Gwynne' and warned you . . . yes?"

"Yes. You are right again. I had finished my work on B. and N. 666 and, that accomplished, didn't much care what happened. I came up to town to get into touch with Armitage. Mrs. Eversley followed me and once again proved my salvation."

"The flat . . . we traced you there from your somewhat peculiar and original ideas concerning the disposal of dead bodies . . . belonged to a friend of Mrs. Eversley's?"

Traquair smiled a little. "Yes, that is so. When I left there I at once connected with Department X2." He turned and bowed to Miss Armitage. "This is another lady to whom I owe a tremendous debt."

Anthony nodded. "Thank you, Doctor." He swung round to Beryl Armitage. "Why did your brother assume your identity for the interview in Dr. Traquair's house on the evening you shot and killed Reicher?"

"We knew that Halmar meant ransacking the house on that day. I went there early—I always had my own key—because we weren't sure what Dr. Traquair might have left behind, and to forestall, if necessary, whomever Halmar sent. He sent Reicher. Reicher fired at me. My aim was better than his. As I was to be occupied with Reicher and Company, we arranged that Paul should play my part. We are terribly alike as you can see and have often exchanged jobs for one another. But Paul makes a much better girl than I make a boy."

Paul Armitage interposed. "What made you suspect me, Bathurst?"

Anthony smiled at the directness of the question. "Firstly something physical. Your hands. They were inclined to suggest the masculine. The face might have been the face of Beryl . . . the hands were the hands of Paul. Her voice I knew not, but yours certainly deceived our two inspectors. Secondly—something psychological. You didn't know the locality of your own bedroom in Dr. Traquair's house. That fact was reported to me by Inspector Rudge just after you had left us."

Paul Armitage laughed. "I know. I messed that up badly. I was afraid that might have caused you to suspect me. But in all other respects you'll admit that I acquitted myself well—what do you say?"

Anthony laughed in return. "Jolly good show, chaps, jolly good show."

"Now I've another question," declared MacMorran—"who killed the man at Miss Fleetwood's flat . . . and why was he killed? This is all very well . . . but I've my duty to do." He glared at Traquair.

"I shoved his body on the train, but beyond that I know no more than you, Inspector."

Beryl and Paul Armitage looked at one another.

"His name was Stuermer," said the latter; "he was Halmar's right-hand man in succession to Reicher. He was killed in fair fight. For further details I must refer you to Department X2."

"Sounds all right," grumbled MacMorran. "I don't know what the Commissioner will say about it."

"Am I under arrest?" asked Traquair . . . "If I am, I will willingly surrender."

"Am I?" asked Miss Armitage. "Or is the Inspector like an eagle cheated of his prey?"

"I must ask you all to accompany me to Scotland Yard. I must consult Sir Austin Kemble. It seems to me that if I've still got my job by to-morrow morning I can call myself a damned lucky fellow."

"It may seem absurd," smiled Dr. Traquair, "but if we're all going to the Yard together I shall be happy to drive you there."

"In my car," added Miss Armitage.

"Yours," queried Anthony, "or Department X2's?"

"How right you always are," murmured Miss Armitage sweetly.

About a month later, Dr. Stuart Traquair leant from a carriage window at Victoria. Helen Eversley, from the platform below, looked up at him. Her hand was in his. "How long will you be abroad?" she asked him quietly.

"I don't know. Some years, I expect. When I feel how much I owe to you, Helen . . ."

At that moment their eyes met and each knew the secret of the other's heart. Traquair bent down and kissed her lips.

"Even the angels will forgive me that," he said. She nodded, her eyes wet with tears.

Traquair felt his sanity deserting him. "Don't . . ." he said quietly, "don't . . . I can't bear it. . . ."

Helen smiled at him through wet lashes.

"I will be brave. But I love you! In all the years that come to me, no other man shall ever get from me a word, a look, or even a thought of Love. I am yours, Stuart, all of me, always. Now you know! I am glad that you know. I think I loved you the first time I ever saw you. I go back to Lifford, thinking only that."

Traquair shook his head. "My love for you must be left unsaid. Good-bye . . . before we 'break the high bond we made and sell Love's trust, and sacramented covenant to the dust'." He knew little of what he said. She nodded again. Their hands were tight-clasped.

The whistle went. Helen Eversley shivered . . . before she looked again at the man she loved and who she now knew loved her. There stretched between them not days or weeks or months . . . but years! Years of desperate emptiness and bitter waste.

"Who knows," she cried with clear courage, "but one day a Love-ship may come home . . . and then . . ."

Traquair bent down and whispered:

"And then, in the words of Charles Wogan: 'There may come a black horse on which I may ride into my City of Dreams'. Till then . . ."

The train started. The last he saw of her was a brave figure . . . waving.

Anthony Lotherington Bathurst spoke to Inspector MacMorran and Sir Austin Kemble.

"It's rather ominous," he said, "that Traquair should have numbered his drug '666', seeing that three people have already died by reason of their contact with it."

"Why?" asked the Commissioner with a puzzled air. "What's the point?"

"Well," replied Mr. Bathurst, "doesn't it happen to be the number of 'The Beast'? Six hundred, three score and six?"

"Which beast?" inquired Sir Austin Kemble frankly. It is clear that revelation had not come to him.

THE END

Printed in Great Britain
by Amazon

55459610R00126